A Charter to That Other Place

Sean Boling

Published by Sean Boling, 2015.

A CHARTER TO THAT OTHER PLACE

First edition. January 5, 2015.

Copyright © 2015 Sean Boling.

ISBN: 979-8224158881

Written by Sean Boling.

Chapter One: Dale

People used to smile at them when he took his son out to lunch, back when Jonathan was a child. Some still smiled, but only to cover the tension or sadness that looking at the two of them now seemed to inspire.

He watched Jonathan line up packets of hot sauce on the tabletop and scan his freshly laid-out collection with his face hovering inches above it, rearranging the order every few seconds and blurting out "That a baby" each time he did.

Their number had yet to be called. This was the part where they would talk, if that was possible, where they would exchange stories while they waited for their food, slight moments about something they had heard or done. But Jonathan always heard too much, could hear everything around him. So while his son found relief in shrinking the world down to a tabletop, Dale glanced around the restaurant and marked time by observing the expressions of the others, whether they were looking at the two of them or not, marking not only the minutes until Jonathan's cheese nachos were ready, but the years since people regarded their relationship as something endearing rather than pitiable. The thought bubbles that clouded every space they entered had gone from "You sweet man" to "You poor man".

He was pleased with how close Jonathan had come to placing his own order. They had brought a takeout menu with them so he could point at what he wanted, and technically he had done so, but with a substantial amount of guidance from Dale before they had arrived. The goal he and his wife had set for Jonathan was independence, or something bordering on it, and they were confident in their ability to get him there. For the past decade, Dale had supervised the Special Education programs in the local school district following a previous decade in the classroom. His first years of teaching were in general education, until he started his degree in Special Education not long after Jonathan's birth. And while his wife had no formal training, Alma had been their son's primary caregiver all twenty years of his life, and as far as Dale was concerned, she was far more skilled in most areas compared to himself.

They had planned on a big family, the birth of their daughter inspiring them even more so, but after Jonathan arrived, they lost their nerve. Their daughter had been a very good sport about the attention her brother required, but Dale and Alma were determined that she wouldn't have to take care of him when they no longer could, and beyond.

They also wanted to make sure he didn't become a ward of the state, so while they felt they could teach him to function, they needed to set him up in a place of his own. It would be small, easy to maintain, a home base for simple routines that required little communication, and it would be paid for. And if they were going to pay cash for a house, even the modest one of their dreams for their son, they needed to make more money.

The nachos were ready. Their number was called. Jonathan had memorized it on the receipt, so he punctuated the announcement with a "That a baby."

Dale chuckled and fetched the order. Any embarrassment he experienced over his son had evaporated within days of Jonathan making his public debut as a toddler. It was the way life was going to be from then on. Shame required too much energy.

Today he was feeling especially light, though, as he had received good news concerning his interview to be the principal of the new charter school opening in their community. It would not only be an opportunity to apply some innovations he had learned about and speculated on over the years, but if it worked, he imagined serving as a consultant on subsequent charter projects, as their district was the first one to grant approval within a fifty-mile radius. Theirs was still a predominantly rural county, trapped between respect for tradition and suspicion of public programs. During the school board meeting devoted to voting on the charter, several local leaders of private industries stated how much they would appreciate a chance to help finance an effort to beat the state at its own game.

Dale already knew this. He had spoken with many of them over the years, had grown up with some of them, and if he could deliver them a victory, his earning power would become more than he had ever imagined up until last year, when the charter committee first formed.

He kept his distance while they chose the founding board members, scouted locations, and compiled their case. He didn't want to appear too eager. The founders were mainly parents and retired educators. Hardly any people who worked for the district were associated with the project, as many considered it a threat, and any sympathetic coworkers as mutinous. So avoiding the founding committee was hardly conspicuous. The trickier part was navigating the frequent bashing of the project by his colleagues. He couldn't very well join in, all the while planning his application and coming out as a turncoat when he finally submitted it. Nor could he defend the effort too vocally and invite suspicion. He wanted to come into the interview as fresh as possible, and not give the committee too much time to form opinions of his candidacy before he arrived. He had no major enemies that he knew of, but he also knew that the fears of those who resist change are often turned into anger against those who embrace it. And even though the charter members wouldn't likely seek opinions from resentful members of the status quo, words traveled quickly in a community where so few were spoken. He sought recommendations from those he safely assumed were sympathetic and able to keep a secret, kept track of the committee's progress through their website and articles in the free local monthly so he could tailor his pitch to their needs, and by the time the interview was over, left them no choice but to hire him.

He playfully stole a chip from Jonathan's plate. When he didn't seem to notice, Dale slowly moved his hand toward the dish again. Jonathan grunted and flapped his hands this time.

"Aw, come on, son," Dale pulled back. "I've earned it."

He had told him about the good news right after receiving the call in the parking lot, and what this could mean for them, but he would have to wait until they arrived home to get any sort of read on Jonathan's feelings. In the meantime he just shook his head at his Dad, and Dale enjoyed thinking that his son was teasing him right back.

On the drive home, Dale celebrated by taking the back roads and treating himself to some scenery. It was yet another room-temperature sunny day in a line of them that had grown far too long, the spring of the second year of drought conditions. It was late March and the hills were tan. The oak trees offered some scattered green, but very dusty shades of it. Sparse herds of cattle were visible on some of the slopes. The only crops allowed to flourish were those that could be dry farmed. The almond orchards were filled with pink buds and some of the vineyards were shiny with leaves, but in between such showcases were fallow fields shriveling with cracks. The only things rising from some of the parched lots were extra-large real estate signs nailed between wooden stakes as thick as telephone poles. The air kept still most of the time, as still as the dormant parcels, the occasional breeze coming across as a dry cough. It had been a while since anyone was able to truly enjoy weather that would be spectacular if it had not been so relentless. Sunshine had become a source of melancholy. Even in the afterglow of the phone call, Dale could only soak up the warmth for so long, as it dawned on him that his opportunity only existed due to the conditions he was driving through. The loss of income from the loss of crops led to lower property values, which led to less money for the schools, which led to frustration with the district, which led to a willingness to experiment.

By the time he crossed back into the city limits and pulled onto their street, he was once again humbled by the sun, and feeling more grateful than triumphant.

"So what do you think about Dad's new job?" Alma asked Jonathan as she slid the letter board across the kitchen table between them. She had developed the device herself, a wooden board with raised puzzle pieces glued to it that she rearranged for months until settling on the layout that seemed to work best for Jonathan. He took to calling it "the instrument". Dale watched in admiration as Alma maneuvered the board and confirmed each letter out loud as their son ran his hands over the bumps and tapped on one every few seconds, as though the spirit of Jonathan was contacting them, the part of their son that wasn't visible to the material world. She was much faster with the system than Dale, thanks to her greater familiarity, so if they were both talking to Jonathan, he let her handle it.

"C..." Alma announced. "O..."

She and Dale glanced at each other, already able to predict the word. She helped him complete it, anyway.

"O...L...Cool?"

Jonathan nodded.

"Anything else?" Dale asked.

Jonathan shook his head.

"Is anything not cool to you?" he followed up.

The sharp look Alma gave him seemed in part to keep herself from laughing as much as it was an admonishment.

Jonathan started to run his hands over the board again. This time he spelled "room".

"Sure," Alma sighed. "Go ahead. We'll celebrate without you."

He got up and walked down the hall, the sound of his door shutting serving as a cue for Dale.

"Those books and articles that inspired you to create that system," he said, "do you ever get the sense maybe they were embellishing a little bit?"

"It works," she answered.

"I mean the results," he explained. "Maybe their kids aren't the poets they're made out to be."

"They took liberties with the transcribing?"

"It would be tempting."

"Maybe Jonathan is just the strong, silent type," she smiled. "Destined to be a great athlete had his mind and body been able to play well together."

"You're an optimist, and I love you."

He leaned over and kissed her.

"Kind of," she said.

"I kind of love you?"

"I'm kind of an optimist. How many great poets would have bothered if they had to rake their hands over a Ouija board instead of just writing or typing?"

"Not many, I imagine."

He sat down next to her and kissed her again.

"But a few. So maybe there is an author in there somewhere. Now," he whispered. "are you going to give me a proper congratulations?"

Alma accepted his kisses but still had things on her mind.

"Did you ever feel like calling him John, or Johnny?" she asked. "Even once?"

He sat back and thought about it.

"No," he realized. "Not once."

"Me neither."

"It just doesn't fit."

"It's too informal," she proposed. "You have to get to know someone better to shorten their name."

She was approaching a familiar conversation from a new angle. Of course they knew him, but on occasion they allowed each other to fret over just how well. Some personal emotional precedent was always possible with their daughter. They could re-visit relatable degrees of heartbreak when she did not get invited to a certain birthday in third grade, or to a prom by a certain somebody in high school. Her frustration with Math was familiar to Dale, with History to Alma. Sometimes it seemed her victories were sweeter to them than to her. But raising Jonathan could often feel like a spectator sport.

They knew everything about him, as the member of a fan club knows everything about their hero, their likes and dislikes and achievements and schedule. But just as a fan can never really know their idol, Dale and Alma worried that a similar gulf separated them from their son. Instead of security gates and bodyguards keeping them away, it was a daunting swirl of unfiltered stimuli. They read the literature, quite possibly every article published on the subject, and in theory comprehended what it was like to be him. Only that's as far as they could go. They understood the need to adjust expectations, to revel in small moments of accomplishment: completing a lap rather than winning a swim meet, solving a problem rather than acing a test. But even as they learned to do so, and enjoyed the feeling, they were still so often left to wonder if Jonathan was enjoying it, too. According to the research, he was.

At times Dale felt as though worrying about how close he could get to his son was the closest he could come to understanding him, so very overwhelming were the thoughts.

"You're thinking too much," he said to her.

"I'm my son's mother."

She smiled at him and at last kissed him back.

Minutes later as they made their way through the hall toward their bedroom, Dale peeked into Jonathan's room to make sure all was well.

He was lying on his side on the floor, his cheek pressed onto the carpet, running a comb through the bristles, watching each tooth of the comb bend back at random moments and then flick forward, perhaps looking for a pattern, listening to the disjointed tinkling of the plastic spikes snapping into place, feeling the vibrations in the carpet make its way past his skin and onward to a place where they would finally disappear.

Chapter Two: Candice

She knocked on the door again and muttered to herself that the best part of the new school was that her daughters wouldn't have to go to school with these losers' kids anymore. She had seen movement in an upstairs window that had yet to be broken. One of the faded floral bed sheets hanging askew as a makeshift curtain had swayed. She stepped back and cased as much of the house as she could without entering the backyard. It was against the law, but even more against her better judgment to wade into a herd of deranged dogs barking that sounded like the last thing an elk hears before being set upon by a pack of wolves.

Candice knew they had the money. She had checked in with the One Stop market down the street and the kid behind the counter mentioned that the teenaged son and the little girl, who attended second grade with Candice's younger daughter, had come in five minutes apart from one another the day before, each with a different EBT card, and bought dozens of cases of energy drinks. That meant the parents had already sold the drinks to the deli out by the fairgrounds at half the price a distributor could offer, and pocketed the cash.

She wished she didn't know all the tricks. She wished she wasn't so compelled to learn about them. But she was. She needed to know. Other tenants would offer the stories and she would accept them. The tattlers wanted her to know that they weren't like that. But from where Candice stood, even their honesty was suspect. They may pay their rent on time, but faked a disability to get the check to do so. She wondered if they thought she was that stupid, or if they had been on the dole for so long that their rationalizing had become their truth, or if they figured as long as they got her the money, she wouldn't care where it came from.

Such was the case with her boss at the property management company. He didn't care. Candice had shared some of the stories with him before, and in some of the more insidious cases wondered if they should call the sheriff's department, when for instance a unit had become a meth pipeline or unmarked massage parlor or cock fight training camp. Her boss would just ask if they paid on time. And when she told him they did, because the criminals always did, he would ask if she liked her job. She needed it, so she would nod, and then look at local job postings when she got home to no avail.

Nothing else paid enough. She was raising two daughters on her own, with nothing but a monthly pittance coming from her husband. Not that he was struggling. His salary was officially small. There were baggage handlers for bigger airlines making more than he did as a pilot for a short-hopping regional carrier, but thanks to the woman he met on a trip who had experienced a financial windfall from her divorce, Candice's husband was able to carry on as though he owned the fleet. Whenever her daughters spent the weekend with him, she braced herself for the tales of kiddie decadence that would follow them home, the trips to hotels in the big city with atrium restaurants inside where they ate sundaes and drank hot chocolate after a day at a baseball game or on a boat tour or down a zip line. She would act very excited for them, and then scream into her pillow after putting them to bed. She vowed to wait him out, for the girls to come to some conclusions regarding why Dad danced around the question of whether they could live with him, or for his sugar mama to dump him. Whichever came first.

The charter school was the best thing to happen on her side since the divorce. At the information meetings she attended, she had yet to recognize any of the disastrous parents from her daughters' school or from her property management rounds. And she figured even if there were some kids from the rentals who ended up at the charter, their parents were at least paying enough attention to notice that another option had become available.

Unlike the food stamp scammers she was forced to badger.

"I know you're in there!" she hollered up at the second story. It wasn't going to make a difference, but she wanted them to know.

The house was part of a small development of newer homes that was supposed to stretch for another quarter mile. The curbs, sidewalks, and driveways had already been poured. But the market clattered after the first phase was complete, so the developers foreclosed, the homeowners fled, and the remaining sidewalks and driveways led nowhere. Eventually a faceless speculator swooped in to buy the abandoned houses of the first phase and turn them into rentals, and here stood Candice.

She looked over at the row of driveways that fed into the row of vacant lots. She thought of the new school that would be starting from the ground up, and the hope that it would provide for people like herself, who wanted some distance from people like this, people who slithered into houses that once meant something to someone.

There was an orientation meeting that evening. She was going to bring the girls and learn about what sort of help the charter needed from the parents to prepare for the following school year. She was looking forward to getting involved.

"Go ahead," she smiled this time as she called up to the bed-sheet laden windows. "Stay in there."

She turned to go, but once again caught sight of some movement. She looked back up and saw the girl from her daughter's second-grade class standing in a part of the window where the sheet couldn't reach. The girl stared down at Candice with no discernable emotion. Before Candice could decide whether to wave at her, a hand reached out from behind the sheet and yanked the girl behind it.

The girl was still on her mind as she drove to the orientation with her daughters. She almost asked her youngest what she knew about her classmate, but didn't feel like providing an explanation for Zoey should her daughter ask why she was curious. Candice wanted this evening to be about looking forward.

And indeed her conscience was sprinkled with pixie dust as they pulled into the recreation center where the meeting was scheduled to take place. Visions of catatonic children starting from unkempt windows were replaced by little girls in horse riding pants and little boys in soccer jerseys flowing through the play structures.

Candice stood to the side and beamed as Zoey ran to join the climb. Her older daughter, Mia, stayed by her side, feeling a bit too grown up for a playground, but wanting a comfortable place to survey the small groups of fifth and sixth graders that huddled randomly around the park. Mia was the one who had not protested at all about transferring to the new school, as whatever ties she had to any kids in her class were quite loose, while Zoey had howled about the change, thanks to her conviction that her classmates were friends for life. And now it appeared to Candice that the same sociability that attached Zoey to her old school would lead to an easy transition, while Mia's apathy would impede her embrace of the new.

"Recognize anyone?" Candice asked.

Mia shrugged. "Nobody exciting."

"Are you bringing any excitement to the party?"

The eye roll Candice expected didn't happen. Mia actually seemed to be considering what she said. Candice would have been less stunned had her ex-husband called and begged her to take him back. She wanted to keep up the momentum.

"A fresh start," she said, hoping her words echoed what her daughter was thinking.

Mia drifted away from her side, not in the direction of any particular clique, but to create some distance in the interest of drawing an invitation from one of the circles.

Candice smiled and winked at her. Mia returned a suppressed smile that she then used as the basis of a pleasantly preoccupied expression she maintained as she scanned the horizon of peers, looking for a signal.

One group apparently gave her one, as her smile broadened and she headed in the direction of a gaggle filled with girls Candice didn't recognize, which put Candice's mind at ease since the people she knew best in the community were those she wished she didn't know. One of the girls wore a pair of shorts that Candice would never let Mia wear, but the others provided a sound enough first impression.

Candice inhaled with deep contentment that grew even deeper as she exhaled, then turned her attention back to the playground, where Zoey was already hanging from the center of the geodesic dome of monkey bars, dangling face to face and enmeshed in conversation with one of the girls who had just come from horse riding lessons. Zoey saw Candice looking at them and dropped from the bars so she could wave and gesture.

"Mom!" she hollered. "This is my new friend Madison!"

Candice waved back and tried not to look too excited over the fact her playmate wore jodhpurs and a polo shirt rather than the variations on dirty pajama pants and frayed hoodies that summarized the fashion at their current school. She was calculating the number of days until the academic year ended and the new one would start when a woman's voice interrupted her math.

"Yet another gorgeous day," the voice said.

"It certainly is," Candice turned into the conversation and deduced that the woman was Madison's mother.

"Is it ever going to rain again?"

"We sure need it."

"The dust at the equestrian center," the woman shivered. "You'd swear it was August."

"I'll bet."

"It's like the kind of weather you see in movies after humanity has been wiped out, or just before the meteor hits."

Candice chuckled, nervous that she couldn't keep up. She was relieved when the woman switched to introductions.

"Jo Jo," she extended a hand.

"Candice," she shook it.

"Your daughter is very friendly."

"So is yours."

"Only if the other kid initiates."

"That's like my older daughter."

"Is she coming here too?"

Candice nodded. "She's in sixth grade."

"Hopefully they can get a charter high school started once the elementary settles in."

"That would be nice."

"We got tired of commuting to St. Bonnie's, but we'll do it again once Maddie hits freshman year if we have to. It's a shame the only good private school is thirty miles away."

"What about Trinity?"

Jo Jo sniffed. "I said *good* private school."

Candice played along.

"Oh," Jo Jo put a hand over her heart as though about to recite the Pledge of Allegiance. "My God. Do your girls go to Trinity?"

"No, no," Candice assured her, then changed the subject. "So I guess they're going to talk about the location tonight, how they're getting it ready."

"Ugh," Jo Jo grunted. "I hear about that every night. My husband is one of the contractors helping out with the renovation."

"That's nice of him."

"It really is a stretch. He's so busy during the week with the prison construction. He's got the contract to do the electrical work. I hardly see him. Maybe that's the whole idea."

Jo Jo laughed. Candice joined her, and steered away from the subject of husbands.

"Kind of funny how they're building another prison," she said. "You'd think one would be enough for the same area."

Jo Jo looked confused for a moment before realizing what Candice was referring to.

"You mean the state hospital?"

"Whatever they want to call it. Looks like a prison to me."

"I guess that's nicer than 'insane asylum.'"

"Or 'loony bin.'"

"A lot of electrical work to be done out there, too."

"Shock therapy?" Candice kidded.

Jo Jo smiled, but didn't quite laugh. Candice decided she had better follow up with something less sarcastic.

"I can certainly see why your husband would want to work on a school for a change."

Jo Jo was happy to be talking about herself again.

"Fortunately it's not totally pro bono. He's volunteering his time, of course, but at least Rod Pluma's paying for the materials on the school project."

"The produce guy?" Candice had seen the Pluma logo on some trucks and hats.

"Rod's way beyond that now," Jo Jo emphasized. "He sold all his local businesses to become a Vice President of some international ag corporation. I forget the name."

Candice was impressed. "And his kids are going here?"

"His youngest, Arturo."

"Wow."

"He'll be in sixth grade, with your older daughter."

"Great."

The news just kept getting better.

"So needless to say," Jo Jo circled back to her original point, "I'm looking forward to hearing more about the philosophy of the school. As fascinating as converting an abandoned tractor dealership into a school may be, I'd like to know what's going to be happening inside of it."

"I've come to all the information meetings," Candice said, proud to know something that Jo Jo didn't. "So I've heard Dale talk about the curriculum before. But I never get tired of it. He does such a great job."

"Dale Copeland. He was head of Special Ed in the district, right?"

"Yes."

"I imagine it's going to be difficult to offer much of that right away."

"Special Education? He hasn't really mentioned it."

"There are so many basics that need to be in place first."

"I suppose."

Jo Jo looked out at the playground and seemed to be measuring her next statement. Candice joined her, turning her attention to the pulse of children streaming through all the levels of the playground equipment. She didn't want to find herself agreeing with what Jo Jo might say next, so she decided to keep from hearing it.

"He's done a lot of research on other charter schools and private schools," she said. "He has some great ideas on what works."

"Good," Jo Jo said, appearing to let go of whatever she was thinking.

They didn't sit next to each other during Dale's introduction. Jo Jo saw some friends who called her over into the far corner of the conference room when the adults were summoned in for the start of the meeting, but Candice couldn't imagine anyone being disappointed in what he had to say.

As he often did, Dale started out by unrolling a reproduction of the Declaration of Independence which borrowed Jefferson's vocabulary of the need to "dissolve the political bands" with a public school system rife with a "long train of abuses". He read his script with enough levity to earn some giggles from those who may otherwise find the analogy rather melodramatic, but still inspired plenty of nodding heads and furrowed brows on those who owned a lot of t-shirts featuring eagles and calligraphy.

Upon rolling up the prop, he spoke in more specific terms of kids having a say in their school and their education. He envisioned a student panel that would help formulate some of the rules, and have a vote on disciplinary measures, a jury of peers in a sense. He wanted each student to always be working on a long-term project of their choice that would run parallel to the standard subjects, something like a Master's thesis that would require planning and many stages of development: constructing a piece of furniture, publishing a web comic, recording a video series. And as each one finished, they would present it to the school before starting a new one.

He ignited the room with the prospect of what the school could be, and it didn't come across as egotistical, at least not according to Candice. It was about the ideas, not him, ideas he had found that excited him, ideas he wanted others to be excited about, too. As if to prove that the enthusiasm was already spreading, he announced that over two hundred applicants had applied for the nine teaching positions available, and that interviews would be conducted over the upcoming weeks.

There were approving murmurs in the audience, grunts of recognition and sighs of epiphany. When he asked if there were any questions, there were none. Instead there were statements of approval and gratitude.

Dale was humbled, and seemed embarrassed by the praise after the initial offerings. He got them to start asking questions by bringing up the student uniforms and the parent volunteer hours that were required.

Some parents wanted ideas on how they could fulfill their volunteer obligations without being on campus during school hours.

"Can you send my child home with some stapling or copying you need done?"

"Can I type up some documents?"

"Can I just volunteer at fundraisers?"

"Can I water the plants on the weekends?"

But most of all they wanted to know what kind of accessories their children could wear as part of their uniform.

"Is a scarf okay?"

"Can my son wear a long-sleeved shirt under his school polo?"

"Does the long-sleeved shirt have to be a certain color?"

"Are colorful socks okay?"

"What color jackets can they wear?"

As cool as Dale was trying to play it, the amount of uniform questions did seem to take him by surprise. When it was clear that he was starting to make up policies as he went along, he chuckled and announced that this would be a good topic for a student panel to handle over the summer. A stocky woman with a voice twice her size volunteered to organize such a panel to applause and laughter.

Dale made a show of asking for her name and assuring her they would talk after the meeting. Then he took advantage of the merrymaking to yield the floor to Rod Pluma.

Rod and Dale exchanged a hug as they switched places. Pluma launched into his portion right away in order to capitalize on the energy in the room, and gain some volunteers for the renovation project. He appealed to people's good old-fashioned desire to see the fruits of one's labor, along with a just-as-old-fashioned competitive streak by playing the renovation against the prison under construction just a bike ride away.

"What do we want the focal point of our community to be?" he asked, finding a rhythm of his own once enough time had lapsed from Dale's display and he could no longer borrow from the residual buzz.

"Which space will our lives revolve around? That John Deere sign above the tractor dealership stood lit for longer than many of us have lived here, longer than many of us have lived, period. But that building is not being torn down, thanks to us. I've spent my life growing things. Lettuce, strawberries, almonds, grapes, you name it..."

"A fortune!" Dale chimed in, drawing some laughs from the audience.

"I've grown some businesses..." Rod grinned and nodded, appreciating the moment as he silently regained the tempo of his speech.

"...And now I want to grow a school, grow a future for our kids that doesn't include metal bars. Let's keep them out of that new space by working with the old one."

Candice felt as though she was at a tent revival meeting, and salvation was reached by building this school, and donations were in the form of time rather than money. She stood to be included. She wanted to be involved.

She wanted to pick up her kids from school and remember when she had been inside the building back when it was an abandoned tractor dealership. She wanted to be a yard duty who helped build the yard. She wanted to be a tutor in Zoey's class (rather than Mia's class, because the thought of a sixth grade classroom intimidated her), and be able to glance around the room at all the bulletin boards she helped install. So she volunteered her name for every weekend that the girls were scheduled to be with their father. She would be over the amount of required hours before the school even opened, but would keep volunteering anyway.

When the meeting concluded, she tried unsuccessfully to catch Jo Jo's eye before rounding up Mia and Zoey for a trip to the frozen yogurt shop.

The shop was a couple of shuttered doors down from the grocery store that tried to anchor the unmoored shopping center with the unnecessarily large parking lot three blocks from their house. The girls were pleased, even Mia, since they associated even the most humble luxury with their dad.

Candice thought there would be a bit of a rush there after the meeting, but there was only an elderly man paying for his yogurt, and both of the wobbly Rubbermaid tables were available for seating. She warned the girls not to load up on too many candy toppings and wondered where everyone else could be.

They claimed one of the tables and Candice tried not to gush over how excited she was about Live Oak Charter Academy, estimating that if she pushed it too hard, there would be some pushing back, at least from Mia. She stuck to one of Dale's talking points to keep her tone level.

"Did you notice what the initials of Live Oak Charter Academy spell?"

Zoey took a moment to visualize it. "LOCA?"

"That's right. And do you know what that means in Spanish?"

"Crazy," said Mia.

Zoey repeated the word "crazy" in a high-pitched voice, several times in succession.

"Smarty," Candice complimented Mia. "And do you think life is going to be crazy good there?"

Zoey gave two thumbs up and a wide-eyed grin with yogurt brimming from her lips. Mia nodded with reserved approval, which compared to her usual reactions, was the equivalent of her little sister's exuberance.

"We'll know who your teachers are by next month," Candice said. "Mr. Copeland said they've had over two hundred people apply."

Mia opened her eyes as wide as her little sister's for the first time in months, stunned that anyone would be interested in where they were.

"Some are probably from local districts who want a change," Candice acknowledged. "But with that many, some are bound to be from other parts of the country, or at least the state."

"Or the world!" Zoey raised her arms.

"Times must be tough," Mia muttered.

"I like all the different colors for the shirts," said Zoey. "Can I get one of each?"

Candice laughed. "Just like the parents. All they wanted to talk about was the uniforms."

"But I'm six," Zoey said.

"Exactly," Candice agreed. "I don't know what their excuse is."

"Did anyone ask how high we can wear our skirts?" Mia asked.

Candice was delighted with how bright her girls were, how observant, and how the evening was playing out.

"No," she said. "But you would think the parents of that girl in the group you were hanging out with might want to know."

Mia scoffed. "Brit? She's nothing. She'll obey when school starts. We were thinking of Kimmy Althouse."

"Who's Kimmy Althouse?" Candice asked.

"I played on a soccer team with her in fourth grade. You don't remember her?"

"It was a bunch of kids wearing the same jersey all chasing after the ball."

"She had a big mouth. Now she has big boobs, too."

Zoey giggled.

Candice scowled. "How do you know?"

"One of the girls showed us Kimmy's Instagram feed on her phone. It's like a thousand selfies with the same pose."

"And she's coming to Live Oak?"

"Yup."

"Why wasn't she there? Or her parents?"

Mia shrugged.

"How are they going to register?" Candice asked. "How will they know the rules?"

"I don't know, Mom. But our class isn't full, so Mr. Copeland probably isn't going to be turning anybody away."

"It isn't full?"

"Nope. The younger grades are, but not from, I think, fourth grade up. At least that's what some of the kids were saying."

Candice nodded and told herself it was still early, there was still time, that really busy and successful families often don't pay attention to local news items.

Zoey once again bellowed the word "life" in her slow foghorn voice, long enough for Mia to snap at her to stop. Candice asked Mia to be nice to her sister, but also let the word "stop" echo in her thoughts, and remind her to not project too much into the future.

Chapter Three: Rodrigo

He preferred "Rod".

And as far as he was concerned, the rich were just as guilty as the poor of not wanting to work hard.

For over a decade he had donated money to the private school his kids attended, and it was clear to him that the foundation board members wished his name wasn't on the checks. Both the elementary school and the high school campus were festooned with plaques and bricks commemorating anyone who had contributed so much as a dollar, and he was no exception. But he should have been.

His name was fastened to the rear end of the Ring of Honor, the part facing away from the high traffic area, the part occupying the side of the circular planter box that faced the empty lawn marked with a sign that read "Keep Off The Grass". He once did some research into the names engraved on each side of his. Neither had donated any money.

The name to his left owned a small concession supply company that kept the school snack bar stocked with trail mix at just above cost.

The name to his right had operated the rider mower for half the twentieth century.

Both worthy contributions, from Rod's point of view, but hardly comparable to the number of digits he had infused into the foundation budget during his children's tenure. And for all its venerability, the school had proven to be not so great after all, at least for Magdalena and Antonio.

Lena had maintained a GPA in the high 3.0 range right up until her senior year, but no private universities accepted her, and the only UC campus that took her in was UC Merced. It was as though having St. Bonnie's on her application was some sort of warning to the admissions boards, an academic biohazard decal. Then Lena validated the boards' stringency by flunking out of Merced by the end of her first quarter. Not that academic ability had much to do with it. She admitted to hardly attending any of her classes, much less study for them. She made frequent trips into San Francisco and claimed to be forging a modeling career. Rod and his wife, Rita, sensed some exaggeration of her prospects, but also thought it best to let her live a life of no regrets or resentment, so they supported her move to the city.

Meanwhile, Tony was having a hard time luring any scouts to his baseball games. St. Bonnie's was in a league of likewise small-pond schools, and there was no club team within a forty-five minute drive, so it was hard to gauge whether his statistics meant much. He was hoping to be a walk-on player for the team of whatever college accepted him. Rod and Rita therefore figured they were going to have to nurse two failed dreams in the near future, but at least baseball would keep Tony in school for a while. Hopefully long enough to finish, or close enough to where he only had to be a regular college student for a dozen units or less.

Then there was Arturo. If the charter school had not been approved, Rod still would have paid for Artie to attend St. Bonnie's. He didn't want to stigmatize him. But as their youngest grew closer to the high school phase of the St. Bonnie's experience, he appeared on his way to getting even less out of it than his older siblings. Artie was a bright kid of no discernable useful interests who came across as two years younger than he really was. He was as petite as his sister, as easily distracted as his brother, and shared their passion for attention.

Rod wasn't bothered much by the role that getting attention played in his children's aspirations. He was hardly in a position to criticize anyone for wanting accolades, much less those who treaded water with him in the same gene pool. What bothered him was that they wanted the attention to come so effortlessly: through looks for

Lena, athletic ability for Tony, and something yet to be determined for Artie. For even if Rod considered himself gifted in any way, he had disliked most of his time spent earning money. His working hours were a dim, sour dribble of memories.

Every job he held felt as though it had to be withstood, the office as much as the fields. The fields for more obvious reasons: heat, cold, mud, dust, snakes, spiders, flies, wasps, cramps, cuts, exhaustion, thirst, hunger, disrespect, disdain, and of course wages. But it did offer a kind of inspiration to move up and away from it that the office did not. The fields left no doubt that there was something better. The office made him wonder if that was all there was.

There was a clarity to his rise from laborer to foreman to manager to owner. The math was easy. So many hours led to a certain amount of money, a certain amount of effort led to an impression on management, an impressive amount of saving led to land of his own. The office was harder to quantify. It was recognizing cues and hitting marks with enough subtlety to win before anyone else knew they had lost. It was hard to know who was worth befriending. He had a formula in the fields: if someone tried to forget the job during off-hours by dousing their free time with alcohol, loud music, and bad jokes, he had no use for them. Rod did not want to forget where he worked. He used it as motivation.

He had yet to find a reliable white-collar equation. Professional relationships were developed as much during free time as they were during office hours. Blatant ambition was uncouth and aroused suspicion. The complexity of this more lucrative phase in life led to his interest in charity as a means to establish some purity, with St. Bonnie's as his primary beneficiary. In his more honest moments, he admitted to himself that his initial reasons for focusing on his kids' school had a lot to do with mixing in his money with the more established pot. But when his frustrations mounted and he got wind of the charter, he re-evaluated why schools appealed to him.

Rod saw them as more emblematic of the office jockeying that had been so challenging for him, which he perhaps could have started to understand as a child if his schooling hadn't been so spotty thanks to his family's perpetual movement, driven by the seasons and the farming cycles they dictated.

He also felt schools provided a filter that revealed which families were worthy of charity. Not so much at St. Bonnie's, whose students would have ample opportunities to fail if necessary before finding their place in life. But such distinctions would definitely emerge at the charter, which he knew would be populated by plenty of kids with a razor thin margin of error.

Other community institutions offered no such test. Parks struck him as watering holes for his old co-workers from the fields to drink beer at the picnic tables and exchange crude stories. Libraries, recreation centers, and playgrounds were dumping grounds for their kids to tumble and shriek under the beaten gaze of their wives. He didn't want to be associated with that. School was revelatory. If a kid could see the value in it and motivate themselves to make it through and rise above the dusty chaos, that was the kind of person he could get behind. There would be plenty who wouldn't cut it, of course, but Rod calculated that at least his money was funding an effective method of sorting them out, and not just paying for a miniature circus in one of the glorified tents scattered throughout the rest of the county.

Besides, his contributions had so much to do with the fun parts of campus. The state would pay for the personnel of the charter, while Rod would give them a place to work, and the students a place to play.

He had submitted the plans for the renovation before the charter board had found all of its members, so they would have the design ready to roll out as part of their lobbying efforts should the plans be approved. And they were approved rather quickly. First by the property owners, who were so pleased to have a bold new tenant who generated such good publicity that they practically waived the lease, then by the county Board of Supervisors, eager to fill one of the mounting number of empty buildings, especially along the frontage road so visible from the freeway.

Rod had explained the plans at many a meeting over the previous year, and was growing tired of hearing himself talk about it. So the first weekend of having all the volunteers on site ready to make it happen was just what he needed to revive his gusto. He toured the old dealership with the crew in tow, some of whom had no construction experience whatsoever, which inspired Rod even more.

He could tell by the vehicles. The bigger white pickup trucks, and they were all white, belonged to the professionals. The smaller pickups and SUVs, most of them white as well, were the dilettantes.

They were all white because white showed the dirt and made it look like someone was working hard, which came in handy when someone didn't feel like working. His first job in a field inspired this belief, as he was bossed around by a foreman who never got out of his truck, his white truck, except when the owner was around. The foreman would then use the dusty veneer of his hood to draw crude maps with his finger and do math problems in answer to the owner's questions, in order to send a not-so-subliminal message about his efforts. Rod thought of it as finger-painting with bullshit. The only task the foreman executed with any diligence was rinsing his truck at the end of every shift, so as to clean the slate for the next show.

He recalled that first foreman whenever he was able to attend one of Tony's baseball games. His son always looked for an excuse to slide headfirst early in the game, so that the front of his uniform would be dirty and everybody would therefore conclude he was hustling, and fail to notice when he decided not to run out a grounder or go hard after a ball hit in the gap. Rod kept waiting for someone to catch on, for a coach to bawl him out and claim the dirt on his jersey was performance art, but no one ever did. On the way home after a game, Rod finally called him on it, and Tony freely confessed. They laughed about it until Tony said he suspected a lot of people were onto him, but didn't dare say anything because they were hoping his father would include the baseball program in his campus largesse. Rod stopped laughing and told his son that was nonsense, but meanwhile swore to donate money to the team the day after Tony was once and for all scolded for lack of hustle.

That day never came.

Rod turned away from the dirty white pickup trucks and proceeded with the walkthrough he had dreamed about for months.

He led the volunteers along as though he should have his arms spread wide apart the whole time, perhaps a staff in one hand. At each stop he didn't just explain the future layout and purpose of the space in which they stood. He described a scene from the future.

"Imagine a room full of third graders in their bright-colored shirts," he said as they drifted around an empty sales office, having already told them the wall separating the office next door would be knocked out. "About six wearing yellow, six wearing blue, six green, and six red. The teacher has already covered the lesson, and now they're in breakout sessions, working in small groups as the teacher and a couple of parents work the room and offer them help, or encourage them to expand on an idea, or play along with their jokes before getting them back on track..."

"Imagine a crisp valley morning," he said as they gathered in the middle of the main showroom floor. "The sun shining through the big display window that now has the school logo etched onto it. The kids have put their backpacks and projects on the shelves in the old parts department, each kid has their own designated spot. They gather here for announcements and the Pledge of Allegiance. Dale comes out from his office on the second floor, up where old Webb

Townsend used to steer the ship when this baby was full of shiny new backhoes and rider mowers."

Rod paused and softly cackled. "They propped him up there even after his son took over. Remember? Let him look through the window and glare at everyone. I thought for sure he would die in that office."

"I'm glad he didn't," Dale shivered for effect. "Webb would make a very scary ghost."

The volunteers laughed.

Rod smiled at Dale and took his cue to get back on track.

"Dale, Mr. Copeland, calls a few of the kids up to the catwalk to acknowledge their achievements. They race up the steps and get their certificates, or trophies. But most of all they can see their classmates, they see all the colors. And they can see the teachers, the staff, and the parents who care about them. All these people who have their back, they're all right there in front of them, looking up at them…"

Rod stopped himself from getting too emotional by announcing that his favorite part was next, and then guided everyone over to the abandoned service area. He unlatched one of the garage doors and pulled the long oval chain that rolled it open until it reached the top with a metallic thud. He stood in the opening with his back toward the rising sunlight and let it shine around him.

"Imagine the kind of playground we used to play on," Rod announced to his squinting audience. "Not the kind at school, the kind you order from a catalogue, but the kind we created ourselves in vacant lots and the big backyards of those dads who liked to putter around and tinker with stuff. More of a constant project than a playground, where we used anything we could get our hands on to make our own structures and make up games, conduct experiments, challenge ourselves and each other. Inner tubes, tires, pieces of plywood, two-by-fours, boxes, crates, barrels, oil drums, old bicycle parts, that was our equipment. Those were the moving parts of an adventure that never looked the same for more than a day. Do your kids ever play those video games where they build a town, or create a ship or a vehicle of some sort?"

Many of the volunteers nodded.

"Well this will be the real deal. And here, look outside..."

He led them through the garage door and across the pavement to the edge of the lot.

"The property extends out into this meadow," he gestured across a field of brittle grass dappled with scrub brush and a dry creek running through it. "The kids will not only have a variety of materials to work with, they'll have a variety of space."

"So we're just going to let them run around in a meadow full of gopher holes and in a garage full of old junk?" Candice asked.

Dale spoke up from the back of the tour. "Adventure playgrounds are a concept that gained traction in England and then other parts of Europe. It's starting to spread through the states with great success."

"Sounds dangerous," she said.

"There's growing research that demonstrates we're over-protecting children," Dale moseyed around the edge of the group, working his way forward. "Allowing kids to have a sense that they're facing obstacles on their own and creating worlds of their own fosters problem solving and provides a healthy way for them to act out on their natural need to feel independent. When kids are watched so closely for so much of their lives, they're left with a weird combination of wanting independence more than ever, but being really terrible at knowing what to do with that freedom when they get it. We'll be sure to keep an eye on them, of course. But we'll try not to intervene unless someone is about to do some serious damage."

Most of the crowd responded with appreciative chuckles.

Candice shrugged. "You're the experts."

"But we're not the last word," Dale reached the front and stood next to Rod. "We'll try things, and if you as parents decide that a certain idea isn't working , then you have the power to make us get rid of it. This is a partnership."

Candice nodded, but apparently only to keep time while she considered whether to pursue the matter further.

Rod veered away from Dale's research and got promotional again before Candice could form another question.

"And there's other ways our kids can use their free time," he headed for the front of the building, beckoning the tour to follow him around the corner. "If your kid is more the quiet type, a little more laid back, we've got perpetual landscaping going on."

He had to speak a little more loudly upon reaching the main entrance, as the freeway just beyond the frontage road made its presence felt, with as many big rigs as cars roaring past.

"The Townsends kept the same landscape design pretty much since they opened the place," Rod bobbed his head in the direction of the standard grass-and-shrub layout that used to welcome customers. The grass was baked, but the shrubs had deep roots and enough shade against the building to survive the drought. "It's nice enough, all well and good, but nothing like what our kids can come up with. I've got deals with nurseries and seed distributors, and we'll divvy this plot into several different parcels and constantly reinvent them. You'll never know what to expect as the seasons roll on, but if you have a kid who's involved with this, one thing you can expect is that they'll end up being a master gardener."

"If your child is more *The Secret Garden* than *Lord of the Flies*," Dale added.

Rod didn't get the reference, but neither did many of the others. One of the contractors laughed politely.

"Stop pretending like you get it," his buddy chided him.

"Anyway..." Rod milked the awkward moment for a laugh of his own.

"See?" Dale surrendered. "If something doesn't work, we admit it."

His confession got the reaction he was initially hoping for.

Rod caught his eye and teased him with a broad swipe of his brow to signal a sense of relief, then signaled the start of the renovation.

"Let's do this!"

The cheers were throaty but for a moment, as it seemed to suddenly dawn on the non-professional help that they didn't know what to do.

Rod had already been working with the contractors who were involved, so they knew their jobs. Finding tasks for the rest of the volunteers was more complicated. He wanted them to come back, so he had to locate procedures that were neither too menial and boring nor too intricate and frustrating.

The first move was to wave the volunteer hours under their noses. He wrote down their names, and their children's names, and told them he would get the list to the parent who had volunteered to log everyone's hours. She had developed a system that involved everyone receiving an ID number, so Rod told them they would get their numbers the following weekend, and that they would be the first to officially bank some time. The volunteers were as pleased as he hoped they would be. Even Candice seemed to have moved past her skepticism over the playground and was back on board.

Rod asked each of them if there was a part of the tour that interested them. After they named their spot, he asked them what skills they had to offer, or if they couldn't think of any, asked them what they would be comfortable doing. He then matched their abilities with whatever was needed in that particular part of the property.

Once everyone had a place and a project, Rod managed to stay involved and keep moving. He delivered tools on request, braced beams, held boards, and brought lunch. He sensed when someone was getting tired or frustrated and talked to them for a while about their kids.

His strategies worked, at least for the laypeople, as attendance for the following weekends remained steady amongst them. It was the pros who started to fade, as the prison construction had fallen behind schedule and the firm started to offer weekend overtime pay. Some of the fathers had already fulfilled their contract to the prison, so not all of them were eligible, but Rod could feel the thinned out ranks in his muscles, which would finally heel by Wednesday after a weekend of labor that reminded him of his days in the fields.

The parts of him that weren't sore appreciated the reminder. Spending so much time at a desk, on a computer, in business casual suits, and behind the wheel of a company car often added a dash of guilt to his days. He was confident he had earned the right to soften up his schedule after all he had accomplished. He considered it back pay for all his previous work. But it never quite fit. When sitting in conferences rooms and scanning the other executives in attendance, it was obvious who had worn the white collar most of their lives, and who couldn't help but tug on theirs, trying to hide the blue one underneath. Sometimes he was the only one, and when he did spot a fellow climber, they were inevitably able to spot him back. They would dine or have a drink together after the meeting and wonder if the others could classify them as well as they could detect themselves.

So he embraced the tightness in his shoulders and forearms that weekends at the old dealership wrought, and grinned a little bit when his lower back seized up, knowing it was temporary, that when the renovation was over, he was not due back in the fields, that the wind and sun and rain would bounce off the windows he now worked behind.

He did hire some extra help when the modular buildings arrived. They could only squeeze four classrooms out of the old dealership, which would serve Kindergarten through third grade, so a portion of their state funds went into the modular rooms. They were well-preserved leftovers from the nearby Army base, and the only input Rod and Dale offered was to request that they form a right angle in the farthest corner of the pavement from the main building, creating a semi-courtyard for grades four through eight. Nobody associated with the charter had any experience hooking up such a unit, and even if Rod did, he would not have been interested. The main building was his baby, and he was a doting father.

Sometimes when a section was complete, when two sales offices had been converted into one classroom, or the rusty shelves in the parts department had been replaced and painted in bright colors, Rod would stand by himself in the middle of what had been done and admire the work, turning slowly, hands on hips. After this proud rotation, he would hold his ground and stare at nothing in particular, letting the satisfaction throb.

When the name of the school had been professionally engraved on the big showroom window, and he thought everyone had gone home, he stood in the middle of the main floor and watched the sunset shine through the letters and the logo, a silhouette of an oak tree that the engraver had reproduced beautifully.

Dale's voice startled him, but not enough to distract his gaze.

"Abby did a beautiful job on that window, didn't she?"

"Is that her name?" Rod said, keeping his eyes on the orange and purple glow rising from the hills that bordered the valley. "She kept calling herself 'Siena's Mom.'"

"We've got some talented parents."

Dale came up beside Rod and patted him on the back.

"We certainly do."

Rod returned the gesture.

Dale joined him in admiring the view for a moment.

"Final walkthrough tomorrow," Rod said out of appreciation rather than as a reminder.

"We'll nail it."

"They'll find some little things," Rod smiled. "But that's okay. We covered the big picture."

And as they proceeded through the inspection the next day, Rod barely paid attention to anything the inspector had to say. Dale was at the man's elbow taking notes, so Rod hung back and imagined the best places to mount a plaque with the name "Rodrigo Pluma" on it. Almost every wall seemed to suffice. Above any doorway would work, too. On the grounds outside, he pictured some of those short cement pillars with the slanted tops holding aloft his commemorations, one in the landscaping area, another at the threshold of the meadow.

He was able to camouflage his daydreaming with responsive nods when Dale would ask him if it was possible to address the latest announcement by the inspector, who seemed to point out issues for the sake of listening to his own voice. It wasn't until they reached the signpost in front of the building that the inspector asked a question that required more than a yes or no answer.

"Any plans for the sign?"

The inspector looked up the pole at the big John Deere logo with the Townsend name above it.

Dale and Rod looked up, too. Rod had some definite ideas, but couldn't remember if he had shared them with Dale.

"Rod?" Dale asked.

Apparently he had not shared them.

Dale and the inspector looked back down in Rod's direction, who kept his eyes on the sign.

Webb Townsend and his son had been big donors at St. Bonnie's. Their names were all over that campus, including the front part of the ring of honor, the part facing the center court of campus, where everyone walked.

"We're taking it down," said Rod, still facing skyward. "And keeping the pole."

He finally lowered his sights and looked at Dale and the inspector.

"I'd like to raise a flag."

"Good idea," the inspector nodded.

"Sure is," Dale grinned.

And when he took the sign down the following weekend, he would tell people that he was just excited about school starting when they asked him why he couldn't stop smiling. He made sure no contractors were part of the crew. He told them that weekend was for installing white boards and bulletin boards, for moving desks and furniture. He told them it would be a good weekend for some of the other parents to get in some volunteer hours.

He rented a cherry picker that he rode to the top of the sign before anyone could form a plan on how to take it down. Some of the parents finally realized this when the sign started to wobble and Rod braced it with both hands.

"Mr. Pluma!" one of them called up. "We don't have any ladders long enough to come help you!"

"And I don't think you can hold it long enough to get another cherry picker out here!" said another.

"Oh well," Rod played dumb. "I guess I'll just have to shove it off. Look out below!"

Once all the people at the bottom were out of his way, he pushed on the letter 's' in "Townsend" and sent the sign falling to the sidewalk. The steel frame screeched, the plastic casing shattered, the light bulbs inside exploded. Rod looked down at the small-scale destruction and thought it would be best to suppress his latest smile.

But the volunteers started to cheer, so he smiled more broadly than he had all day, since he could pretend it was in response to them.

He lowered himself to the continued ovation, and his smile ran out of room and became laughter.

Chapter Four: Mia

She was fascinated by Kimmy Althouse in the way some people chase tornadoes. Mia was determined to find an answer as to why Kimmy held so much sway over so many people, especially given that most of those people didn't even like the girl. She pledged neither fealty nor disdain for her. Kimmy was a field of study.

It was easy to assume that a large part of her subject's appeal lay in the novelty of her body, which had developed earlier than the rest, and once the other girls' figures caught up, there would be a shift in power. But there had to be more to it, Mia believed. The physical draw had such obvious limits, yet she seemed to have so little else to offer. Everything about her fell into blatant patterns. She wore the same high skirt no matter the weather, always showed up toward the end of morning announcements with a ten-inch tall travel mug she claimed was full of coffee, and forever posed for pictures by looking upwards at the camera with the same slight pout of artificial innocence. When she spoke, it was of conflict, constantly telling stories of spats with everyone from people at her old school to people who worked at Walmart. Every tale involved a moment in which she would bark "Fine!" at someone.

"So I just said 'Fine!' and walked away."

"And then I go, 'Fine, be a school secretary the rest of your life.'"

"I'm like, 'Fine, work at Walmart till the day you die.'"

"So I'm all 'Fine, Grandma! I'll be in my room.'"

"Fine...!"

"....Fine!"

"Fine!"

Her words and actions were so repetitious, so embodied by the bottomless collection of selfies she took, that she reminded Mia of how a word starts to sound weird if you say it over and over, how it seems to lose its meaning.

So she couldn't understand the strong emotions Kimmy inspired, particularly in those who clung to her. Perhaps they hated themselves for caring.

As appeared to be the case with the girl in front of Mia during morning announcements on around the twenty-fifth morning. They stood in their line of fellow sixth graders, minus Kimmy, who was due to sashay in around the middle of the Pledge of Allegiance. They listened to Mr. Copeland speak from above. It was Tuesday, which meant it was Great Trait Tuesday, and the Great Trait for that Tuesday was "Compassion." He asked if anyone could define it. In the line next to them, a fifth grader who looked like a miniature middle-aged man formulated a close enough answer, stating it was "Like when you see a lost dog and you feel bad for it. Or a person." Mr. Copeland called him up to give him a prize, a coupon for free tacos at Jack in the Box, and as a mixture of polite applause and embellished yelping echoed through the showroom and accompanied the modest boy's journey up the stairs, the girl in front of Mia started to stare over her shoulder into the space behind them where Kimmy would fall in at any moment.

The girl's name was Corinne, and her wide open features would have been very expressive had she anything to express. She looked back constantly, with no particular face, until Mia could tell Kimmy had entered. Corinne then scowled and turned around. She wore her hair a little shorter than Kimmy's and her skirt a little longer, and as she faced forward, replaced her frequent glances backwards with frequent checks that her hair and skirt were in place.

Mr. Copeland finished his further explanation of compassion as Mia heard Kimmy slurp on her travel mug.

"What's he talking about?" Kimmy asked Mia, barely bothering to keep her voice down.

"Great Trait Tuesday," Mia turned her head just enough for Kimmy to hear her quiet reply.

"That's a thing?"

"Every Tuesday."

"Never heard of it," she sipped.

"Why would you? You're never here on time."

Mr. Copeland asked the prize winner to lead the class in the Pledge of Allegiance. Kimmy snorted.

"I made it for the Pledge this time."

Mia kept looking ahead and saw Corinne shoot a rueful glance backwards. Kimmy picked up on it.

"Keep your eyes on the flag, Corinne."

"Fine!" Corinne scowled as they all turned to look out the showroom window at the flag flying from the top of the pole planted in front of the school.

Mia stifled a giggle throughout the Pledge of Allegiance. Disguising her laughter was easy while she could submerge it into the words and pass off her smile as love of country, but when the Pledge was over, and each grade waited their turn to walk in a line to their classroom, she was exposed.

"Something funny?" Kimmy asked with more insecurity than Mia was accustomed to hearing from her.

Mia leaned closer to Kimmy to keep Corinne from hearing her. "Corinne does a good imitation of you."

"It takes more than a skirt and a hairstyle," Kimmy scoffed.

Mia started to laugh again. She was about to explain what she meant, but their line was about to move, so she didn't bother. Kimmy shrugged and invoked her second most commonly-used word: "Whatever."

Which further goosed Mia's giggling, but she was once again able to conceal it, this time thanks to the movement of the line. They walked single file, behind the fifth graders and in front of the seventh graders, out of the main building to the 'upper cluster', as they had taken to calling the ninety-degree angle of modular rooms. By the time her class climbed the ramp up to their door, Mia was sufficiently settled down.

So far the only thing that seemed to differentiate the charter from her old school was that Mr. Benton, their teacher, was awesome. The subjects were the same, and he didn't seem to use any revolutionary methods, other than a sense of humor and energy. Mia had heard the other teachers and the parents call him by his first name, Isaiah, which struck her as fitting, as it sounded like the name of a wise person.

They were only on the cusp of their second month, and their room was already filled with original works of art and sample projects from the students. Not a single item hanging on the walls or from the ceiling was printed by a textbook company. The historical timeline spanning the great ancient civilizations was captioned and illustrated by the class, as was the checklist on when to use a period or a comma, the multiplication table, the periodic table, and quotes from Shakespeare. They had yet to fully study all of these subjects, but Mr. Benton organized the room décor project to establish what they would be covering during the first half of the year.

He was also very good when dealing with disruptive students: patient, but not with the contrived calm that Mia noticed in so many adults. He let them know they were being obnoxious by asking them sincere questions about what they were doing or talking about. Asking questions was the main way he communicated. Someone would ask what they were supposed to be doing on an assignment, and he would ask what they thought they were supposed to be doing, and let them know if they were on the right track.

"But I really have no idea," said Artie when Mr. Benton employed this tactic as everyone was finalizing their proposals for their Major Projects, a long-term assignment that was supposed to take them at least a few months to work on.

"You have some idea, Arturo."

"Artie."

"Until you give it a shot, I'm calling you Arturo."

The class laughed and Artie talked over them.

"I guess what I mean is I don't know what to put for the part that says 'date of completion'. Mine never ends."

"Yeah," cracked Josh, the closest thing the boys had to a male version of Kimmy, "because your parents never stop buying you Legos."

"Oh, like you're so poor," Artie snapped back.

"All right," Mr. Benton drifted into the middle of the room to obstruct their view of each other, "you've each taken a shot. Let's move on. Artie, what's another way of saying 'never ending'?"

"Ongoing," chimed in Delilah, whose disheveled appearance went well with her nebulous sense of boundaries.

"Artie..." Mr. Benton reminded her without looking her way.

"Ongoing," repeated Artie, earning some giggles.

"Have you considered 'ongoing'?" Mr. Benton played along and heightened the laughter, then told everyone to change the question to 'date of presentation' rather than 'date of completion', as it dawned on him that Artie's may not be an isolated case, which turned out to be true upon polling the class.

Mr. Benton's willingness to acknowledge his mistakes was another point in his favor. He actually seemed to enjoy being corrected by students. Mia suspected some of his errors were by design, to assess their awareness and reward them if they were indeed being attentive.

Artie's project not only lacked a definitive end, but had started years before. He starred in his own web series, in which he would take a Lego set designed for a specific outcome, like a Star Wars Imperial Destroyer or a Hobbit dwelling, and demonstrate alternative creations with the defined parts. Each episode had hundreds of thousands of hits, and his channel had almost three thousand subscribers. Some thought it was unfair that he could use his online videos for his Major Project, that he should have to propose something new, but he claimed each episode was in fact new, and that he also planned on adding some special effects to liven up the parts where he was connecting the pieces. There was also the fact that his father built the school. That slant went unspoken, but it hovered over anything that involved Artie.

His mother had helped him start production on his videos when he was eight years old, and when Mia watched some episodes after hearing about them the first week of school, she was struck by how little difference there was between second grade Artie and the sixth grade version. His voice had hardly changed, he was only slightly bigger, and his spastic energy was exactly the same. He acted young for his age when he was eight, and the meter had not risen much from its arrested position since.

During recess, Artie acted as though he didn't mind being the butt of jokes. He appreciated the attention, and played up whatever awkward mannerism he was being teased over. When Josh, or one of the boys who attached themselves to Josh like lampreys, would laugh at the way Artie was running, Artie would tuck his elbows into his sides and swing his forearms like a flailing Tyrannosaurus Rex while kicking his legs out behind him as though on a treadmill that was set way too fast for him. Artie was always the first one willing to subject himself to the riskiest ventures on the adventure playground. He would crawl into the center of a tractor tire or empty oil drum and let others roll it along until either he fell out, it fell over, or it ran into the scrub brush upon reaching the meadow. Some eight graders liked to put him in the shopping cart and push him over the dirt grades they had developed in the meadow, and the wooden jumps they had made in the garage. And when he seemed to be injured, all it took to cover up the incident was for a student to mock his grimacing and Artie would pretend to cry like a cartoon baby and throw a fit.

Initially there were plenty of kids ready to jump in and oblige Artie's willingness to make fun of himself. But by the end of the first month, their interest paled. They seemed to conclude that if they couldn't break him, then it wasn't worth teasing him. He wasn't the kind of victim that could sustain their practice.

So their spotlight searched for someone else, and Artie tried a broad variety of acts to convince them to train it back on him. He had to try to engage them rather than respond, since they no longer initiated. He came across like a desperate street performer at recess, turning the playground equipment into props for his slapstick routines, darting from one area to another in a frantic hunt for a sympathetic audience. His attempts started to work their way into the classroom and assemblies, which led to him spending more time in the office, and being put on work duty at recess and lunch.

He was supposed to pick up garbage and sweep, but there was little supervision to make sure he followed through. The dust bin became his shield, while the broom became his lance, or his guitar, or his horse, or a Godzilla-like phallus. The call for yard duties had gone mostly unanswered. The rare parents who did volunteer for yard duty hovered near their child and their child's friends, and not simply because they were overprotective, from what Mia could tell. What really drove them to stalk their own was the number of problem children who wound up at the charter academy, for whom LOCA was their latest and possibly last landing spot, having bounced around the rest of the district creating piles of paperwork based on stories that grew more alarming with each whispered revision.

The yard duties were from the go-getter group, while most of the kids who disturbed the duties were products of those mysterious households from which family members would only surface when they had no choice, when their child was getting suspended or expelled. The volunteers seemed content to let all situations reach that extreme, to let everything become an administrative matter, so great was their discomfort at intervening on the ground level.

"Live Oak Reform School," Mia's Mom would mutter after helping out with recess. She was actually pretty good about not lingering near Mia or Zoey, and not being afraid to mix it up with the wild bunches. But she was a bit overzealous in pursuing them, at least when it came to the younger grades. Just like all the other volunteers, she was intimidated by the hard cases who were older, from about fifth grade upward.

"If they would just train us," she would further mutter after lunch service as she checked in with Mia before going back to work. "Give us some direction, some tips on how to deal with these gypsies."

There didn't seem to be any average students at the charter. They were either children whose parents felt as though they weren't being challenged at their previous school, or children who were a challenge. And unlike the parents, the children themselves mixed together pretty well.

The first friend Mia made, Beatrice, by her own admission should have flunked just about every previous grade due to all the time she missed, but was bright and funny enough to charm her way into passing as each year drew to a close.

Now that Beatrice was older, her Mom was able to hold a steady enough job to separate from the father, an itinerant worker who had dragged them all over the state. Beatrice's Mom worked at the shipping warehouse for an online retailer which had opened four years earlier on some foreclosed farmland. It was a massive building that the company wanted people to call a "realization station". Mia was always curious about it and was glad to finally meet someone who had seen the inside. Beatrice would ride her bike out to it after school and do her homework in the break room while waiting for her Mom's shift to end, since they rented a room in a house occupied by a family who expected Beatrice to help babysit their children when she was around. She doused Mia's vision of the "realization station" as being like a giant Toys R Us or Willy Wonka's factory. Beatrice described it as the world's largest messy closet, filled with stacks of hodgepodge, a fluorescent catacomb of whatever, being picked at by robotic arms and placed on conveyer belts that passed by the humans who were there to put it all in boxes.

"For now," Beatrice joked. "I'm sure they'll find a way to get rid of the rest of the people. I told Mom she should learn robot repair if she wants to keep working there."

She and Mia often didn't look at one another when they spoke at school. They would sit on the table of a picnic bench on the perimeter of the upper cluster and watch the play unfold in front of them while they conversed. Mia set her sights on Kimmy holding court with the hoi polloi. Beatrice apparently did, too.

"Speaking of robots," she said. "How does Kimmy do it?"

"Speaking of random piles of stuff," Mia said. "I'll give her one thing: she doesn't discriminate. If you adore her, you're in."

Beatrice exhaled a quick laugh.

"Sometimes I think my little sister Zoey might end up being like Kimmy," Mia continued. "Hopefully a nicer one."

"There's no doubt she'll be nicer," Beatrice assured her. "How could anyone be less nice?"

"That would be a good test," Mia said, still looking over at Kimmy's circle as she assumed Beatrice still was. "Like a personality test."

"Yeah," Beatrice agreed. "Like one of those signs at an amusement park that says you have to be this tall to ride. If you are less nice than Kimmy, you can't be a member of society."

"Please report to the nearest mental hospital."

They laughed at their own material, loud enough for someone in Kimmy's world to notice. It was Corinne, whose eyes flared.

"Uh oh," Beatrice saw it too.

"Funny," Mia said. "I though they didn't like each other."

"I'm not sure any of them really like each other."

"True."

Corinne directed Kimmy's attention their way, but the great leader appeared unperturbed.

"I'll bet I know what Kimmy said," Beatrice narrated.

"Whatever," Mia said.

"Fine!" Beatrice added.

They laughed again. This time Kimmy looked pissed at them.

Any trepidation on their part was interrupted by Artie banging together two metal garbage can lids like cymbals behind them.

"Dammit, Artie!" Beatrice glared back at him from around her slumped shoulders.

Even Mia felt like cursing at him, and she usually felt sorry for Artie.

"Shouldn't you be picking up garbage instead of playing with the cans?" Mia said instead.

Artie shrugged. "Like anyone checks."

"Maybe we'll tell on you," Beatrice said.

"Seriously?" he asked.

"Of course not," she sighed. "They're all inside the garage and I don't feel like walking over there."

"Poor women," Mia said. "They're scared to death of us. My Mom's probably in there trying to rally them to come outside and do a sweep, like a yard duty SWAT team."

Artie didn't seem to hear them, which was surprising since he liked to be included in anything, even a conversation. He looked past them with more fear than neediness, and it was usually the other way around.

Mia and Beatrice turned to see Kimmy leading a leisurely charge toward their picnic table.

"Hey Artie," she called out as she entered their space. "Is your dick as small as the rest of you?"

She came to a stop and her team reared up behind her, giggling like whinnying horses.

Mia had seen Artie gape at Kimmy in class, and was outraged that she should be so cruel to someone who appeared to truly like her.

"At least he does things," Mia heard herself say before she could form the words the way she would have preferred. She tried again as everyone reprogrammed their expectations for the encounter.

"He has talent," Mia annunciated. "What is it that you do, Kimmy?"

"Well I don't act like a retard."

"I'm not so sure," Mia said. "I've read your posts that go along with your selfies."

She got a laugh and was inspired to expand on her point: "I'm bored", "I want frozen yogurt", "I'm tired", "I want Starbucks".

The laughter bloomed larger. Kimmy stared at Mia, who was planning to grab one of Artie's garbage can lids should Kimmy strike.

"Something's gonna happen," Kimmy finally said. "It's just not gonna happen now."

Mia found that comforting. She relaxed and almost smiled, but decided not to push her luck. Kimmy read Mia's instincts. Rather than seethe even hotter, however, Kimmy studied Mia as though through a pair of binoculars. When one of the yard duties ventured from the garage and blew her whistle to signal it was time to line up, it actually rescued Kimmy more than Mia.

When Kimmy's pawns went to line up in front of the classroom, she hung back a ways and lined up just ahead of Mia.

"I've got your back," Beatrice murmured, who was indeed right behind Mia.

Kimmy, meanwhile, leaned against the wall and rolled her head in Mia's direction.

"You really don't give a shit, do you?" Kimmy asked.

Mia pretended to think about it for a moment before shaking her head.

Kimmy contemplated the situation while Mr. Benton opened the door and let them in.

As they walked up the ramp, Mia and Beatrice exchanged looks that were as marked by confusion as Kimmy's had been.

Between looking away from Beatrice and entering the room, Mia noticed her Mom had been the one who blew the whistle. Mia nodded at her. Her Mom nodded back, but very absent-mindedly, apparently more interested in who surrounded her daughter in line.

Chapter Five: Dale

In his promotional speeches, he often vowed to spend very little time in his office, and that vow proved easy to uphold. Dale liked to visit the classrooms and walk the grounds, but most of all he loved to mingle with the parents as they picked up their kids after school. It reminded him of the pitch meetings he had grown so accustomed to. He had come to know many of the parents quite well leading up to the opening, and appreciated the chance to maintain the relationships. They were trying some unique strategies, some that might inspire griping amongst the kids, so he figured cultivating the parents' goodwill would buy him some leverage in letting the experiments proceed. The more parents taking his side at the dinner table when the kids complained, the better.

Most of the parents picked up their kids, or were part of a carpool, out of concern over how fast the traffic moved on the frontage road. The small parking lot in front of the building would fill quickly, and the overflow would park parallel for a quarter mile in each direction on the road that was separated from the freeway by a chain link fence.

There were soldiers who came from the base in uniform, one of them a woman, another who walked with a cane; there were parents who were barely old enough to vote, who could be confused for an older brother or sister of the child they were picking up; there were some who looked quite a bit older than they really were, who had been students in Dale's classes when he taught Independent Studies at the continuation high school, before he had taken over the Special Education program; there were women who spoke no English, pushing strollers along the frontage road for what must have been great distances, as there were no homes in the immediate area; there were men in mesh baseball caps and cowboy hats who had been baked in the sun so long it looked as though a knife or needle could not penetrate their skin, women in yoga pants and shiny sweat jackets with their hair pulled back tight enough to give them a makeshift facelift, heavy grandparents who seemed dazed to have to do this again; there were dusty passenger vans with windows smudged by fingerprints and dog noses, luxury cars, and the ubiquitous dirty white pickup trucks with tool boxes and tool racks; there was a father who rode a homemade motorized scooter with a wooden platform big enough for both him and his son. Dale would joke with him that his balancing act reminded him of his own.

Each adult required a tone all their own, and navigating through them was a series of adjustments. As it was with the kids, too, he believed. The motto of the school was "Each Child, Every Day". But working the lot at pick-up time meant seconds, maybe minutes, with each adult. Each child meant hours a day. For all of his spinning about learning styles and tailored lesson plans, Dale was beginning to think it may just come down to the teacher. The classrooms he enjoyed visiting were the ones managed by teachers who seemed like they could start a cult if they were so inclined. And having been in session for a matter of months, it appeared as though he really only had two such teachers, maybe a third on her good days.

He would stop by Shirley Ojeda's Kindergarten class first thing after announcements for a dose of inspiration, then head up to his office to take care of some business before resuming his daily morning teacher tour. He liked to conclude with a dose of Isaiah Benton's sixth grade class.

If there was a rainbow over the storms that blew through his visitations of the other classes, it was the proof they offered of how helpful programs could be in a curriculum. How else would these people be able to teach anything absent talent? They had interviewed so well.

He had the power to fire them at will thanks to the lack of a union in the charter. But where would he find another Shirley and

Isiah? He had stumbled into them. They almost didn't hire Shirley. It was down to her and someone else, and the board deliberated for so long that he started to steer them in her direction simply because he wanted to get home in time for dinner. The runner-up was immediately hired by another school. He had looked her up as soon as he realized some of the Live Oak hires weren't working out as hoped, so the pool was already a little more shallow.

So as he watched Alicia Unser try to pander her way into the approval of her seventh graders, or Delilah Pico slowly go insane in the jungle being cultivated by her first graders, he started to dream of devising a fool-proof method. He realized that even a pristine program needed a competent delivery system, but if he could just get close to something resembling a useful set of hoops for students to jump through that his faculty merely had to hold up, his opinions would be in demand and his consultation fees would reflect it.

He was convinced the answer was tied to technology, but in a way that didn't give people the impression they were members of an endangered species. He imagined poor Delilah being able to check on her students rather than hide from them in plain sight inside her catatonic shell, Alicia tailoring her jokey flattery to each student at their work station as she visited them to see if they had any questions. And those who had the charisma to hold the room could still do so, could use a student's question to call everyone's attention up front and moderate a discussion.

Wiring the classrooms would cost more money than they could procure from the state with even the most eloquent grant proposal. There weren't enough fund-raising miles that the kids could run, enough proof-of-purchase seals that the families could save, nor votes in the valley to win one of those online contests that rewarded schools for rallying the clicks necessary to be photographed receiving a check from the sponsor.

Dale had traveled with Rod to a couple of conferences already, since they had plenty to say about the opening of a charter. Not that Dale had participated in much of the early work, but those who had been part of the initial push either weren't as comfortable presenting their product to a crowd, or had grown tired of doing so. Dale still had the energy for it, and had become the face of school besides. Even if there were moments when he couldn't quite bring himself to unfurl his mock Declaration of Independence, or other times he had to strain a little to lift up the same old aphorisms about 'building for the future', he ultimately found it refreshing. Being on stage reminded him of how much fun it was to build the school and to promote it, how much more fun it was to campaign for the school than to actually run it.

The first conference had been driving distance. For the two hours each way in Rod's car, Dale never spoke of the school, and mainly asked Rod about himself, which had the effect Dale hoped it would. For when they started to plan for the next conference, Rod suggested they take his company plane.

Attendees referred to themselves as being part of a movement, usually with the word 'choice' attached to the name. Academics seemed to regard 'Choice' and 'Movement' as euphemisms for 'Freedom' and 'Revolution'.

"That's a fair assessment," said a man made of dandruff with whom Dale felt comfortable enough to share his hypothesis. "Those words have been commandeered by right-wing media and interest groups. We want school choice to sound rational, not unhinged."

"But we're talking about schools," Dale gestured with his aluminum bottle of Bud Light. He wasn't much of a drinker, but his presentation had gone over well, and there was a big plastic punch bowl of ice filled with them. "We're not talking about guns or taxes."

"Yes, and next thing you know, we're attracting those types and being lumped together with them."

"We already are," Dale chuckled. "At least where I come from."

The man laughed and seemed to think about his laughter at the same time. "Well, I guess if you built a school out of a tractor shop, I shouldn't be surprised."

Dale grinned and took a swig from the aluminum bottle. He looked around the banquet room at the other conversations taking place. A portion of the people were clearly talking about him. He pretended not to notice, which he had done before out of modesty, but this time his nonchalance was charged with panic. Maybe their project was becoming a running joke, and people were approaching him on a dare from friends.

The man had asked Dale a question, but Dale was too busy scanning the room for Rod.

"I'm sorry," Dale said. "What was that?"

"I said have you had any problems with them?"

"Problems with whom?"

"The fringe," said the pillar of dry skin. "Any protests about what's being taught? Evolution? The more sordid bits of our history?"

"No," Dale spotted Rod in a circle of men who looked more like sales reps than academics. "But it's still early, I suppose."

He patted the man on the arm and excused himself.

On his way over to Rod's group, an assortment of people leaned his way and congratulated him on the presentation, which started to revive his confidence. They wouldn't seek him out just to be condescending, after all. They would ignore him. So the spasm of worry dissolved and his breathing filled him with ease.

He prepared to do some networking as he drew closer to the shiny gathering that surrounded Rod. Just before he made it there, however, Rod caught his eye and halted him with a quick head shake.

Dale altered his course but didn't know what to do once he had taken steps in a new direction. He jiggled his beer and acted like he needed another, and by the time he reached the long folding table with the bowl of aluminum bottles on ice, he really did feel like a fresh one.

He opened it and turned to face the room. Rod's group was hidden from his field of vision for the most part. Only one of its members was visible through the mingling. Dale took a sip to help settle down, but instead the cold bubbles filled him with static, as though he was between stations on a radio dial, and the next clear moment would involve him doing something stupid. He took one more sip just to confirm how anxious it made him feel, and left the room to duck into the first breakout session he could find so as to avoid any more conversation.

The room he crashed was hosting a presentation that was winding down. The woman up front was asking the measly crowd to fill out their feedback cards. Dale skulked to an empty chair in the back row and nodded at people along the way, mumbling that he was arriving early for the next session.

They were all gone within ten minutes and Dale had the room to himself. The doors remained open, so he could hear the cacophony from the corridors and the main banquet room. He sat there chiding himself for being so naïve.

A woman with a very small head came in and asked if the "Choosing School Choice" session was scheduled in the room, and Dale said he thought so. She appeared to doubt his answer and left to double check. After another minute of silent self-admonishment, Dale sensed someone coming back in the room, and assumed it was the cautious woman.

It was Rod.

"Here you are," he said.

"Just waiting for the 'Choosing School Choice' session," Dale tried to rally. "I hear they really bring it."

"Sorry about that back there."

"That's okay," Dale said without conviction.

"No, it's not…"

"I should know my role by now."

"But those guys," Rod continued. "They get a little uneasy around the academic types. They're business folk, and they feel like the teachers don't like them. Like they make fun of them behind their backs."

"And do they like the teachers very much?"

Rod paused. "They appreciate them. And they don't feel like it goes both ways."

"Who are *they*, anyway? These business folk?"

"Tech industry."

Dale shifted in his chair. Rod proceeded into a more detailed account.

"Our company uses their products. Mostly software. They throw in some hardware to run it on, some cheap knock-off crap from a supplier they hold hostage. But their work is great. I only recognized one of the guys, from this seminar we had at the headquarters last year when we contracted with them, and he introduced me to the rest."

"What are they doing here?"

"What do you think they're doing here?" Rod smiled.

Dale leaned back and smiled too, but once again was seized by doubt.

"I don't imagine we're a big enough fish."

He slumped a little and wondered why this pesky inability to ward off reality had suddenly become such an issue.

"Don't think of us as a fish," Rod came to his rescue. "Think of us as bait."

Dale stared in Rod's direction without really looking at him. He was already formulating a pitch, but wanted to keep Rod in sight for when he expanded on the plan.

"They have an extra room at their hotel," Rod obliged. "The Biltmore. I'm going to stay there tonight and play some golf with them in the morning. I'm terrible at golf, so they'll kick my ass and feel really good about themselves. By mid-afternoon I should have them ready for you."

Dale stood up and felt like giving Rod a hug, but contained himself by extending his hand.

"I'll be ready."

"Remember," Rod pulled Dale a bit closer to him. "Don't act too much like a teacher."

They shared a laugh, bid goodbyes until the next day, and as Rod left him in the empty room, Dale thought more about the half-serious reminder to refrain from acting like a teacher.

"Not a problem," he half-joked aloud.

He prowled through the conference for the remainder of the day and the following morning on the hunt for specifics to apply to his ideas for the fool-proof classroom. He sat in on any session with a title that blended the words Classroom, Technology, and Future into some sort of smoothie. He jotted down jargon that caught his ear, copied floor plans that presenters had hastily drawn on white boards as they realized their powers of verbal description weren't as good as they imagined they would be once they found themselves in front of a crowd, and lurked after meetings to ask pointed questions about elusive points.

Dale was energized both by his impending meeting with the investors, and by how rapidly people seemed to be forgetting his presentation from the opening morning. Their charter had definitely achieved something unique in the construction of the school, but it wasn't a process that could be emulated. It amounted to a fun story, and his colleagues in the movement needed something they could use.

Part of the challenge was finding a way to borrow ideas rather than steal them, to combine parts of what he was observing into a copyrightable whole. The notion that technology is only as good as the teacher using it haunted him through the banquet rooms and buffet lines, but Rod's golf buddies wouldn't worry about that. Their job was to promote their products, not question them. All Dale had to do was get those classrooms wired, and then he could work out the kinks in his ideas with the help of his teachers. Not just the gifted ones like Isaiah and Shirley, but the albatrosses as well, since they would have keen interest in anything that would allow them to pull a string rather than have to supply a voice.

The fun construction story that he had brandished did come in handy at the lounge just off the lobby and at the breakfast bar. Comforted by the knowledge that he was moving past the story, and would not be defined by it, he enjoyed fielding boozy requests to expand on his adventures in tractor dealership conversion. And though he had never been confident in his ability to recognize flirting, even before marriage took him out of the dating scene thirty years earlier, he got the impression that more than one of the requests was of that timbre.

Dale enjoyed the feeling without being the least bit tempted. He had heard from multiple sources that one of the reasons people stray is thanks to their love of the pursuit, and their dissatisfaction with the protocols of a relationship. Even if he wasn't satisfied with Alma, or wasn't worried about upsetting a family that provided him with so much purpose, he still wouldn't be interested in any of the implied offers. He already had a pursuit he loved, a professional one.

And while he felt a little bit like he was about to sing for his supper on his way to the Biltmore Hotel upon receiving the call from Rod, he thought about his family, the people in his life who brought him permanence, and how his love of the chase was in their name.

Chapter Six: Candice

The Word of the Day was "responsibility", or the Tuesday Trait, or the Weekly Waltz, or whatever Dale called it. Candice was weary of all the catch phrases that Copeland threw around. Everything he said and did came across as a living rough draft of a book he was writing on running a charter school. She didn't even like to call him by his first name anymore. She did when she spoke to him, because he insisted. Whenever she addressed him as Mr. Copeland, he would interrupt her with a "Call me Dale", which was of course intended as homespun charm, but really just interfered with her memorization of how she wanted to recite her thoughts. And articulation was important to her, because she had concerns that she wanted to air in measured fashion, which wasn't easy given her distress. She always complied with his request, because she didn't want to get sidetracked by an argument about formalities, but in her mind she just thought of him as "Copeland" at this point, without the "Mr." in front, much less the "Dale".

Copeland had Artie Pluma up there with him on the catwalk to talk about "responsibility" to the students gathered below, which presented a great opportunity for some winking comedy directed at the teachers and parent volunteers standing around the perimeter of the gathering, but he was utterly sincere in using Artie as an example. Even Artie seemed aware of the irony. When Copeland put a hand on Artie's shoulder and asked him who was responsible for maintaining the quality of his online video series, Artie answered "My Mom", which inspired a burst of laughter from all corners of the showroom.

Even Candice chuckled a bit, at least until Artie started to admire his little feat a little too much. She was well-acquainted with that self-congratulatory grin, and it induced brief nausea whenever she saw it. Artie never owned up to anything he did, and with every denial came that grin. He thought that acting innocent was cute.

The other disturbing children took responsibility for their actions. In fact, they seemed to take pride in what they did. Their disruptions and disrespect functioned as misguided kill marks on the sides of their doomed fighter planes. They compared notes, shared their exploits, tried to outdo one another in being the biggest nuisance. But Artie was an island of irritation. He went his own way, pretending he was somehow different from the rest of the lineup.

Copeland's approach to discipline only augmented Artie's perception. While his fellow troublemakers spent hours in the office or days on suspension, Artie never served any time beyond being benched at recess or being assigned clean-up duty that left everything dirtier afterwards. The first several times Candice approached Copeland about the Artie Rules, he would look serious but then pass her a mindless hiccup about boys being boys or Artie being starved for attention from a very busy father. And when Copeland seemed to sense that his stiff arming was growing limp, he told Candice that maybe it was time to take a different approach with Artie, to make him feel included rather than shunned.

So Copeland started to invite Artie up to his perch at least one morning per week, put his hands on his shoulders, and make sure the grinning little meal ticket felt wanted. Candice had grown fed up enough to feel bold about calling out Copeland on his protectionism, but she never bothered because she already knew how he would respond. He would drop a version of the school motto at her feet, improvise a mishmash of "every child is different."

She looked around the room at some of the other faculty and parent volunteers as Copeland once more thrust Artie into the spotlight. None of the faculty revealed any disgust, as their jobs depended on pretending not to notice the swelling double standard, but a trace of the parents were clearly rubbed in the same wrong way as she was. But not enough, or at least enough who were willing to show it.

She wished she had greater numbers to back her up, and had felt that way from the second day of school.

The first day was as inspiring as the months leading up to the grand opening. Every parent must have been there. The campus was a festival. Unfortunately, they were only there to take pictures and videos of their kids. By day two, they were down to Candice and a handful of others who mainly seemed to show up for lack of anything better to do. The rickety crew asked Copeland to remind the Live Oak families of their volunteering obligations, and he complied with their request practically every week, but still the hours lagged.

The younger grades represented well, at least when it came to clerical work and assisting in the classrooms, because the classes were full and the school had some leverage over them by claiming they could be replaced with someone on the wait list. But the older grades had space available, and were half-filled with kids whose families had always been unconscious when it came to threats or cajoling, with no sign of adapting to a new environment. Meanwhile, the same financial constraints that prevented the board from hiring any full-time yard duties also make them reluctant to take any action when it came to the more challenging students. They needed the bodies. If enrollment dipped below a certain point, a magic number that the board kept to themselves, the contract with the district would be voided.

So in addition to the kids who celebrated their offenses, Candice had to keep an eye on the likes of Xavier, who neither rejoiced nor wailed over what he did, who instead remained expressionless during his deeds and the ensuing reprimand.

"Can you even hear me?" Candice finally asked Xavier as she stood between him and a large girl named Viv, who was still sniffling and snorting from the fight between them that Candice had just broken up in the meadow with help from some nearby students.

She had started to break it up herself. They may have been the two biggest kids in fifth grade, but they were still kids, and Candice stood a head taller than either of them. Grabbing someone else's children gave her a jolt of the willies, though, and reflexive thoughts of accusations and lawsuits, so she played meek and asked for help, which plenty of kids were eager to provide.

Xavier avoided eye contact with Candice and everyone else, finding an unoccupied spot just above the circle of curious faces that surrounded them.

"Hello?" she followed up. "Do you hear me, Xavier?"

The encircled students joined her. A chorus of 'Hello?' and 'Xavier?' and 'Are you in there?' gained volume, along with some giggling and improvised scary movie themes. She waved them off and asked Viv if she was okay. Viv nodded and looked hard at Xavier, wanting to glare at him and show him she was bent on revenge. But he held his gaze outward, without the slightest sense that anything was happening inward.

"Who made the first move?" Candice asked Viv.

A smattering of students chimed in with "He did" before Viv confirmed their accusations.

"Come with me, please, Xavier," Candice gestured, not wanting to touch him.

He complied, as usual. It was never clear what would set him off, but his response after the chaos had settled was always reliable.

They broke through the circle and walked over to the gaping entries of the garage, then up the stairs to Copeland's office.

The office administrator, Wendy, greeted them with a sigh.

Candice liked Wendy. She got the impression that Wendy was as disappointed as she was with how LOCA was turning out, perhaps even more so, since she had given up a fully vested position in the district based on friendship and trust in Dale.

"Hello, Xavier," she said as though speaking to someone who is hard of hearing.

He nodded at her, which was more than Candice had managed to wring out of him.

"What happened this time?" Wendy asked.

Xavier decided against communicating anything beyond the previous nod.

"He got into a fight with a girl," Candice chimed in.

"A girl?" Wendy was incredulous.

Xavier glared at Candice.

"Well..." Candice saw his point. "It was Viv."

"Ah..." Wendy understood.

Xavier walked over to the chair next to the door with the 'Mr. Copeland' nameplate.

"Thank you, sweetie," Wendy said to him. "You know the drill."

"Should I get Viv?" Candice asked.

"Let's let Xavier tell his side of the story first. Then maybe we'll fetch her later."

The notion that Xavier would tell a story prompted a quizzical look from Candice.

"Dale has his ways," Wendy answered her expression.

"So he's here?" Candice asked.

"For now. He has some investor meetings lined up for later on."

"Of course he does."

"Just trying to get the local blowhards to put their money where their mouth is."

Candice admired the way Wendy could deflect a gripe and commiserate with the griper at the same time.

Copeland sprung from his office.

"Candice!" he greeted her.

"Dale," she remembered to use his first name.

He looked over at Xavier sitting in the chair by his door.

"I see our Most Valuable Yard Duty is continuing to run away with the title," he said as he tried to catch Xavier's eye.

Candice wasn't sure how much of a compliment that was. She looked at Wendy for a hint, who smiled back at her noncommittally.

Dale squatted down in front of Xavier. "Good morning, sir. Can you tell me what happened?"

Xavier looked everywhere but at him.

"Can you tell me on paper or into a microphone?"

The boy nodded.

"Paper?" Dale followed up.

The boy shook his head.

"Microphone?"

The boy nodded again.

"Okay, then," Dale stood up. "Come on in."

They went into his office and left the door open. Candice watched as Xavier sat in the chair in front of Copeland's desk. Dale took his cell phone from his back pocket and put it on the desk in front of Xavier. He tapped the screen a couple of times.

"I'll leave you alone and you tell me all about it, okay?"

The boy nodded.

Dale tapped the screen one more time and a single high note popped from the speaker.

"You're on, kid."

He walked out of the office and closed the door behind him. Within seconds a muffled voice could be heard slowly expounding on recent events. Candice expected a triumphant strut from Copeland. He had earned it, she had to admit, and frankly that's what she would have done. Instead he stayed by the door for a brief while, listening not only to Xavier, it seemed, but to something more.

Dale came out of his trance and walked over to them.

"Thank you for all you do," he said to Candice.

She stammered humbly before saying, "I wish I could do more. I wish I could do stuff like that, what you just did."

"That's not something you should have to worry about," he said. "We'll hire some specialists once we raise the funds. And on that note…"

Wendy took her cue. "Knock 'em dead."

"And then take their wallets?" Dale teased.

"Maybe you should just wow them instead," Wendy said.

"Will do," he waved as he made his way toward the door. "Thank you again, Candice. We need about twenty more parents like you around here."

She nodded and started to wave back, but he stopped and turned his attention to Wendy.

"Let Xavier stay in there when he's done, then let him go to lunch. When I get back we'll listen to his version and decide if we need to bring in Viv."

"Got it," Wendy replied as Dale darted out onto the catwalk and down the stairs.

Candice stood by Wendy's desk for a moment. She was about to say "Who was that masked man?", but wasn't sure if Wendy would get the reference. Besides, she wasn't necessarily ready to make superhero allusions just yet. She was conflicted more than reassured when it came to Copeland's priorities. There was no way his sheen could be reapplied in her eyes, but maybe she could come to understand what was truly underneath it now that it had been scraped off.

She thanked Wendy for her assistance, and climbed back down into the showroom. The whistle had blown, and the kids were back in class. She drifted into the garage and sat on an enormous tractor tire that always needed a small team of kiddos to move it. An older kid could move it on their own, but older kids rarely played in the garage area despite all the equipment available. Clear distinctions had arisen. Indoors for the smaller ones, outdoors for the bigger ones. If it ever rained, Candice thought, maybe the boundaries could be breeched as naturally as they developed. But it never did, and no matter where they were, the bigger kids liked to act as though they were above it all, anyway. They were beyond playing. Their games had grown to be mental.

From her vantage on the tire, Candice looked through one of the open garage doors at two mothers at the edge of the meadow. They each wore shapeless jeans and hooded sweatshirts branded with the name a local youth sports league and probably would have been smoking if it wasn't against the rules. She couldn't hear them, but they were clearly complaining about something. She was tempted to join them. It was fun to complain about things. That's why she did it so often. Even if all of her concerns were addressed, she would find new ones.

She resisted and stayed put on her tire. Instead of thinking of all that bothered her, she decided to wonder. She wondered what the goal was for a kid like Xavier, and those like him. The kids who needed a team of adults just to teach them how to use the silent 'e' or multiply a single digit number by two, and who had a hard time functioning not only in school, but in the world. Even if they got the help they needed as a child, what would become of them as adults? Where would they go when they had outgrown school but still needed guidance?

During the lunch recess, she found herself grumbling a little less about the kids who drove her crazy as she imagined their future. She imagined them looking back and talking about the crabby lady who worked yard duty. Some would laugh as they told her story, others would be bitter. None would be flattering.

Patience came easier as she wondered. She considered the source of the insulting behavior, and tried to think of ways to explain why it was a bad idea, rather than just bark at them. Her explanations would take time to formulate, so until they were ready, she decided in the meantime to just sigh and try to make the little culprits feel guilty.

The exception was Artie. The sight of him and his impish antics still made her want to scream in his face until she ran out of breath. For while the other problem kids were sabotaging what could be their best path to a better life, Artie had no such risk. He could act with impunity, and would be just fine when he grew up. The fact that he never confessed to anything nor was forced to follow through on any consequences symbolized his future all the more, as he would eventually join the rest of the plutocrats and continue to live above the law.

With regard to Artie, she thought the best course of action was to coerce the other volunteers to deal with him, as the more empathy she felt for some of the troubled kids, the more resentment she felt toward him. She was afraid of what she might do the next time she caught him making mischief. More to the point, she was afraid of what she might do when he denied his actions.

First she had to get the parents out of the garage and into the yard. They were so wedded to standing around watching the little kids play with the flotsam and jetsam littering the "adventure playground" that the thought of hazarding a trip out into the wilds of the upper cluster never occurred to them. And now that she was bringing it up, they agreed to help, but with panic in their eyes.

Their progress was slow. At first the mothers dawdled near the garage doors and looked past the outdoor cliques of children to the fields and hills beyond. When even slightest whine or shout came from inside the adventure playground, they sprung toward the noise and spent plenty of time making sure everything was okay before reluctantly stepping back outside. After days' worth of trying to untether them from the building, Candice asked for Copeland's help to lure them further out, and he indulged her with an effective strategy.

He would give parents tips on how to deal with condescending adolescents while walking them out to a point past their comfort zone, somewhere near the meadow or the picnic benches by the modular classrooms. Each would be so compelled by his advice that they wouldn't notice how far they had come until he stopped talking and turned around to survey the landscape. He would stay with them for another minute, switching to small talk as the parents would waver upon seeing where they were, as though the pilot of a small airplane had just surrendered the controls to them while airborne.

Candice found it easier to call him Dale as they started to gain outdoor coverage. There was more monitoring and less punishment. Best of all, Artie barely made a move under the new system. Plausible deniability was important to him, and the extra eyes made that harder to accomplish. He still darted from group to group vying for attention, but kept his punishable offenses in the classroom, for there were still marches from Mr. Benton's room to Dale's office occurring almost daily.

Sometimes as she was setting up for lunch or taking a break in the showroom, she would see him through the window being banished, and she would walk outside to signal Mr. Benton that she would make sure Artie reached his destination. Mr. Benton would respond with a wave and a "thank you" hollered through cupped hands.

Occasionally she had to leave early to address some rental unit crises that couldn't wait until after lunch, and sometimes her rounds allowed her to drive past the school on her way from one appointment to another, and she would notice that the parents usually abandoned their posts when she wasn't around to keep after them. The frustration she felt was cushioned by her pride in discovering she commanded that much impact.

One such day she was tempted to surprise her yard duty charges by returning after a series of minor calls and false alarms left her with more free time than she was accustomed to having. The first was a dispute that the tenants had resolved by the time she arrived, the next was a complaint that she was able to handle herself with a quick trip to the hardware aisle, and finally she pulled up to an empty house that the people had decided to abandon the night before rather than wait to see if she could negotiate a deal with them for back rent.

Mia and Zoey were each being picked up for a playdate after school, so the surprise inspection would be the only reason for her to head back to campus. She wasn't sure if she could bring up the backsliding of her fellow volunteers without revealing a certain level of snobbery, so she decided to forego the risk and treat herself to lunch, and then some frothy caffeine at the local Starbucks wannabe.

She didn't like the coffee they served, in any of its forms, but it offered a trendy oasis for people who liked to think the valley couldn't hold them. At any given time there would be various tableaus of youth angst posing with laptops that were slapped full of stickers, grey-haired couples sharing a copy of some major newspaper that they had to subscribe to in order to affect their image, younger pairs sporting wardrobes ordered from online catalogues for whom the slender paper cups were a fashion accessory, and a tattooed staff of baristas who appeared to have been flown in from a big-city cafe scrunched into a dicey neighborhood that was in the process of gentrification.

Candice preferred to think that she was people watching, rather than one of the people being watched. She fiddled with her phone, but really just used it as a prop to keep her from staring too long and for cover in case she started laughing. She didn't even know what time it was in spite of all her glancing at the screen, for when Isaiah

Benton walked in, she wondered for a moment why he wasn't still in class. A more purposeful look at the screen revealed that school had been out for half an hour.

They went through their usual paces, waving from a distance. When he received his order and approached her table, they each laughed for a moment at the unfamiliar nearness.

"Maybe I should sit over in that far corner and holler through my hands," Isaiah acknowledged the dynamic. He acted like he was hollering but without the volume: "Hello! What brings you here!"

"Sorry," Candice didn't play along. "Without Artie walking between us, it's just not the same."

They shared another laugh and he asked if the empty seat at her table was taken. She gestured that it wasn't, and he settled in.

"So you like this place?" he asked.

"I do," she said in a very qualifying tone.

"Not for the usual reasons, I take it?"

"Considering I'm not a big coffee fan, no."

"The people," he surmised.

"Where do they come from?" she validated his answer. "Do coffee houses order them and have them delivered with the furniture and the equipment?"

"It reminds me of home," he said. "Well, a few of my homes."

"You moved a lot?"

"Yes, ma'am."

"Military family?"

He smiled.

"Yes...ma'am"

"Ah, I think I get it now," Candice had a revelation. "You spent some time at the base here when you were a kid, had a good year for whatever reason, and came back to teach out of nostalgia."

Isaiah put his coffee down and applauded her powers of deduction. She took a seated bow.

"One thing escapes me, though," she said.

"How I could be nostalgic about this place?"

She nodded emphatically.

"It's a nice little town," he tried to remind her. "I do get the impression maybe I caught it at a better time back then. But I had been in a lot of cities, some of them in parts of the world where I didn't speak the language. This place was just so authentic to me. It was America. And there was this girl..."

"Now it makes much more sense."

"Nah," he waved off the point. "There really wasn't much to it. In fact, there was nothing to it. She didn't give me the time of day."

"It wasn't me," Candice held up her hands. "I didn't grow up here."

"So then what brought you here?"

"My ex-husband. And referring to him as a 'what' rather than a 'who' is very fitting, by the way."

"And your kids are comfortable."

"And it's affordable."

"Speaking of your kids," Isaiah said. "Mia's great. A real pleasure."

"Thank you," Candice nodded. "Not that I had much to do with it. But it's good to hear. Does she contribute much?"

"Besides really good work, well, yes, she's a little quiet. But that's okay. When she does have something to add, it means something."

"She sure goes on and on about you."

"It's a fun group. Easy to work with."

"Even with Artie?

"Artie's all right. A little restless, but harmless."

"Harmless. Unlike...well, I should probably stop."

Isaiah agreed with a slow nod. They laughed again and worked on their coffee in comfortable silence.

"You should see for yourself," he picked up the conversation. "Come work with us in the classroom. Get out of the yard for a while. Change things up."

Candice was pleasantly surprised by the offer, but had finally reached a point of pride in her yard duties.

"I'm not asking you to lead a discussion or anything," he assured her. "Honestly, it would be a lot of busy work. Helping me grade quizzes and stuff that piles up if I don't stay on it. I'll give you an answer key and everything. Meanwhile, you can sit in and check things out while you're plowing through them."

"I suppose I can do that before the first recess. Or between recess and lunch."

"Or both," he grinned. "And as you start to get accustomed to the room, who knows? Maybe you will want to participate a little more. Lead some group work, do some tutoring."

She laughed a bit too loudly.

"Sorry," she said. "It's just that, we want them to actually learn something, right?"

"It's sixth grade," he maintained. "It ain't graduate school."

"All the more reason to get embarrassed if I don't know something."

"You'll know," he looked like he wanted to reach out and take her hand, but he didn't. "You'll know."

Candice hedged. The silence had grown less comfortable.

"It'll be a nice way for you to see the good side of the students," Isaiah persisted. "Instead of always seeing them in their packs out on the playground, looking for ways to bust them."

She laughed softly and felt more at ease again.

"And you can show them your good side, too," he played into her laughter. "Show them you can do more than glare and scowl."

She acted indignant and took a swipe at the air in front of him.

"That's not all I do."

"No?"

"No," she said. "I smile sometimes. When I bust someone."

"Well, that can be fun..."

"And I yell really well. You've heard that."

"Oh, I've heard that."

She took a melodramatic deep breath.

"Okay," she said. "Come to think of it, I probably should help out in the classroom."

"Thank you," he replied with complete sincerity. "Hopefully you'll be a role model for the other parents. The younger grades are crawling with volunteers. Those of us in the upper cluster need help, too."

"Sounds like the yard duty dilemma."

"See?" Isaiah raised his paper cup. "I came to the right person."

She tapped her cup against his, but of course no sound came from the impact.

"Too many things are disposable these days," he said, holding the container at eye level and observing it from different angles.

Candice considered looking at her screen to see what time it was, but decided she didn't want to know just yet.

Chapter Seven: Rodrigo

He stood atop the deck he had built that extended out from their swimming pool. Their house was on a hill that overlooked the entire valley. The view included fields that he used to work in, which was by design, so he could look back on those days he had risen above. He liked to recall the mornings he would ride an old school bus painted white, filled with two dozen other workers, a trailer of portable potties hitched to the back, not knowing what sort of work they would do until they reached the field for that day. Eventually he bought a used Datsun and drove himself to where the work was being held. He couldn't remember what color that car was, since it was perpetually covered in dust.

He could see a white school bus in the distance, parked along the perimeter of a field that was a rectangle of green in an expanse that was otherwise fallow for winter. He couldn't tell what kind of lettuce it was from so far away, but figured that's what it was, which meant a lot of stooping over for those who caught the bus, and those whose battered cars filled in the remaining spaces along one side of the green patch.

Rod's back ached in sympathy, but his satisfaction was even greater than usual. For in addition to absorbing the past below him, he had his ear to his cell phone, absorbing the news from his technology contact that the classrooms would be wired during the upcoming summer break. His networking had come through.

They mentioned how impressed they were with Dale's pitch. They felt the two of them, Rod and Dale, represented the kind of merger between business and education that they had been seeking for sponsorship. There were some structural modifications in the buildings for which the charter would be responsible, but the hardware was complimentary, the software license fees reduced, and the promotional presence minimal.

Rod felt as though he could fly over the valley that he surveyed while they sliced through the details. A tap on his shoulder from behind interrupted his flight. He turned to find nobody there, then spun in the other direction to find Artie grinning with pride. Rod covered the bottom of his phone.

"Wait," he mouthed.

"Can Josh sleep over?" Artie asked anyway.

"Excuse me for a moment, Kento," Rod lowered his phone and glared at Artie.

"Wait," he said out loud this time through bared teeth.

Artie saluted and imitated a robot as he walked away.

The phone conversation proceeded and the deal was sealed, with contracts on their way by the end of the week. As Rod exchanged concluding pleasantries with Kento, his phone alerted him that a call was coming in from his daughter Lena.

But before he could switch over to her, there was Artie's voice again.

"Dad?"

"It's your sister," Rod waved him off again.

Artie sighed dramatically and slumped his shoulders, this time impersonating a penguin as he walked off.

Lena wanted money, which normally irked Rod, but he was feeling celebratory, and suggested they come to the city and deliver it in person over a nice dinner. She didn't do a good job of sounding enthusiastic about the idea, but he laughed it off.

"Just dinner," he assured her. "You can meet your friends afterwards."

She brightened up over the promise of brevity, and warmly suggested a restaurant and a time before saying goodbye.

Artie once more knew exactly when the conversation was ending, and appeared just as Rod lowered the phone and tried to stand triumphantly in front of the farmland lying beneath him. He also knew what Rod and Lena had been discussing.

"Can Josh come, too?"

"Where were you eavesdropping from? It's a good forty feet to the house."

"You're so loud."

Rod made a playful move to push him in the pool. Artie dodged him and asked again if Josh could come with them on the plane to the city.

"I didn't even say he could spend the night yet. How did we jump to him flying to the city with us?"

"Please?" Artie collapsed and walked on his knees toward his father with hands wrapped together in prayer.

"Have I even met Josh?"

"He goes to LOCA."

"I figured as much. What does he look like?"

"He's the tall dude with brown hair that all the girls have a crush on."

That gave Rod an idea of who it was, but his realization confused him even more.

"The one who makes fun of you all the time?"

Artie seemed surprised that his Dad remembered that part. He stood up and brushed off the bottom half of his pants.

"He doesn't do it as much anymore."

"Look, Artie..." Rod searched for a way to articulate his answer. "The company plane is not a toy."

"You're using it to go to dinner."

"To celebrate a business transaction," was the best justification Rod could come up with.

Artie crossed his arms and raised his eyebrows at him. Rod had to agree that his excuse sounded rather pitiful. He went with something more straightforward.

"I'd like to just be with the family tonight."

"Fine," Artie said. "Can Josh still come over?"

"You don't want to come with us?"

Artie shook his head.

"We can't leave you two alone here."

"I've done it before. For more than one night."

"When Lena and Tony were still home."

"No," Artie corrected him. "I did it at the end of last summer when you moved Tony into his apartment."

"But nobody else was with you, Artie. I don't know Josh's parents, but I'm pretty certain they won't go for it, either."

Artie fell silent and looked around, searching for a comeback.

"Can I go over to his house, then?"

Rod exhaled until there was just enough air left inside of him to say "Sure."

Artie thanked him and ran inside to make the call. Rod turned toward the valley and tried to re-live his moment of triumph, but it was gone. He would have to regain it over dinner, and when he delivered the news to Dale, which he decided to do in person the following week.

It was still a pretty view, though. He gazed at it a while longer before going inside to tell Rita and make arrangements for the plane.

He found Artie in the living room sitting quietly on the couch.

"Josh said no?"

Artie nodded his head.

"Did he give you a reason?"

"He said his parents aren't going to be home, either."

"And do you believe him?"

Artie looked stunned.

"Why shouldn't I?" he replied.

Rod regretted asking the question, and tried to spray whipped cream over the situation before Artie could see what it was made of.

"If you come to the city with us tonight, we'll go on a Lego run to Toys R Us. You can get a whole stack of boxes for your shows. Enough for a year's worth of episodes. Isn't there even a Lego store there? A store with nothing but Legos?"

Artie nodded.

"So what do you say?" Rod felt as though it was his turn to get down on his knees. "Come celebrate with us. I struck a deal to wire the whole school this summer."

Artie glared at him. "Wire it to blow up, I hope."

He got up off the couch and walked to his room. There were no imitations of robots or penguins, just one sad step after another.

"So no Legos, then?" Rod called after him, grasping at a last chance for a light moment. The only reply he heard was Artie's door closing.

Rather than chase after him, Rod decided to regain some of his buzz by proceeding with his initial reason for coming inside. He found Rita watching television in their room, and gave her the good news. She was happy for him, and then happy for herself when he mentioned the flight to the city.

"Perfect," she gushed. "I've been wanting to introduce the kids to ikebana in my art classes, and I need some supplies. Lord knows we have plenty of flowers and plants around here, but I just can't find a decent variety of containers."

"You mean the art classes at the recreation center or at the school?"

"Oh, mi querido, you know I stopped teaching at the rec center when I started teaching at LOCA."

"But that's hundreds of containers."

"You just got free computers, Rigo."

She kissed him and since he couldn't stop himself from laughing, he kissed her back. He gave her the name of the restaurant Lena had recommended. She picked up the phone to make reservations and to check which of their pilots was available.

"Is Artie coming?" she asked.

Rod crumpled his lips.

"Could you find out, please?"

He set out back into the hallway, devising a strategy as he approached Artie's room. Rather than converse through the door, he tapped on it to see if he encountered any resistance. There was neither sound nor movement, so he slowly entered.

Artie was lying on his side facing the far wall.

"Your mother and I would really like you to join us tonight."

"At least somebody wants to hang out with me."

"Your sister would also like it."

"That's because you have to. It's the law."

Rod ventured over to the bed and sat down by his side.

"I was thinking," he introduced his plan. "We should bring your whole class out to some of our local operations on a field trip. Maybe one of the processing plants, something with lots of big machines."

"The one with the helicopter?"

"Well, the helicopter kind of gets around. But we can make sure it's at the one we visit on that day. We can't give everyone a ride, but maybe Mr. Benton can put together some kind of contest, and the winners get to go up."

"Hmm. That sounds pretty cool."

"Then at the end of the school year, how about a pool party?"

Artie rolled over and sat up.

"Here?"

"Of course, here. You know a better pool in town?"

"Thanks, Dad."

Artie gave him a hug, and Rod accepted it gratefully. But as Artie characteristically started to overdo it, and rock back and forth while telling him in a goofy voice that he was the best Dad ever,

Rod wondered what he had done, if he was really helping Artie make friends, or only helping to ostracize him further.

At least they could always rely on having a good time in the city. The restaurant was indeed impressive, and Lena was able to maintain her charm since they didn't exceed the two hour window in which she was capable of turning it on. Rod and Artie dropped off Rita at a home and garden outlet so she could compile a collection of containers and have them shipped to their home. Rod suggested shipping it right to the school, but she wanted to deliver it personally. He could relate, since he was likewise so intent on delivering the computer news to Dale in person, rather than calling him.

Artie kept his bounty in hand. He and Rod left the Lego store with several sets of the new Architecture collection. The boxes contained pieces that would create Lego versions of real-world structures like the Sydney Opera House and the Brandenburg Gate. Artie imagined out loud that the collection would raise the maturity level of his show. He just had to come up with some alternative arrangements of the pieces.

As Artie wrestled with some possibilities on the plane ride home and on the living room floor the following day, Rod noticed him pausing more than usual, and not in frustration. He instead came across as more contemplative than Rod had ever seen him. And though he was reluctant to interrupt such a landmark sequence of tranquility, Rod's curiosity eventually ballooned to a degree where he had to ask what was on his mind.

Artie's response was even more surprising than the silence, so much so that Rod didn't process the exact words as they were being spoken. He could only nod and piece together a summary as he walked out onto the deck in a pleasantly-surprised daze, then down the steps to the olive orchard that climbed the hill below the house. He was pretty certain he heard his son suggest that maybe it wasn't such a good idea to toy with reality, that for years the models he rearranged on camera were based on creations that didn't really exist, and to change the Batmobile into a cyborg rocket launcher was one thing, but changing the Chrysler Building into a troll fortress was another thing, something that undermined his wish to come across as more mature. Rod did recall the exact words Artie used at the conclusion of his meditation:

"I'd be taking something grown up and turning it into something childish."

And with that Rod found himself in the middle of the olive trees. He had planted them after buying the house to prevent erosion along the hillside. He had bought the property from the squabbling sons and daughters of a big-time grape grower. The offspring had all left the area the first chance they could get, and used the house maybe once a year for a decade after the last parent died, which left it in a state of disrepair by the time Rod picked it up. He did everything he could to fortify his investment, including the addition of the orchard. The trees were still young and thin, not quite having shed their sapling past. They stood just a couple heads taller than Rod, and it occurred to him that as gradual as he knew growth tended to be, he was always looking for that seminal moment when his daughter would become a woman, and his sons become men.

Over the weekend he had calls to make and reports to draft. In the spaces between, he would quietly open the door to the guest house to check on the production of Artie's newest episode. Rita would smile from behind the camera and put a finger to her lips. She had mentioned while they lay in bed after the first day of filming that Artie was trying something new. He was simply building the structure, starting with the United Nations Headquarters, then offering some history and trivia concerning it when the demonstration was complete. They were still in the process of filming the construction, since there were hundreds of pieces and Artie liked to make each move carefully so that when they sped up the video before loading it, the fast-motion sequences looked smooth, and the audience could see a logical progression to how the parts grew into a whole, despite the high speed.

"Dad?" he asked without looking up from the pieces splayed across the table in front of him during one of Rod's visits to the guest house production facilities.

"Can you talk when you do that?" Rod asked. "Didn't you just screw up the take?"

"This is the fast motion part," Artie said. "And it'll have music in the background."

"Then why does your mother always make a gesture for me to be quiet when I come in?"

Rita chimed in.

"Because we're not always doing fast motion parts when you come barging in."

"Barging in?" Rod defended himself.

Rita smiled and Artie giggled before following through on what he wanted to ask.

"Dad, can you check my research on the United Nations? It's on my desk in my room."

"Um. Sure."

"Let me know if there's anything I should add," he said as he slowly grabbed a piece from the spread and clicked it onto the burgeoning United Nations of Lego. "Just remember that the history part shouldn't last more than two minutes."

"Got it," Rod was about to duck out. "What if I find something that I think should be deleted?"

"I'll consider it," Artie said, still focused on the pieces.

Rita and Rod exchanged raised eyebrows.

"Okay, then," Rod offered a casual salute and left them alone.

Artie's history of the U.N. had the plagiarized look of something that had been written by a committee, rather than a person. Rod's only suggestion to Artie was to write the passage himself, rather than copy and paste it from the web, and to mention the sources he used at some point in his presentation.

He presumed his son's attempt at word theft was innocent, since it was so blatant and Artie had asked him to proofread it. Unless of course he thought his Dad was too stupid to notice. Either way, the incident had Rod thinking about the ramifications of a school utterly aligned with the internet, and how plugged in to temptation the students would be.

He asked Dale about this issue on the morning he planned to break the news to him, caching up to him on the catwalk right after the Pledge of Allegiance and announcements.

"Well," Dale straightened up and shifted into a one-on-one version of an investor pitch. "Education is about meeting challenges, and teaching intellectual honesty is a challenge that the brightest educators will lead the way on."

His response sounded as plagiarized as Artie's great moments in Lego history. Rod smiled.

"Sorry," Dale dropped into a more casual mode. "It's an answer that was floating around the conference. I need to put my own spin on it."

"You'd better," Rod smiled even more broadly.

"Wait..." Dale caught on. "Do you mean to tell me...?"

Rod nodded.

Dale yelped and gave him a hug.

The Kindergarteners were almost to their classroom, the first graders just starting to make their move, while the rest of the students were still on the showroom floor. Everyone turned around to face the sound above them.

"One more announcement!" Dale beckoned everyone back together. Within seconds all were once again present, but the confusion caused by their principal's excitement and his sudden orders to reverse course erased the manicured lines as the colored shirts coalesced into a bright mob.

"Mr. Pluma has some great news!" Dale swept his arm in Rod's direction, catching him by surprise.

"Yes," Rod hemmed while lobbing a good-natured glare at Dale. "We have secured a deal to get the whole school online this summer. By next fall, we'll have computers in every room, a computer at every desk..."

The students, faculty, and volunteers bunched together below started to buzz. They looked stunned, at each other and up at Rod, who got the sense that one more exhortation might help the news sink in.

"We're going to be the future of education!" he raised his fist.

It sounded like a teen idol had just taken the stage as a swell of high-pitched voices shook the windows and seemed to raise the catwalk.

Rod and Dale nodded at one another. Dale then put an arm around Rod and got in on the hyperbole.

"Get ready to be the envy of the county," he shouted. "Maybe even the state! Maybe even the nation! We are leading the way, people! Welcome to the cutting edge!"

Dale's motivational screed maintained the bedlam a little while longer. He used the arm he had draped around Rod to pull him into a full embrace and the youthful roar reached yet another crescendo.

"I know the applause is fun," Rod whispered loudly in Dale's ear. "But I'm afraid of what you might do next to keep it going."

Dale cracked up and as Rod joined him, their laughter inspired one more great howl from the little voices.

When they quieted down enough for Dale to re-excuse them, and the showroom was at last clear, reality swooped in quickly in the form of Rita holding a box of containers at the bottom of the stairs.

"Congratulations, guys," she said. "Now if you don't mind, there's still five more of these in the back of my car."

"Just when I think you couldn't possibly give anything more..." Dale said.

"I'm putting these in the supply area behind the shelves, yes?" Rita started walking toward the old parts department that held the backpacks.

"Perfect," Dale confirmed. "Thank you."

"You don't know what they are," muttered Rod as Rita faded from sight.

"Art supplies, I assume."

"They're ikebana containers."

"What's ikebana?" Dale asked.

"It means you need to get a real art teacher in here once and for all."

"Speaking of art..." Dale chuckled.

"I'm not kidding," Rod deadpanned.

"I know you're not, and I agree," Dale gestured for Rod to follow him down the stairs. "Not that I don't think Rita is doing a great job."

"Ikebana is flower arranging, Dale."

"And how many other schools will be doing that this year?" Dale insisted on seeing the bright side as they reached the floor and turned toward the front door.

"How many schools would want to?"

"We'll get an art teacher, Rod. We'll get whatever we want once the donations start flying in. Thanks to your help..."

He led Rod out the door and stopped halfway down the cement path to the parking lot. He turned to face Rod with an expectant smile and took a big step toward one side of the walkway. Rod got the impression he was letting him pass.

"Rita's car is still a ways out there," Rod reminded him.

"You didn't notice anything here on your way in this morning?" Dale asked, still beaming as he moved closer to a leafy section of landscaping.

"I took the side door."

"Well take a look," he said, jerking his head toward the bushes.

Rod noticed a thick wooden post standing about three feet high, driven into the ground beside the walkway.

"That wasn't there before?"

Dale laughed. "I thought you knew this place inside and out."

Rod drifted in to get a closer look and saw a plaque bolted to its top. Then he saw that his name was on it. He caught his breath and read the whole inscription aloud.

"'Dedicated to Rod Pluma, whose hard work and generosity provided the foundation for this campus and the ideas it fosters.'"

He stared at it a while longer, trying not to get too emotional. Dale seemed to pick up on his wishes and provided some verbal cover.

"And that was before today's announcement," he offered. "We just might put one in every classroom next year. On the wall, of course. We won't stick any posts in the floor."

Rita pushed through the door and looked ready to ask why they weren't unloading the boxes, but then respected the moment even though she wasn't sure what it was about. She approached the two of them to figure it out.

Taking her place by Rod's side, she read the post.

"How did I miss this?" she admonished herself and gave him a hug.

"You've got Ikebaba on your mind," Dale kidded.

"Ikebana," Rod corrected him while still hugging his wife.

"Wow, Rigo," said Rita over his shoulder. "A memorial. And you're not even dead."

All three of them shared a laugh, and Rod stopped laughing first as he peacefully considered the reference to death. He was comfortable in knowing his time was limited, as long as he left a trail of accomplishments that led to his name.

Chapter Eight: Mia

She and Beatrice agreed that age difference wasn't the main reason that their class started a mentor program with the Kindergarteners. They could have worked with the first or second graders, and the Kindergarteners could have apprenticed with any of the grades in the upper cluster, but there was a mutual respect between Mrs. Ojeda and Mr. Benton.

"I hear that some teachers might be replaced next quarter," Beatrice said as they walked toward the main building to put in an hour of mentoring along with a half dozen of their classmates.

"Me too," said Mia. "You heard any names?"

"All of them except for Ojeda and Benton. You?"

"Same. They're the only safe ones."

"Not gonna happen," Kimmy caught up to them and walked next to Mia, who glanced over at Beatrice. They shrugged at each other with their eyes.

"Nobody's getting fired," Kimmy continued.

"How do you know?" Beatrice asked.

"I have to go by the office every morning so Miss Wendy can measure the length of my skirt. I hear things."

"And Mr. Copeland said all the teachers are coming back?" Beatrice pressed her.

"Nah," Kimmy said. "He's just totally convinced the computer thingy he's working on stops teachers from being shitty."

Artie materialized behind them.

"Shitty?" he repeated, the word apparently calling to him like some sort of beacon.

"Yeah," Kimmy crackled. "Rhymes with 'Artie.'"

"Kind of," Artie rolled with it. "You need more than just the last syllable for a good rhyme. Two is better. Like 'fartie' or 'Bacardi' or 'party.'"

"Or 'pity' or 'ditty' if we're talking 'shitty'," Beatrice jumped in.

They all cracked up, even Kimmy.

"Or 'titty'," blared Artie.

The girls stopped laughing and sighed. They veered away from him, while Josh caught up to Artie and put his arm around him as if to explain something.

"Good to know, I guess," said Mia as they re-established their trio.

"What rhymes with 'shitty'?" Kimmy joked.

"That nobody's getting fired," Mia clarified. "I feel bad for them. A lot of it's just a bunch of parents bitching and moaning."

"Not ours," Beatrice said. "Everyone loves Mr. Benton."

"Especially Mia's Mom," Kimmy teased. Beatrice joined her in making some 'oohs' and 'ahs'.

Mia paused at the door to the building and spun a look in their direction.

"So she's helping out with the class," she narrated her exasperation. "So what?"

"Hey, I'm rooting for them," Kimmy said. "How cool would it be to have Mr. Benton as a stepdad?"

"I'd say that would be very cool," Beatrice replied.

"It wasn't really a question," Mia said to Beatrice as she held open the door to the dealership for her and Kimmy. "You're not supposed to respond."

"Thanks, but I felt like it."

Beatrice gave her an air kiss as she and Kimmy accepted her offer of an open door.

"Close it before the boys get here," Kimmy told her.

Mia obliged with a giggle and the three of them made their way across the showroom floor toward Mrs. Ojeda's class.

"Speaking of people getting it on..." Kimmy said.

"Would you stop it already," Mia groaned.

"What's with Artie getting all fresh these days?" Kimmy finished her thought.

"Oh..." Mia backed off.

"I know, right?" said Beatrice.

"He is?" Mia asked.

"You haven't noticed?" Kimmy added yet another question to the exchange.

"It's like he's trying to be more mature," Beatrice offered a statement. "And he thinks being some sort of player is the way to show it."

"Only he's got no moves," Kimmy snorted.

"What, grabbing butts and pulling bra straps doesn't do it for you?" Beatrice laughed.

Kimmy joined her and Mrs. Ojeda appeared at her door with a gentle signal to keep the noise down.

While the two girls tried to lower the volume on their laughter as they waited outside the room, Mia tried to recall any perverse incidents involving Artie that she may have overlooked.

Artie and Josh caught up with them, along with the other sixth graders who were scheduled for mentoring. As they lined up waiting to be called in, Mia stole a glance at Artie. He didn't seem capable of the kind of behavior Beatrice and Kimmy described. Perhaps, she thought, he just didn't act that way around her. And if that was the case, was it out of respect for her, or because he didn't find her attractive?

He caught her looking at him and she turned away. After a few seconds, she checked to see if he was still looking at her. He was. Only instead of making a goofy face back at her, which she had come to expect, he was smirking. His cocky expression wasn't exactly a butt grab, but nonetheless provided a hint that Beatrice and Kimmy were not guilty of slander.

During their time amongst the Kindergarteners, however, Artie acted like his old childish self, but in the best possible manner. He related to the kids beautifully, his sense of humor just their speed. It helped that the kids in his group had all seen episodes of his web series. Mia kept looking over at him and his little cult, a bit jealous of how fun he was able to make the lesson. Artie didn't have a chance to practice any more of his steely new stares on her, as he was so absorbed with the silly voices and sound effects he utilized to hold the kids' attention on the chart showing how to spell out the numbers one through ten.

Kimmy, meanwhile, played on her group's worship of older kids. She complimented the little girls on their most flattering features, while giving them age-appropriate beauty tips, like how to add a splash of color to their hair by wrapping a piece of yarn into it. The little boys did whatever she said, because they wanted to make sure they had a chance with her when they grew up, even if they weren't yet conscious of that hankering.

Mia borrowed a voice from Artie and some flattery from Kimmy and had a productive session. When Mrs. Ojeda called her students' attention back to the front of the room for a five-minute class-wide exercise that would lead to some more individual work, Mia spent the break in satisfaction. She was proud of herself for learning something from two people she considered the two most annoying in the school. She saw it as a sign of growth, evidence of a maturity that they all wanted so badly but chased in so many bad ways.

This glint of development motivated her to raise her hand right away when Mrs. Ojeda asked for two volunteers, before she even knew what she was volunteering for. She was the only one to submit at first, but then Mrs. Ojeda explained what she needed, and more hands rose, including Artie's, whose hand she chose.

She wanted them to set up an obstacle course in the "adventure 'garage'" (as she called it) for their next task, which would involve each kid pausing at an obstacle to answer a question before they could move onto the next hurdle upon providing a correct response.

"I'm glad she picked you," Mia said to Artie as they walked over to the play area. "You'll be good at this."

Artie responded with nothing but a quick nod, which she assumed was part of the new image he was crafting.

"You're so good with the kids," she added, trying to poke through the screen.

"I know," he said mournfully.

"Oh, come on, Artie," she scolded him. "It's nothing to be ashamed of. I think it's wonderful."

"Me, too," Artie said. "Or, at least, I do now."

They reached the adventure grounds and he started pulling items to use.

"We should make two courses," he spoke as he tossed and rolled the recycled bits of industry toward the middle of the garage. "That will keep more kids on the move at the same time."

Mia was still too baffled by his tone to jump in with wholehearted help.

"What's up?" she asked.

"Nothing," he shrugged as he rode the back of a shopping cart into the expanding mass of obstacles.

She grabbed a refrigerator box and flung it into the center, not far from where he came to a stop on the cart. He turned and glared at her. She held his gaze.

"Having some regrets over the new cool routine?" she sassed him.

"I don't know what you're talking about," he said. "Cool routine?"

"Never mind," she shook her head and made her way to the pile in order to start construction.

"But I do have some regrets," he confessed.

Mia was stunned. She may have been the first in her class to witness him in a sincere moment, adrift between wacky and snooty.

"About what?" Mia proceeded with caution.

Artie stared at the gathering of discards as though it were on fire.

"I made some new episodes," he said.

"So?"

"The kids don't like them. They told me."

"Why don't they like them?"

"I tried something new."

"Really?"

"They're about real buildings. I play it straight, build them and talk about them. I thought maybe my audience could grow up."

"I'm sure some of them have. You're widening your audience. Playing to all ages."

Artie blew a short laugh through his nose and finally looked over at her.

"You know what kind of older people like it?" he asked.

Mia shook her head.

"Social lepers," he answered himself. "Just like me, when I get older."

"You don't know that," she said.

"Oh, I know it," he explained. "They send me emails and leave comments."

"I mean you," Mia clarified. "You don't know you're going to be like that."

"Everyone knows that," he said.

He returned his attention to the pile, then set upon it to start building the course.

Mia said "Nonsense" as she joined him, and tried to think of something more to say as they proceeded to fulfill their obligation.

"You did a nice job of not letting the kids see your disappointment," she decided on as she strung together a line of obstacles next to his. "I had no idea until we came out here."

"It's not their fault," he said, remaining focused on the project. "I'm actually grateful to them. Now I know what's up."

She would have liked to learn more about what he meant by that, what exactly was 'what', and what exactly was 'up', but Mrs. Ojeda brought out the class, and Artie fell back upon his expertise as a clown.

He had created the most involved obstacle for himself. The other sixth-graders merely stood by their section and asked their question, then let each kid pass when they got it right. Artie tied a rope through the hole of an oil drum lid, and when each kid earned their ride, he would pull them as they sat on the lid as though wakeboarding over the cement floor. The kids ended up as exhausted from laughter as Artie was from pulling them.

All the mentors from Mr. Benton's class stayed behind to break down the course before the morning recess. Mia spent some time lying alone inside her refrigerator box, contemplating the Artie Paradox. Each end of the box was open, creating a cardboard culvert that the kids had crawled through. There was a knock on the roof that wiggled the flimsy tunnel, then Kimmy's head popped into frame on one end.

"I've got a question," Kimmy said.

"I already know how to spell numbers one through ten," Mia snapped, a little miffed at her quiet time being interrupted.

"Wanna come over Friday after school?"

"To your house?" Mia tried not to sound astonished.

"No, to the next obstacle," Kimmy smirked.

"Um, sure...let me check with my Mom."

"Cool."

And she popped back out of frame. Mia sat up and processed what had just happened.

"It was weird hearing her say 'cool' instead of 'fine,'" she told Beatrice later on as they sat on their preferred picnic table at recess.

"And that's the only thing that struck you as weird?"

"Should I go?"

"Why are you asking me?" Beatrice looked at her askew.

"I don't want to hurt your feelings."

"We can have other friends."

"I know..."

"And besides, I'm really curious. Aren't you?"

Mia smiled.

"Very."

"Good," Beatrice bobbed her head once in a conclusive nod. "I want a full report. Behind the scenes of The Kimmy Show."

"You think she's trying to turn us against each other?" Mia asked.

They turned their attention to Kimmy and her current crew as they fended off some boys who seemed to be on a sugar high from flirting with them.

"She might be," Beatrice said. "But it doesn't matter, because it won't work."

Mia was relieved, and wanted to tell her that was the nicest thing anyone besides her parents had said to her, but figured it was safest just to smile. Beatrice smiled back, and they continued to watch the boys perform for Kimmy. They had run out of tricks, and were down to weird noises and sudden movements.

Asking her Mom for permission to go to Kimmy's house turned out to be fun. Like any parent volunteer, her Mom was not a fan of Kimmy. But like any parent, she didn't want to come across as uptight, either, so there was an entertaining struggle that led to her saying yes.

As an added bonus, her Mom still had to pick up Zoey on that Friday, whose second grade class was late being excused, so Candice was stuck for the arrival of Kimmy's grandmother, who dressed like a mother who was hoping someone would ask if she and her daughter were sisters. By the brevity of her kiss goodbye, Mia could tell her Mom was trying to duck out before introductions were inevitable, but Kimmy's grandmother caught her.

"Hey there!" she extended a hand and when Mia's Mom haltingly reciprocated, gave it a masculine shake. "I'm Kile, but the kids call me Grandma i."

"Candice," Mia's Mom introduced herself.

"They call me Grandma i because my husband's name is Kyle, too, but he spells it with a 'y' and I spell mine with an 'i'. So we're Grandma i and Grandpa y. G.I. and G.Y. for short. Kimmy made that up."

Everyone looked over at Kimmy, who smirked and curtsied and asked if they could get going.

"I'll have her home by dinner," said Kile.

"Thank you," replied Candice.

"And when is that?" Kile followed up.

"Oh, um...six?"

"We'll be there. And what are we having?"

Kile laughed heartily enough at her own joke so as not to notice the brief look of panic on Candice's face. Zoey's class filed out and her Mom power-walked over to greet them while waving over her shoulder to tell Kile it was nice to meet her.

At first Mia couldn't figure out why Grandma Kile turned on the radio in her truck to a talk station, because she rarely stopped talking during the entire drive. She would ask Mia a question, and Mia's answer would remind Grandma i of a story of her own, or a point she wanted to make. Mia rode next to her in the front passenger seat, so she wasn't able to gauge Kimmy's backseat reactions to her Grandma's one-woman show. But it wasn't hard to imagine.

Eventually Mia learned the purpose of the talk radio. When one of Mia's replies didn't inspire G.I., she could respond to the agitated voice blurting on the radio, sometimes with her own burst of temporary rage, or at the very least with a shake of her head and some muttering along the lines of "those people these days in this country," which served as something of a breather for her while still allowing noise to come from her mouth.

They lived off the grid on a ranchette, a couple of acres littered with piecemeal projects of metal and wood that baked under the sun in a variety of broken angles, weeds sprouting through every opening. Two dusty ruts carved more of a path than a driveway, leading to a modular home that was surprisingly well-manicured, especially in consideration of what surrounded it.

"Can you tell which part of the ranch I take care of and where Grandpa y does his thing?" Kile chuckled as they bounced along the trail. "I tease him. I tell him, 'Don't worry, hon. Just get out there and finish something. Nobody from the state disability office is gonna take videos of you.'"

She upped the intensity of her laughter, then felt obligated to explain. "He used to work at the state hospital. Got jumped by a child molester. Twice! The same guy! I told Kyle, 'You should be flattered. He must have thought you looked really young.'"

Her laughing turned to wheezing as they pulled in front of the house, and with a final throaty coughing fit, she yanked on the emergency brake and bid them farewell.

"See you in a bit, girls. Keep an eye out for G.Y.. Never know where he might pop out from. Don't let him startle you."

Kimmy jumped out from the back seat and beckoned Mia to follow her. Mia thanked G.I. for the ride and caught up to Kimmy, who was on her way around to the back of the house.

"See why I didn't invite you to sleep over?" Kimmy said once they were side-by-side.

"What do you mean?"

"My Grandma."

"She's nice," Mia maintained her manners.

"She talks too much."

"Maybe a little."

"She does it so she doesn't have to think."

Mia found the statement odd.

"About anything?" she asked.

"Let me show you something," Kimmy said, and veered away from the house toward a line of scrub oak and willows on the other side of a field where some of her grandfather's projects peeked through the tall grass.

The line of wispy trees marked the shoreline of a dry creek about the width of a four-lane highway. There was a slightly deeper trench carving its jagged way down the center of the sandy plain that made up most of the thirsty bed. The girls hopped from the miniature cliff face into the grit.

"Over there," Kimmy nodded upstream.

Mia saw an abandoned car far enough ahead to be imperceptible if it hadn't been pointed out. Kimmy led the way toward it. The loose footing heated up Mia's calf muscles by the time they reached the car, which turned out to be a Honda Civic of no discernible color thanks to years of sunlight and dusty wind. Apart from the rinsed-out body, it appeared to be in decent condition.

"It was my Mom's," Kimmy announced. "She and my Dad lived here after I was born. They were really young. Grandpa put it here when he got tired of asking her family to come get it. I think they liked her better than their son. My Dad."

She looked up at the tree line and Mia followed her gaze. There was a section of shrubbery half as high as the rest, and as wide as the car, with a dent in the ridge just below it.

"So she died?" Mia asked.

Kimmy nodded. "Car accident. Her friend was driving. There were four of them and they were heading home from a Girl's Night Out, some barn dance thing that used to happen in an empty section of Dos Santos Ranch, sort of a redneck rave. Some of the families tried to sue, but they had no case since everyone brought their own alcohol and drugs, and the driver wasn't even high. Just going too fast on a crooked back road."

"How old were you?"

"Still a baby. Which is good, I guess, since I didn't really know them."

"What happened to your Dad?"

"Went downhill. Ended up in prison after about a year."

"Don't you have any contact with him?"

"My grandparents tell me they try to get him to keep in touch, but he says I would bring back memories. I don't think they try too hard. I can tell they're ashamed of him. He married a new woman, some skank who gets off on being part of this prison wives group. They post pictures on visitation days and write lame little notes to each other on their web site about how people just don't understand them and how it doesn't matter, because they're so strong. When I search my Dad's name online, that's what I get. At least the other women were already with their guys when they got busted. I don't know what the deal is with this bimbo."

Kimmy stared in the car window and seemed to have forgotten Mia was there.

"Sorry," Mia said.

"It's okay. Like I said, I didn't know them."

She looked over at Mia.

"I just wanted to explain my grandparents to you. Or at least my Grandma, so you know why she won't shut up. Who knows if we'll see my Grandpa."

Mia focused back on the car.

"Why don't they sell it? Or give it to charity?" she wondered aloud. "I get why they don't want to see it, but this doesn't make sense."

"What happened to their son and daughter-in-law doesn't make any sense either," Kimmy answered. "That's what Grandpa said when he drove it in here."

Mia noticed that the front was bent upward a bit from the impact. She imagined the car pushing over the scrub oak and diving into the creek bed. A breeze ruffled the leaves lining the shore and made a sound like water flowing.

"Does this creek ever run high enough to wash it away?" Mia asked.

"Grandpa said it would take the storm of the century."

"So it does."

"Yeah," Kimmy seemed to have never considered it. "I guess it does. Once a century."

They contemplated the car a while longer before Kimmy interrupted the silence.

"You wanna paint our toenails or something?"

Mia shrugged.

"Sure."

The two of them walked back through the tall, brittle grass, retracing the trampled route they had left behind on their way in.

Mia followed Kimmy's lead as long as she could in trying to pass herself off as being seasoned in the girly arts, but Kimmy caught on. Mia felt her staring at her as she once again tried to smooth out the globs of polish clumping onto her latest nail. She concentrated all the more, knowing she was being evaluated, and nearly fell off the bed from trying to hold her bent position for that long.

"You've never done this before, have you?"

"No," Mia admitted, relieving the tiny brush back into the tiny bottle.

"I should've known. Your fingernails are never painted, either."

"Sorry."

Kimmy laughed and put her brush back into the bottle, too.

"Why didn't you just say so?" she friend-slapped Mia. "You're usually so honest."

"You just told me about your parents and stuff. I didn't want to hurt your feelings."

"Aw, you're sweet," Kimmy said. She then gestured to the pedicure supplies.

"So, what do you think?

Mia feigned deliberation as she surveyed the spread.

"Still don't see the point," she confessed.

"It's not about the toes, girl," Kimmy said. "We're supposed to be talking, not going for the perfect nail. Here, let me finish for you."

"You don't have to..."

"C'mon. There's just a few more."

"Really, I'm fine."

"Don't hurt my feelings," Kimmy grinned.

Mia sighed and grinned back.

"Fine," she said in a slight Kimmy imitation, then wondered if she should tell Kimmy about the running joke regarding her and the word 'fine'. She thought it best to include Beatrice in that decision, and let the impulse pass.

"What about boys?" Kimmy asked as she started to work on Mia's toes.

"What about them?" Mia was trying to get comfortable with the division of labor that had developed.

"Let's start with the most obvious candidate. Any thoughts on Josh?"

"He can be mean."

"Everyone can be mean at our age."

"That's not true. Artie's not mean."

Kimmy stopped in mid-brush stroke and looked up incredulously at her.

"I guess he hasn't grabbed your ass yet."

"Oh. Yeah," Mia had forgotten the accusations.

"Do you want him to?"

"No!"

"Careful. Keep your toes still."

"I'm disappointed he started doing that. Not that he didn't do it to me."

"Blew that great image of his, eh?"

"Better to be goofy than mean."

Kimmy kept quiet as she finished her work with a small grin. She capped the polish and swept her hands dramatically over Mia's feet.

"Ta da!"

Mia leaned back and lifted them up for a better look.

"It's easy to tell which ones you did. Thanks."

"No problem."

Mia spun around and hung her legs over the side of the bed.

"Ah," she breathed. "I was getting tired of being in that sit-up position."

Kimmy lifted her knees toward her chin and wrapped her arms around them.

"You really like him, don't you?" she asked.

"Who?" Mia replied.

"Artie."

"What?"

"C'mon. You brought him up out of nowhere when we started talking about boys."

"We were talking about being mean."

"Still..." Kimmy leaned back onto her elbows. "Suddenly, there was Artie."

Mia laughed off the probe and avoided eye contact. If it was true that Kimmy's Grandpa could pop up anywhere, Mia hoped he would suddenly tap on the window or burst from the closet holding a broken support rod he had just replaced. Any diversion Mia could self-generate would be flagrantly obvious, so she had to sit there and push through the interrogation. She thought of Kimmy's earlier compliment, how honest she was, and Mia agreed with that assessment without feeling the least bit conceited, because it also meant she was a terrible liar.

"I just had a nice talk with him the other day, that's all," she figured being as transparent as possible was her only way out. "It was fresh in my mind."

"What did you talk about?"

"Nothing much. I was just surprised at how, I don't know, not-goofy he could be."

"Hmm."

Kimmy seemed to plotting her next move. Mia decided to get the jump on her.

"Kind of like with you lately."

"What?"

It worked. Kimmy was caught by surprise.

"I just think it's really cool that right close together, like in the same week, I got a chance to see another side of Artie that's not so ridiculous, and a side of you that's not so bitchy."

Kimmy looked as though she was debating whether to be angry or flattered.

"Thank you for showing me," Mia pushed her in the preferred direction. "I'm honored."

However Kimmy decided to feel, she covered it with an all-purpose smile.

"I still think you like him," she said.

"Whatever," Mia slumped, using that word without applying a Kimmy imitation for the first time since she'd met her.

"Nice try, though," Kimmy crept forward and started tickling Mia's side.

Mia fought back and within seconds they landed on the floor in a heap of laughter. With the wider spaces of the floor to work with, their grappling grew more intense, and the laughter devolved into gasps for air. They rolled over each other several times, and when they ran out of room against the closet door, Mia found herself on top. She had Kimmy pinned.

"I totally get it," Kimmy breathed. "He's rich."

Mia went for her sides.

"Okay, okay!" Kimmy squealed. "I won't say anymore."

Mia collapsed next to her and they caught their breath, each to a different beat. After a dozen or so huffs, their rhythms happened to match for a few mouthfuls, which turned the gasps back into laughter.

There was a knock at the door and Kimmy's Grandma asked from the other side if everything was okay. Kimmy said they were fine, then turned and whispered to Mia.

"Jeez. A little late there, Grandma."

Mia started to giggle harder, doing her best to stifle the noise.

Kimmy kept it up.

"What, was she waiting to see if we broke through the door?"

Kimmy giggled at her own joke and looked over at Mia as if to learn some tips on how to smother laughter, but seeing each other with tears rolling down their cheeks only made them struggle more.

The rest of the afternoon passed easily by, more so than the rest of Mia's weekend. Saturday and Sunday felt like January and February. She couldn't blame the valley this time, or the company of her mother and sister. It was the thought that maybe Kimmy was right. Maybe she did like Artie. Maybe it was more than pity that moved her to think of him so often.

Chapter Nine: Dale

An old friend of Alma's who had been a realtor in the valley through five recessions gave them the combination of some lock boxes hanging from the doors of empty houses she thought might be suitable for Jonathan.

"You told her our plans?" Dale snapped when Alma first told him.

"They're nothing to be ashamed of," Alma leveled her reply.

Dale wasn't responding with their plans for Jonathan in mind. He was responding with their method of payment in mind, which was still precarious.

"Sorry," he relented. "Of course not. I was just thinking maybe it's a little early."

"We would only be gauging how Jonathan responds to the idea, and to certain homes and neighborhoods. So we're ready when the time comes."

He appreciated the vote of confidence implied by her use of the word 'when' instead of 'if', and decided it sounded like a fine idea after all. It also helped that Alma had requested the combinations rather than allow her real estate friend to take them on a series of tours, as they agreed it was preferable to not have any outsiders lurk at their elbow while assessing Jonathan's reactions to each house.

During their first self-guided tour, however, they caught themselves being no more helpful than a vague acquaintance, as they trailed Jonathan while he drifted between spaces as though stalking him.

"Are we going to duck behind a corner if he turns in our direction?" Dale joked.

"I've got pepper spray in my purse," she played along.

The sound of a large truck rumbling onto the block lightly rattled the walls. Jonathan sprinted outside.

"Oh...yeah," Alma remembered something as he darted past them.

"Where there garbage cans outside?" Dale confirmed.

Alma nodded and they walked after him.

Jonathan was standing on what used to be a front lawn with his hands cupped around each side of his face, as though holding binoculars, creating tunnel vision that he focused on a garbage truck as its mechanical arm lifted one bin at a time above its body and shook out the contents into the opening.

The driver waved at Jonathan, like he had so many times before in their own neighborhood when Jonathan so faithfully greeted him. Then he saw Dale and Alma and rolled down his window.

"You moving!?" he hollered at them above the hydraulic hum.

They shook their heads and waved.

"Just looking!" Alma answered.

The driver was confused but nodded anyway. With one last wave in Jonathan's direction, he rolled his window back up and moved on to the next batch of bins down the street.

Jonathan lowered his hands but continued to watch the truck do its job in the distance. He repeatedly gave his head a single shake to the left in satisfied awe of what he was seeing. Dale and Alma watched him watch the garbage truck.

"Who are we kidding?" Alma asked herself aloud.

Dale knew he didn't have to answer, but wanted to anyway, if he could come up with something decent.

"If it doesn't work out for him," he decided to say, "the house can still be an investment. We can rent it out or sell it to help pay for his care."

"Even when this market isn't crashing," she kept her eyes on Jonathan, "it's not exactly Manhattan."

"Which is why we'll be able to pay cash, and not have a mortgage, so any rent or any sale is pure profit."

Alma looked at him and forced a smile.

"The charter is about to take off," he responded. "By the end of next year we'll be the keynote speakers at every conference west of the Rockies. Then the year after that, every conference to the east."

Her smile relaxed, though Dale wasn't sure if it was because she believed him or wanted to console him. Maybe both. But when she made a move, it was toward Jonathan.

She sidled up next to her son and put her arm around him. Jonathan leaned into her and she pulled him even closer and spoke into his ear just loudly enough for Dale to hear.

"Do you remember the time we were using the instrument and talking about what makes people happy?" she asked softly of him. "And you spoke of that other place people always keep in mind, no matter how happy they are?"

She took out two laminated index cards that she always kept in her purse. One said "Yes" in big green letters, and the other said "No" in big red letters. She had equipped Dale with a pair that he had long since abandoned. Using them required asking Jonathan a barrage of questions, which from Dale's perspective felt more like hassling him than talking with him. Alma understood, and for the same reason rarely used them, but decided this was one of those times she was willing to value spontaneity over articulation. She held the cards in front of him and he tapped the "No" card.

"That other place," she reminded him. "Maybe it's on a map or maybe it's a goal of some sort, and they think everything will be better there?"

He tapped on "Yes".

"We're looking for that place," she said. "For you. It might be this house, it might be a different one. But we're going to keep looking. Would you like to help?"

He chose "Yes" again.

She kissed him on the head and led him back to the house. Dale reached for her as they passed by and she squeezed his hand for a moment.

They visited a new house every week, right after Jonathan's life skills class at the recreation center. They enrolled him soon after the house hunt began, realizing his interactions with people had dwindled since he finished high school, and that combining each class with a home tour could provide a tangible glimpse into where the program could take him.

Dale would duck out of the office and meet them for lunch, where they would read up on the features of the house they were about to unlock so they could compare how closely the description matched reality.

A criteria developed as they passed through the houses. It needed to be one story, with as few bedrooms and bathrooms as possible while still being a single family home, so that Jonathan could establish clear and simple paths without sharing any walls with neighbors. They had read about people who stood on roughly the same spot of the spectrum as Jonathan and managed to become self-sufficient adults. Some lived in larger homes left behind by family, wherein most of the rooms ended up in disuse and disrepair from not being included in the routines they carved out for themselves, while others in smaller spaces ran the risk of people above them, below them, or to their sides contributing to the relentless tide of stimuli they were left to strain without a filter.

When a house looked promising upon completing a walk-through, they would drive by it at various times of the day and night to weigh the personality of the neighborhood. After the social calculations came the mathematical ones. They tabulated how much they would have to put away per month to buy it outright, and what sort of future value it may have based on its history and those of comparable homes, which they were able to access thanks to their inside source, Tess the realtor, who had known Jonathan since he was a baby and was delighted to help. Tess tended to be a little too curious as to where the money was going to come from, but they considered that a small price to pay for her assistance. They stuck to a story that featured an inheritance, as they remained sheepish over mentioning the possibility of future consulting fees.

"Why should we feel guilty about that?" Dale asked Alma when the subject came up again as they walked through a promising house and debated calling Tess for further background information.

"It just sounds weird," she replied. "Making money from education. We're not used to it."

"It sounds dirty."

"I find it more hard to believe than dirty."

Jonathan had wandered one room ahead of them and they found themselves alone, surrounded by nothing but bare white walls in the middle of a hardwood floor. An echo seemed possible just from standing still, so Dale put his lips as close as he could to Alma's ear while still being able to whisper into it.

"If I make you feel dirty, will you believe it then?"

Alma laughed quietly. He pressed on.

"Empty houses," he tried not to laugh himself, "the thrill of maybe getting caught."

"I can't believe it took you until the fourth house to suggest that," she said.

He gave in and laughed along with her. They drifted in an echo toward the door that led out of the empty room.

"So you've been thinking about it, too?" he teased.

"From the moment Tess gave me the combinations."

"Why didn't you suggest it, then?"

"Because I knew I didn't have to."

He looked at her with complete satisfaction. She let him. They held hands and restored their moving vigil behind Jonathan as he reappeared in the corridor that tied the tiny house together.

The images conjured by their erotic premise had Dale smiling on the way back to LOCA, thanks as much to the comedic possibilities as the sexual. He bounced up the stairs to his office two at a time, then grabbed the railings on each side of the catwalk and swung his legs toward the door like a gymnast on the parallel bars.

Wendy's expression as he entered tried to stop him cold, but he wasn't ready to surrender. He returned the look on her face with one of his own, to which she jerked her head in the direction of his office.

Artie sat in the chair outside his door, which still didn't faze him, as Artie's visits had become far less frequent.

"Hey," Dale greeted him. "It's been a while."

He stared at the floor and nodded.

"So what broke that impressive streak you were on?"

He shrugged.

"Artie," Wendy cut in. "Could you please go inside Mr. Copeland's office and wait for him?"

He obeyed.

Once the door was shut, Dale looked to Wendy for the explanation.

"Not good," she said.

Dale waited for her to proceed, but she clung to the same stern look she had worn since he arrived.

"Oh?" he prompted her.

"He grabbed Kimmy's butt," she declared.

Dale exhaled and shook his head.

"That's too bad," he said. "He's been doing so well."

"Maybe not," Wendy said, still working hard at remaining calm.

"What do you mean?" Dale asked.

"Candice walked him over. She was helping out in Isaiah's classroom, and Kimmy yelled, 'I'm sick of him doing that.' That's the only reason he got caught. Kimmy got fed up. And she told Candice she isn't the only one."

Dale grew silent and came up with some benign interpretations of what he just heard, but Wendy steered them aloud toward the most inevitable.

"Artie hasn't calmed down. He's just moved on from embarrassing himself to embarrassing other kids…girls…so they're too ashamed to say anything."

He kept the alternatives he was hoping for to himself. His eyes rose skyward then slowly started to sink. Just before his vision hit the floor, he dragged it toward his office door. He wasn't sure what he was going to say. The conversations he had with students often revolved around the future. But it was always the student's future that was up for discussion. His own prospects were never the point.

Chapter Ten: Candice

The town square was the feature that had sold her on the idea she could be happy there. She had never lived in a town with a bandstand and a pond at its center. Neither was large enough to host much in the way of entertainment or wildlife, squeezed into one square block as they were, but small wedding parties appreciated the photogenic backdrop each provided, and children liked to play on one and feed ducks at the other, at least until they reached a certain age.

"What a fitting symbol that small pond is now that I look back on the move," Candice said as she and Isaiah sat on a bench watching Zoey feed the ducks from a long bag of sliced sandwich bread that she was about halfway through.

"Something about a big fish?" he encouraged her.

"If there were any in there," it dawned on her. "I guess it's only half a symbol. But if there were any fish, they'd be my ex-husband. That was his whole reason for moving here. To come in and be a big shot."

"Make a big splash," Isaiah added.

Candice fake-laughed while he waved to an invisible adoring audience.

Zoey heard her Mom, saw Isaiah waving, and darted toward them while twirling the bag of bread above her head like a lasso.

"No, no!" Candice assured her. "False alarm. Not waving at you, honey!"

Zoey imitated the sound of screeching brakes as she stopped, pulling the bag into her stomach as though catching a football, then sauntered back to the anxious team of ducks.

"The energy," Isaiah shook his head. "That's why I don't teach second grade."

"I'm sure you could do it."

"I did once."

"Really?"

"Once."

"How did it go?"

"Tell me more about your husband," he smiled.

"I'm sure it wasn't that bad."

"I'm sure your husband wasn't, either."

"You really want to change the subject that badly," she nodded playfully. "Okay, then. Well...he was more like this whole place, come to think of it. The little town square is cute. So cute it's easy not to notice how many closed businesses surround it. And all the new development is around the outside, all the money sunk into expanding the city limits instead of focusing on what you've got. Wow...look at me riding this metaphor into the ground."

"I'm impressed."

"It's all that time in your class. Even if I am supposedly twenty years too old for it."

"Supposedly? Have you been lying about your age?"

"I mean," she laughed, "I can't believe how much I've learned from a sixth grade class. It seems like something I should be taking, on my own, and paying for it."

"At your age."

"At my age."

"Whatever that is."

She laughed again and pushed him.

"So what you're saying is," he picked up the earlier thread, "your husband put on some weight around the middle, around his outside..."

Her laughter grew.

"...and that represents the new houses on the edges of the city. Am I right?"

She made a buzzer sound to indicate an incorrect answer.

"You're missing the part about focusing on what you have," she said.

"I know, I know," he assured her. "I hear you."

"You know what I'm sayin'?" she imitated some of the kids in his classroom.

"I know what you're sayin'," he followed her lead, then transitioned into sincerity. "He was a nice, shiny ring that was crumbling in the middle."

Candice really appreciated his attention, but as usual held the line at having her gratitude come across as affection. She was relieved to feel a call tremble in on her cell phone, as it provided further camouflage.

The screen read 'Kimberly Althouse'.

She showed it to Isaiah.

"See?" she narrated. "I love your class so much that I'm besties with the coolest girl in it."

Isaiah was perplexed. She allowed the ensuing conversation to explain.

"Hello, darling daughter," she said to the other end. "Did you thank Kimmy for letting you use her phone?"

Isaiah mimed an 'ah-ha' of recognition.

"Yes, I did," said Mia's voice. "And she said you need to get me a phone of my own."

"She always says that."

"She's right."

"Anyway," Candice deflected her pursuit. "What's up?"

"More time?"

"How much?"

"An hour."

"Got it."

"Cool. See you then."

"Nice talking to you."

"Love you."

Candice said "I love you too," but was pretty certain Mia hung up before she heard it.

"No, really..." she cradled her phone as she slid it back into her purse. "I love you so much, honey. There aren't enough emojis on my keypad to express it."

Isaiah chuckled.

"She's still a good student," he said. "Most of the kids I've seen morph into social butterflies kind of toss that aside, at least for a while."

"Oh, I'm happy for her," she clarified. "I've been hoping for this, for her to open up. But, you know...Kimmy."

"Aw, come on, now," he smiled. "She cracked the Artie case for you. Show your star whistleblower some love already."

"Nothing came of it."

"He's on record now."

"He should have been suspended."

"That's not on Kimmy."

"If it was anyone else but her, we could have gotten a suspension."

"Are you saying she was asking for it?"

"Let's start with the skirts."

"Look, Candice," Isaiah turned up his seriousness. "Groping girls is either wrong or it isn't."

"I know, I know," she apologized. "But it just feels like everything has to line up perfectly for Artie to face any discipline. And even then, who knows?"

Isaiah appeared to accept her point. He settled back and took in the surroundings once again. She assumed his next move would be to seize on Dale's lack of leadership on the issue, which was there for the taking, or failing that, he would re-lighten the mood.

Instead he asked, "What if Mia started hanging out with Artie?"

She needed a moment to respond with something other than dumbfounded stammering.

"She wouldn't."

"Would you have thought she'd be buds with Kimmy at the beginning of the year?"

"It's a phase."

"Really?"

"Everything is at their age."

"Ah..."

He extended his exclamation like a musical note that faded into a nod. She waited for the follow up, but he left it at that.

"Ah...what?" she prodded.

"If everything's a phase, that means Artie is no more destined for a life of sexual assault than Kimmy and Mia are for a lifelong friendship."

"Maybe he will be if no one does anything about it."

"You're right," he caught himself getting too loud. "Absolutely right. So maybe we should stop hating Kimmy and Artie."

"When you say 'we,'" she joined him in slowing down the conversation in addition to lowering its volume, "do you mean that you hate them too, or is that a condescending teacher 'we'?"

"They can make it hard not to sometimes," he grinned.

Candice was grateful for the release of tension that had started to build, and as part of her relaxation, risked sharing too much.

"They rub their gifts in everyone's faces," she said. "They had nothing to do with their best attributes, but they flaunt them."

"And we don't want them to become adults who do the same thing, do we?" he added. "And I do mean 'we.'"

"No," she emphasized.

"So we let them know they are more than what they inherited, don't we?"

"Yes, teacher."

"Nah," he shook his head. "It's not like that. We're a team."

She liked the sound of that, but made an effort not to read more into it.

"Meaning all of us," she confirmed. "The whole school, it takes a village."

"The whole enchilada," he agreed, which brought Candice both relief and disappointment.

She shifted to the topic that she had wanted him to chase earlier.

"Have you had this talk with Dale?" she asked.

Isaiah exhaled.

"I never imagined it would be necessary."

Candice didn't expect to prod anything so troubling. Her most devious motive had been to illustrate the strength of their partnership by singling out a fraught teammate.

"He's so good in so many ways," she cushioned her criticism of Dale. "I've been up and down in my opinion since I met him. Mostly up."

Isaiah seemed poised at the edge but still unsure whether to jump.

"I decided to work in charter schools for some pretty specific reasons," he talked himself into it. "I wanted to see the country, do some more exploring. It was in my blood, I guess, from the way I was brought up. So I liked the idea of no tenure, a new contract every year, having an escape hatch even when I decided to settle on one school, just in case."

She thought she did a good job of not looking concerned over what this meant for his future at Live Oak.

"And going along with that freedom theme, I liked not being under the thumb of the state. But now with this board we've got, with Rod Pluma and his dancing computers, I just wonder if we're trading one thumb for another."

She stopped worrying about his plans out of respect for his anxieties, and his willingness to share them with her.

"I agree with you about Dale," he said. "He's a good man. And I imagine Rod is too. But I don't think they're aware of what they're doing to each other."

Candice left him plenty of space to continue. When it was clear that he was done, she felt responsible for the dejection that draped his silence.

"It wouldn't matter who was in charge if all teachers were like you," she said.

He smiled just enough to let her know she had given him a decent shove out from under his apprehensions.

"Thank you, Candice."

They watched Zoey knead the remaining slices of bread inside the bag into a big ball of dough. She tore big chunks from it and lobbed them into the murky water. The ducks had grown sluggish compared to their earlier frenzy, which Zoey had encouraged by tossing them tiny snippets to fight over. The constant reaching into the bag drained her as well, so the late amalgamation served them both. She was able to empty her supply with less motion, and small parties of ducks were able to feed off a single bread buoy. After launching the final glob, she announced "that's that" with equal parts relief and exaltation.

She turned and ran toward their bench.

"Bag!" Candice reminded her.

Zoey took a sharp turn to the garbage can without missing a stride, then resumed her course, stopping directly in front of Isaiah.

"Do you like Mrs. Horst?" she asked him.

He beamed out of whatever remained of his slight funk.

"I don't really know her," he smiled. "But she acts nice at the teacher meetings we have. Do you like her?"

She threw her head backwards and forwards in a theatrical nod. Candice reached over and pulled her in for a hug.

"Zoey's one of those students who always likes her teacher," she said.

Candice then looked over her daughter's shoulder at Isaiah and mouthed the words "I don't."

He restrained himself from laughing. Candice tried to get him to crack by adding barf signals and plunging her thumbs downward. She ceased fire the moment Zoey ejected from her hug with another question for Isaiah.

"Are you going to be my teacher when I'm in sixth grade?"

Isaiah inhaled a breath of diplomacy.

"We'll see," he said, then noticed Candice was also interested in his answer.

"I hope so," he added for her benefit.

"Me too," Zoey said. "Mia loves you, and she's one of those students who never likes her teacher."

Candice shrugged in Isaiah's direction and gestured in Zoey's, as if to say to him "there you have it."

She would have liked to say more, but instead suggested they get a frozen yogurt on their way to pick up Mia.

She was about to invite Isaiah, but Zoey beat her to it. He politely declined, citing some work to be done. Candice was relieved that she wasn't the one who asked, as it allowed for a more comfortable hug goodbye.

There were plenty of spaces, as usual, in the windswept parking lot of the browbeaten shopping center. Zoey recapped how much she loved her school as they walked amongst the tattered paper and cardboard products that skidded across the pavement. They sat at one of the rubber tables where Zoey rocked back and forth in an uneven chair while sharing all the good things she had heard about the teachers she would have as she made her way up the grades at Live Oak Charter Academy.

Candice reminded her every so often to keep eating her yogurt before it melted, but she was grateful to hear her daughter's voice, feeling as though her own didn't have much to say.

Chapter Eleven: Rodrigo

The plan was to let Gio handle most of the tour. He had been a forklift operator at the distribution center back when Rod still owned Pluma Produce. Rod liked to deliver his own goods whenever possible, and Gio would help him unload. A bond developed that led to Rod hiring him to manage the center when he sold Pluma Produce and took over the corporation's regional operations. He looked forward to an opportunity to watch his former apprentice run the show for the LOCA sixth grade field trip, but wanted to handle the words of welcome before handing the kids over to Gio.

He stood on a wooden palette that Gio had lifted a foot off the ground with a forklift to serve as a platform. Rod told the kids he understood how easy it is too feel isolated in a town like theirs, how small the world can seem. He said he used to think the same things. "Just me and the crops," he would mutter as passed the fields, and later worked in them. "More crops than people," he would curse the land around him, and wish for the kind of connections that were possible in a big city. But then he started to learn about where these crops ended up. He asked the kids if they knew. A couple of them raised their hands and guessed some of the nearest big cities. They were right, he told them, but there were many more right answers. Some other cities were named, and he praised their knowledge and asked them to think even bigger. They started to name countries, and as he told each one they were correct, eyebrows started to raise and mouths open. When the buzzing started to summit, he made his final push, telling them that they are more connected to the world than they realize, and that while their town may be small, it plays a big role. He closed with "And you can play a big role, too, if you work hard and stay in school."

He had debated whether to use the line about working hard and staying in school, since it was so derivative, but went with it when the time came, since he figured they were too young to have been overexposed to it. He introduced Gio and hopped off the palette.

"You're not going to tell them to stay off drugs, too?" Gio whispered to him with a grin as they switched places to the requisite applause of the class.

Rod chuckled and settled off to the side to watch his former disciple at work. He told the kids he started out driving the same kind of forklift he now used as a stage, and the image of him rising above his beginnings was not lost on Rod. He looked on with pride, then looked over at Artie, who looked back at his Dad with pride. His son nodded as if to say "thank you," and Rod returned the gesture.

Their exchange of nods stared down any guilt he may still have been confronting over his efforts to keep his son from getting suspended.

Not that it took much effort. More than he would have anticipated, but a brief conversation nonetheless.

Dale had called him in to discuss what happened with Artie, even though Rita was teaching art that day.

"I would be more comfortable talking to you about it," Dale said over the phone when Rod reminded him that Rita was on site. "Or maybe the both of you. But not Rita by herself."

Rod rearranged his schedule and reached the campus within a half hour. He assumed Dale's caution had to do with their business relationship, that he was hesitant to do anything about Artie without first consulting him. And though their phone conversation had been brief, little in Dale's tone led him to believe his son was involved in anything drastic.

His worry grew upon arriving in the waiting area. Artie sat outside Dale's office, and Wendy greeted him as though it was a prison visit. He nodded at her and asked Artie what happened.

"You should wait until the meeting is over," Wendy gravely suggested.

Artie looked down and his lip started to quake, so Rod followed Wendy's direction if only to spare his son's dignity.

She tapped on Dale's door and poked her head in, which added to the tension, as Dale usually came out to greet him. She leaned back out and announced with a chill that Mr. Copeland was ready for him. The chill dropped several more degrees when she told Artie to stay outside with her.

When Rod finally found out what instigated this pall, he started to laugh, and had to catch himself from getting too loud. He didn't want Artie, or Wendy, to hear.

Dale seemed to want to join in, but the most he could manage was a tight smile.

Rod collected himself and leaned back in his chair.

"Boys will be boys," he said.

Dale stopped smiling. He started to say something.

"I know, I know," Rod interrupted him. "That sounds bad. But I never thought I'd be able to say that about Arturo."

Dale appeared to loosen up.

"He has gone through some changes, it seems."

"All of a sudden," Rod agreed. "It's like he got tired of being pushed around."

Dale nodded, and proceeded to do so longer than Rod expected.

"So what has Artie been telling you?" Dale finally said.

"About what?"

"How kids treat him?"

"He's a target," Rod said.

"He said that?"

"No, that's what I gathered. He doesn't tell me anything."

"Well, this isn't the first complaint we've had. Just the first of this nature. Hasn't Rita mentioned anything before?"

"Yes. That he gets picked on."

Dale took a moment and looked away.

"Look, Dale," Rod seized the pause. "We're not holding you responsible for the other kids' behavior. They're jealous. We understand. We're with you on this sort of thing."

"You're with me..." Dale needed clarification.

"We share your belief that kids need to work things out for themselves."

"The adventure playground is one thing," he replied. "This is something else."

"Is it?" Rod posed.

Dale waited, perhaps for inspiration.

"Yes," he finally said.

For the first time in the conversation, Rod felt like he truly was on the visitor's side of the desk.

"So what were you thinking of doing?" he asked Dale.

"Suspension."

He wanted to pull every cent he had donated and cancel the computer deal. But he took a deep breath and instead tried to explain why that was unfair, in a volume still inaudible through the door.

"Everyone is so sensitive these days," he hissed. "So goddamn sensitive. How many butts did you grab when you were a kid, Dale?"

"I might have grabbed a few," he admitted.

"And were you suspended?"

"No."

"There you go."

"Maybe I should have been."

Rod was surprised at how much Dale was pushing back.

"The field trip to our distribution center is scheduled for next week," he reminded him.

"It doesn't have to be a week-long suspension," Dale offered. "Three days would have him back in time."

Since Dale was willing to negotiate, Rod assessed that he could still save Artie with some nuance. He didn't want to dangle the money over him. They both knew it was there.

"Where would you be now, Dale, if you were suspended each time you did something wrong?"

"Nobody is suggesting that should happen."

"But that's the way it ends up going a lot of the time, doesn't it?" Rod sensed he was on to something. "A kid gets suspended once, then when something happens again, people can't believe he didn't get the message, so he gets suspended again. Now he's a problem. He's got a reputation. He starts bouncing from one school to another..."

He stopped there.

More points were waiting to spill out, none of them intended as a threat. But now that he had stumbled upon one, a delicious combination of soft and jagged, he let it hang there.

Dale appeared to weigh the consequences of Artie bouncing away from Live Oak Charter Academy. They seemed to once again switch places around the desk.

"Why don't you take him home today," Dale ended the silence. "And I'll write a report that either you or Rita can sign off on when you bring him to school tomorrow."

"Fair enough," Rod said.

He stood up and extended his hand toward Dale, who rose and shook it. But then Dale sat back down and gripped the handles of his chair, rather than come around and hold the door open, as was his custom. Rod waited for a moment to see if he would relent, but Dale had entered a trance. He caught himself and looked up at Rod.

"I should get started on that report," he said, then started to open his desk drawers as though he had no idea what was inside them.

Rod let himself out and corralled Artie under his arm.

"Let's go home, son."

As they passed by Wendy's desk, she managed to smile at them, but it came across as conditional. She looked past them toward Dale's office.

Rod relieved her suspense.

"We'll see you tomorrow," he said.

He waited until they reached the door to turn and check her reaction. She just managed to refasten her smile as they made eye contact, but it was even less convincing than before.

"See you tomorrow," she attached to her smile.

He wrapped his arm all the more tightly around his son as they left and walked to the car.

The memory of that walk prompted him to re-enact putting his arm around Artie as Gio led them outside the distribution center to look at some the equipment his company made available to any grower who contracted with them. He was pleased that Artie didn't fidget away from his grasp, as he imagined the other kids would if one of their parents tried the same maneuver. His son was proud of him.

Gio gathered everyone around a lettuce harvester they had recently acquired, a newer model that used water jets to sever the leaves from their base before rolling tongs scooped them onto the conveyer belt that guided the greens up and away from their roots to wherever they were destined.

When the jets first came on, most of the kids jumped with a start and laughed at themselves. Then as the gears started spinning the scoopers and belts, Artie started humming a song that Rod couldn't quite place, but fittingly accompanied the whirring mechanism.

"What is that you're singing?" he asked.

"It's from the Bugs Bunny cartoons," Artie looked up at him from the crook of Rod's arm. "When they're running around a factory or stuck in a machine."

He went back to humming and Rod let it vibrate through his body as he kept Artie close until the tune suddenly tapped into some visuals that goosed a laugh out of him, and not only thanks to images from cartoons he hadn't thought of in decades. As Artie's soundtrack implied, the harvester was also rather cartoonish in how specific it was, in its elaborate and ingenious response to a single task. There was no other job it could perform.

He thought of how much he would have appreciated working with such a contraption back in his field days. But maybe it would have replaced him, or pushed him in a different direction. Maybe his resolve would not have been sharpened to such a fine point if he had been spared the thousands of hours stooped over, cold and wet, or hot and dusty. In combining the old with the new, he wished that old sensibilities could be maintained with new amenities, that struggle and want could somehow be programmed into the systems. He hoped such a marriage was possible in their plans for LOCA, that fortitude and ease could run parallel to one another. It would be a challenge, but staying hungry in a kingdom of convenience struck him as the great struggle of their times.

As Gio demonstrated some other cutting edge pieces of equipment, though, and led the flock of small, colorful polo shirts into a massive refrigerated warehouse filled three stories high with food that was on its way to their tables, Rod surrendered his dream of a tougher America.

It wasn't a fair fight.

Chapter Twelve: Mia

She had the window seat on the bus ride back from Mr. Pluma's company, since Kimmy had it on the way there. That was the deal. They felt it was worth compromising to sit in the back row, as it put them the farthest away from authority.

Beatrice sat in the seat in front of them, and had the window round-trip, since she sat next to a girl who preferred the aisle.

Artie sat in the center of the back row, so Mia had been next to him en route to his Dad's display. She had wanted to talk to him more than she did, and Kimmy kept nudging her to do so, but the kind of conversation she wanted to have with him was not possible. She wanted to pick up on what he had said to her the day they found themselves alone, setting up the obstacle course for the Kindergarteners. That wasn't going to happen on a noisy bus filled with noisy kids, though, particularly in the back of it.

Kimmy had no trouble talking to him. The chaos and shallow chit chat fostered by their surroundings was the way she liked it. Any animosity she held over recent encounters with Artie had either passed or was lying dormant in the interest of enjoying the moment.

She harped on his size, as she often did, but this time in a manner that played up how cuddly and cute it made him.

"Look, Mia," she sung above the clamor.

Mia pulled her attention away from the tawny valley that passed by the window. Kimmy had Artie on her lap.

"I made him at a Build-A-Bear Workshop," she rested her head against his. "It's an Artie. Isn't he cute?"

Mia smiled and was about to look back out the window.

"And watch," Kimmy continued. "When you tickle him..."

Artie pretended to dread what was coming next. Kimmy followed through.

"He giggles and wiggles!"

He indeed did all of the above. Some of the other kids noticed and took time off from the rest of the adjacent goofiness to laugh along with him, or perhaps at him.

"There's like a computer chip inside him or something," Kimmy added. "Ooh, the things they can do nowadays."

The noise level rose to a point where the bus driver and Mr. Benton snapped at everyone to quiet down.

Enough of them obeyed to bring down the volume.

Kimmy stopped tickling Artie and pinched his cheek before shoving him back into his seat with a "Stay there, Artie Bear."

Mia was finally able to return her gaze to the countryside, and noticed Beatrice looking back. She smirked and shook her head for Mia's benefit, who silently agreed. Mia thought the aisle seat next to Beatrice was looking pretty good.

The back of the bus soon started to regenerate its rolling circus, with each clique once again establishing their rings.

"Why don't you ever grab Mia's butt?" she heard Kimmy ask Artie.

Mia was blinded with adrenaline as she pretended not to hear. There may as well have been nothing on the other side of the glass for her to see.

"What?" Artie said, sounding as surprised as Mia felt.

"You heard me," Kimmy pressed on. "You're either afraid to, or just don't want to."

"Why would I be afraid?" Artie quivered.

"Because you like her."

Mia glanced around as best she could without moving her head, trying to see if anyone else had taken an interest in the conversation. Everyone seemed to be preoccupied with their own contributions to the bustle, which provided a flash of relief.

"I don't like her," he said, then qualified his answer. "In that way."

"Aw, come on," Kimmy volleyed. "Her butt's even nicer than mine. She just doesn't flaunt it like I do. I'll bet that's why you don't grab it. You respect her too much."

"Kimmy…" Mia decided to get involved.

"It's nothing to be ashamed of," Kimmy put her arm around Mia. "Admit it. Your butt is better than mine. And I'm fine with it."

She lowered her arm down Mia's back.

"Fine," she said as she brought her hand across Mia's waist.

"You hear me?" she passed below the belt. "Fine!"

Mia jumped and laughed before Kimmy could reach the topic of discussion. She wondered if Kmmy was always conscious of her relationship to the word 'fine', or if she had finally caught on thanks to spending more time with the likes of her and Beatrice.

As Mia calmed down, she noticed how Artie was looking at her. He was wide open, not a trace of buffoonery or bravado on his face, appearing to have finally met an object of his affection whom he had only seen from a distance.

Mia had never had this effect on anyone before, and never imagined she would. The adrenalin that had blinded her now filled her with a warm awareness. She felt as though her body was growing bigger and lighter at the same time.

"And I totally get it," Kimmy narrated the moment Mia shared with Artie. "I totally get the attraction. She's got a lot more brains than I do, to go with that tight little bod."

Mia lapsed back into a thin layer of discomfort, but only out of modesty rather than a desire for Kimmy to stop. She was feeling too beautiful to want it to end.

"We don't have to test the smarts," Kimmy proceeded. "I mean, the results have been in all year. Can we agree that Mia is smarter than me?"

"Yes," Artie smiled.

Mia turned away and felt herself blush.

"So all we need to do is prove the body part," Kimmy said. "Since she doesn't show it off like I do, we need a test."

Mia didn't remember what followed with as much accuracy as what preceded it.

She remembered Kimmy switching places with Artie so that he was in between them.

She remembered standing up and turning around and thinking he was just going to look at each of them from behind.

She remembered Beatrice making an effort to not look back.

And she remembered being relieved that Kimmy was blocking everyone's view of what happened, whatever it was.

Chapter Thirteen: Dale

He was running a P.E. session for Jay Quintero's fourth grade class when he saw the bus drive by on the frontage road.

The fourth graders were playing capture the flag in the most trampled-down part of the meadow, where Dale and a gang of Dads had cleared some brush for just such an occasion.

"Wrap it up and bring it in!" he hollered as Jay emerged from the upper cluster to collect them. Quintero was a young teacher who had little else to offer besides energy when the school year had started, but was starting to show signs of fulfilling the promise of his interview.

Dale could hear the bus shifting into a lower gear as it turned into the parking lot around the front of the building, and decided to jog over and greet them.

With a high-five from Jay as he hit his stride, Dale made it in time to wave like an ecstatic tourist pulling into port on a cruise. He got some laughs and some imitations from the faces in the windows before they stood up to disembark. Moving over to the door, he held out his hand for two dozen more high-fives as he welcomed them back and intermittently asked the passing line how it went. They responded with either a 'good' or a 'fine', with an occasional over-the-top "awesome!" from one of the boys trying to be funny.

He expected Artie to be one of them, but he was unresponsive.

Since Artie was one of the last to exit, Dale only had to wait for a couple of girls to pass before Isaiah came down the steps with a discreet announcement.

"We may have a situation."

Chapter Fourteen: Candice

There weren't many apartment buildings in town, and Candice knew them all, their interiors and exteriors, thanks to her job. One of her fellow property managers joked that everything you needed to know about renting an apartment in their territory could be found in the real estate listings.

"If you can't get into a house here," he wheezed between sips from his 64-ounce soda, "You might as well give up."

With some exceptions, she considered it a fair portrait.

She walked the inner courtyard of The Oasis Apartments and wondered if she would ever meet the owners of the building. She was certain they had never seen the place. An occasional dead palm tree teetered high above the complex, trying to lend credence to the name written in bamboo font above the street address, but the dehydrated fronds at the top clacked in the wind and undermined the effort. The back patios were enclosed by cinder block walls painted light brown that stood waist-high to an adult, making it easy to steal the items gathering in the corners, if they were worth stealing. Some residents did complain of theft, of things undeniably worthless. Candice supposed the only reason anyone would take a Big Wheel with a missing big wheel, or a rusted toaster oven with a missing door, was to feel as though something, anything, had been gained.

The only possessions in good shape were the satellite dishes mounted on the tops of the short bunker walls, and nobody stole them because everybody had one. Many of the walls had stains running down them, remnants of when a potted plant stood on the ledge leaking soiled water, or a tenant emptied their grease pan.

Candice sat on a bench in the center court along the weathered path that was the same color as the dried grass that it passed through. She reviewed the report she was going to file on behalf of a resident who had not been able to completely turn off the bathtub spigot for two years.

Nothing ever came of these requests, however, and once again she found herself growling, "Three days."

She thought burying herself in work would sublimate her anger over recent events, but she kept falling into the same disgruntled mantra.

"Three days."

The owner of The Oasis took money from the people who lived there, whose money came from whatever government subsidy they were on. There were profits for the top, and help for the bottom, and she was stuck in the middle, where there were no profits and there was no help.

As it was with everything.

As it was with Live Oak Charter Academy.

She didn't dare come to campus. She texted Isaiah and told him she was out for a while, maybe for good. He kept his reply simple, "I understand," and left it at that.

She even avoided the parking lot. She was afraid of what she might do or say if she got too close to the building. She picked up Zoey and Mia in the same spot that she had been dropping them off every morning, as she had for the past week. They stood on the sidewalk several paces down from the parking lot entrance, and even Zoey looked tired of this routine.

"Hello, ladies!" she put on a cheery face as Mia climbed into the front seat and Zoey the back.

While they responded by rote and buckled their seat belts, Candice scanned the campus for signs of the Pluma family, found none, and noticed that Dale was still avoiding his old routine of mingling with the parents after school.

"Has Mrs. Pluma been teaching art?" Candice asked as they pulled away from the curb.

"Yes," Zoey answered from the back seat.

"I haven't seen her car," said Candice, glancing at Mia.

"She leaves early," Zoey continued to do the talking.

"Isn't Artie back?"

"She takes him with her," Mia finally joined in. "They come late, after morning announcements, then leave after her session with the eighth graders."

"That's about an hour before school ends," Candice noted.

"Lucky Artie!" Zoey chimed in.

"I'll say," Candice muttered.

"What?" Zoey asked.

"Nothing," Candice said, and looked over to find Mia glaring at her.

"What?" she addressed Mia's disdain. "They obviously know they got off easy. Otherwise they wouldn't be sneaking around."

"Got off easy for what?" Zoey asked.

"Nothing," Mia said to her sister.

"Nothing," she then said to her Mom.

Candice lifted her fingers above the steering wheel in mock surrender. They spent the rest of the drive home in silence.

As they pulled into their driveway, Zoey asked if she could check for eggs and feed the chickens. Their house was within the city limits, but in a small development of homes on the edge of town built on quarter-acre parcels that provided enough space to allow their father to pursue his dream of being a gentleman farmer, the same dream that motivated his purchase of the used Jeep Cherokee that Candice still drove after his dream reached its morning after.

While chickens remained in the coops, the livestock pens stood empty. Mia raised a lamb as a 4-H project the first year they moved in, but was heartbroken over having to sell it for meat, and their father left before he got around to filling the property with any other animals. Zoey had heard the story of selling the lamb, and decided to stick with eggs as the sole sustenance provided by their layout.

"That would be very helpful, Zoey," Candice said. "Thank you."

Her youngest daughter was out of the backseat and through the back door of the garage the moment they stopped. Candice was proud of being the only person in the neighborhood who was able to park in her garage. Mia liked to remind her it was only because they didn't have a boat or jet skis, not because they were any more tidy than the others.

Candice was surprised that Mia remained seated as the garage door closed behind them. She wanted to try and get her to talk some more, but was expecting to have to chase her down to do so.

Not only did Mia stay, she initiated the conversation. Granted, it wasn't the same one Candice had in mind.

"Nobody knows what happened," she snapped at her Mom while continuing to look through the windshield. "Only the people involved. So why would the Plumas need to sneak around?"

"Whoever told on Artie knows," Candice pointed out.

Mia looked her way.

"Beatrice would never tell anyone," she said.

Candice took advantage of being the one who could look askance this time.

"Never tell anyone besides Mr. Benton," Mia clarified.

"I'm sure people noticed Artie was missing for three days, and I'm sure Beatrice wasn't the only one who saw something. She was just the only one brave enough to do anything about it."

"And you're the only one making a big deal about it."

Mia got out of the Jeep and passed through the door that led into the kitchen. Candice followed her. Mia took advantage of her head start and was almost to her room by the time Candice caught up and blocked her way.

"If it's not that big of a deal, then why won't you tell me what happened?"

"Ask Mr. Copeland," Mia looked down.

"He said he would be willing, but wanted to give you the opportunity first."

"I don't want it."

"Yes, you've made that clear, but I really, really, really don't want to talk to Mr. Copeland about anything right now, much less this."

"How about Mr. Benton? You two get along."

"Mia, please..."

"I don't know!" Mia shrieked. "I don't remember!"

Candice tried to hug her, but Mia squirmed away.

"Can I please just go to my room?" she said, clearly on the verge of tears that she clearly didn't want her mother to see.

Candice nodded and stepped aside.

She was hoping that Mia would slam the door, right in her face, so that Candice could get back to feeling angry. But instead her daughter gently shut the door, and when the latch struck into place, the small sound of its click tore through Candice and left an echo that only she could hear.

She floated back down the hall as she reconsidered every decision she had ever made, and arrived at the kitchen in time to meet Zoey entering from the back door with an egg in the palm of each hand.

"Double whammy!" Zoey proclaimed, thrusting the eggs forward.

"Great," Candice managed to say.

Zoey lowered the eggs.

"Are you okay, Mom?"

"Fine."

"Is it the thing with Mia?"

"Well...yes."

"You should talk to someone about it. That's what all the adults say."

Hearing the advice coming from her second-grade daughter elevated it above the cliché, and made her realize there was a good reason it was repeated so often.

"You are absolutely right, my love," she kissed Zoey's forehead. "I'll do that. Now why don't you add those eggs to the carton in the fridge and get started on your homework."

Zoey kissed her back and complied, bouncing over to put away the eggs, then trudging in an exaggerated slouch over to her backpack on the kitchen table.

"In your room, please," Candice said.

She slid her backpack off the table and remained true to her performance all the way to her room, as the sound and rattle of her overstated stomping filled the house until her door closed, bringing a temporary halt to the youthful dramas.

"At least hers is fake," Candice mused.

She didn't want to talk to Isaiah, to expose herself even more. But all of her other friends were in cities she had left behind, and she hadn't done a good enough job of keeping in touch with them to maintain the right to call them all of a sudden to vent about a situation that she would have to explain first.

She started with a text.

Can I call you? she wrote.

She remained standing and stared out the window at the front yard next to the driveway. Replacing the lawn with drought-tolerant plants that were leftovers from a landscaping project contracted by her employer was a great idea. She had made at least one good decision in her life, after all.

Isaiah wrote back. She imagined him in the classroom doing some grading.

Certainly, he typed.

Now?

Yes.

She tapped on the number and he answered before the first ring completed its note.

"I'm sorry to bother you," she said.

"I was looking for an excuse to take a break," he assured her. "What's up?"

"You probably know."

"Probably."

She was glad that they were talking on the phone rather than in person. She could pace and hide her facial expressions as she struggled to choose her words carefully. And if she chose wisely, she had a chance to come across as being interested in a civil discussion rather than a rant.

"She won't talk to me about it."

"About how she feels?" he asked. "Or what happened?"

"About anything."

"She's embarrassed."

"Was it that bad?"

She realized that sounded like a hint.

"Not that I'm asking you to tell me what happened," she clarified.

"It's okay."

"Oh," she wondered if that meant it was okay to ask.

And if that was the case, she wondered if she wanted to hear it from him.

"I really don't know much, anyway," he said.

"Oh," she said again, and bared her teeth at herself for being so repetitious.

"Beatrice came to the front of the bus on our way back from Pluma's field trip," he explained. "She told me Artie was back to his old tricks with some of the girls, and I sent him over to Dale's office when the bus pulled in."

"Old tricks?" she quipped. "More like a pattern."

"You're right. Poor choice of words."

Candice hadn't thought that a detailed account of the event was what she was after, but now that such a direction was crossed off, she wasn't sure where to go next.

"Candice?" Isaiah said after the pause had grown lengthy.

"Sorry."

"What did you want this conversation to be about?"

She wasn't sure how to answer the question, so she said the first thing that came to mind.

"It must have been pretty bad if she's that ashamed."

"It certainly wasn't good."

"How are the kids interacting with each other?"

"The kids in general, or Artie and Kimmy and Mia?"

"So Kimmy was the other girl?"

"You didn't even know that?"

"Perfect," she reared back then bent forward. "Just perfect. Mia must think I know. She hasn't asked for permission to spend time with Kimmy lately. Then again, she hasn't wanted to go anywhere. How is she doing at school?"

"All right. A little quiet. Kind of like the earlier version of Mia this year."

"But her work is okay?"

"It is."

"What about Artie?"

"What about him?"

"Any remorse?"

"He's not proud of himself."

"Why would that even be an option?"

"I've seen lots of kids wear a suspension like a badge of honor. You've seen it, too. He's not doing that."

"I guess I had him all wrong."

"Candice..." Isaiah sounded like he was trying to reboot the conversation. "You said you wanted to talk. So let's get off the kids and talk about how you're feeling."

"Isn't it obvious?" she was veering into a rant, but couldn't stop. "And what makes me even more angry and frustrated is that no one else is angry and frustrated. Three days? Three days? That should have happened weeks ago. Months. He should be gone by now. Maybe I shouldn't be talking to you. Maybe that's the problem. I should be talking to everyone. If everyone knew, maybe they would feel like I do."

"I'm frustrated too, Candice."

"Are you?"

"Yes."

"You could have fooled me."

"I'm resigning."

The phone may as well have blown up in her hand. The silence after the blast was deeper than the noise before it, then it rose to the surface of a normal hush.

"Maybe resigning isn't the right word," Isaiah said at last. "I'm finishing this year, but not coming back. You know I've been concerned about the way things are going here, and this incident pretty much sealed the deal."

Candice wasn't able to say anything. The news was still ringing in her ears.

"I've sent out some applications," he continued. "If I get any interviews, they'll be in the spring. That's when I was going to tell you, and the kids, once I had a sense if there was any interest."

"There will be interest, Isaiah."

"I've moved around a lot. That may scare some people away."

"All it takes is one," she said. "If one of them interviews you, they'll hire you."

"That's nice of you to say. And I know you're not feeling like saying anything nice right now."

"I feel like telling the truth. Some truths are nice."

The quiet this time was shared. Neither seemed capable of breaking it. Perhaps out of habit, Isaiah was the one who did.

"I wanted to be more prepared when I told you," he said. "I wanted it to be under better circumstances."

"But I wanted proof that you were on my side," she said. "And I got it."

He exhaled.

"Could you please do me a favor and not tell anyone? I'd like to deliver the news myself when the time is right."

"And because you still need Dale as a reference?"

There was a pause in which Candice assumed he was debating whether to respond to what she said. If that was the case, he decided not to.

"Do I have your word?" he asked.

"Of course you do, Isaiah. Who am I to stand in the way of greatness?"

"Thank you. I'm sorry."

"I'm sorry, too. You're welcome."

She heard him hang up.

"Good talk," she said anyway.

Candice was more grateful than ever for having had the conversation over the phone. She was able to sit on her couch and fall onto her side and smell how musty the cushions had grown before she started to cry.

She kept reaching for anger, and kept finding sadness.

Chapter Fifteen: Rodrigo

Rita was more sensitive than he was.

Her family traced their lineage to the Spanish ranchos, and when they were dating, she would perceive slights no matter whose family gathering they were attending. If it was her family, she would rail over how snobbish they were in their conviction that Rod was beneath their station. If it was his family, she would decry how boorish they were in cloaking their insecurity with crass remarks meant to make her blush. Rod would rarely notice until Rita took him through a detailed account of what happened at the party they had just left. Then he could start to see her point.

When they were married and started to attend corporate events as Rod made his way upstream, she would try to convince him that they were being racially profiled by the moneyed stiffs even as they drove up in the same type of car as his colleagues and tipped the valets just as much.

"I can see it in their eyes," she once complained. "They imagine you in a big belt buckle and El Norteno shirt, and me in big hair and fake nails."

He had a harder time being persuaded by her point of view when it came to the work world. She told him that was because he didn't want it to be true. He needed to value the opinions of his business associates so that he could keep working his way up and keep chucking the opinions of his family or her family back in their self-righteous faces. Professional respect was the most important kind of respect to him.

So when she first became convinced that there was backlash building amongst the Live Oak parents over Artie's suspension, Rod decided to take her suspicions seriously, as the LOCA folk were closer to being colleagues than they were family, and held power over his charitable legacy.

Rod and Rita assumed that most of the resentment, however much there was, revolved around their money. They still believed their wealth made Artie more of a target than a favorite, but they had to try and see the alternative, for they couldn't undermine what they didn't understand. Each agreed to imagine the stereotype that had developed about their relationship, and in turn Artie, and come up with ways to combat those projections.

They wanted to get their ideas aligned and lay out a plan before sharing it with Artie, who had a penchant for eavesdropping at their bedroom door. So they tried whispering in Rita's walk-in closet, which felt silly, and talking in the master bathroom with the water running, which was a waste of water, so they decided on a quick lunch date at the Taco Bell off the freeway exit during a break between Rita's art class commitments.

"Let's start with the most obvious accusation," she got the session started as they sat down with their trays full of wrapping paper, paper napkins, and paper cups. "He's spoiled."

"Not a lot we can do about that one," Rod unwrapped his first item.

Rita kept her jaw from dropping, but all the stunned energy went into her eyes.

"We can stop," she reminded him.

"That doesn't do us any good."

"Maybe it will do Artie some good."

Rod hesitated and would have scratched his head if he wasn't holding a crunchy taco.

"I thought the goal was to generate some good P.R.," he said.

"Well, yes. But..."

"So how is anyone going to know we've stopped spoiling him? Do we make sure he complains out loud about us not buying him as many things as we used to? Whine to anybody who'll listen? How does the message get out?"

Rita sucked on her straw before offering a reply.

"If we do the right things, then it will show. It will come across natural."

Rod waved her off while swallowing his latest bite.

"We need to polish our image right away," he said as soon as his mouth was empty. "Before whatever they're thinking about us becomes cemented in their minds. That cement dries fast. We can worry about all the long-term goals you want once we get past this."

Rita released her cup from an inch above the tray, letting it drop into place.

"Okay," she increased the tension before releasing her sarcasm, "How about a special episode of his show, where he delivers all of the Legos he's used to the Salvation Army. Or maybe right to the doors of some struggling families."

In spite of her delivery, Rod was pleasantly surprised by the idea.

"Just one problem," he said.

"Just one?"

"Aside from how quickly we could get it out there, and whether it would cross over into the kind of audience we need..."

"And if one of those struggling households is a meth lab and they answer the door with a shotgun..."

"It punishes Artie too much."

"Yes," she agreed. "Getting shot is a bit much. And on camera. Oye."

"I'm serious," he leaned in. "It's all about blaming the parents these days. Whenever a kid goes bad, it's all eyes on the parents. Even when the story goes that he played too many violent video games, or listened to scary music, that only happened because the parents didn't do their job. Your whole life is supposed to be wrapped up in your kids. God forbid you should have any other interests."

"You're starting to sound defensive, Rigo."

"I know what people are thinking. They see you volunteering around school, but they see me throwing money at it. Then they hear about Artie. So they think he's acting out because I'm not there for him. They say I buy him things because I'm always working. That's what people who don't have money like to tell themselves. They claim to be more loving, more caring, because that's all they've got. It has to be one way or the other for them. There has to be a sacrifice, they say, you have to choose, your kids or your career. They don't want to admit you can have it all."

Rita seemed to think there was more to come. He felt like taking a bow to signal he had said his piece, but took another bite instead.

"So what's your plan?" she asked.

He grunted and raised a finger to let her know he meant to follow through on that part, then skipped a lot of chewing to get down to it.

"Yard duty," he announced.

"You?"

"Of course me. I'll show them who's there for their kid."

"What about work?"

"I'll tell them I need do some work from home to spend more time with my son," he took a sip to help lubricate the mouthful he had rushed. "They'll think it's beautiful. Business is all mobile now, anyway. We barely need the office space. It's for meetings and to impress clients, like a stage."

He went into greater detail about how he could bring his work with him and pick at it during the breaks between each recess, and how he could serve as the new destination for Artie when he was ejected from the classroom, rather than Dale's office.

Dale was just as enthusiastic about the plan when Rod ran it by him, and went so far as to say that the new procedure would likely cut down on the number of times Artie was asked to leave in the first place. Rod would set up camp at one of the picnic benches near the main building and serve as a sort of lieutenant.

As they concluded their meeting with the most agreeable handshake they had fastened in weeks, Dale said out loud what Rod was feeling, that they were back in business.

"Just do me a favor," Rod said as Dale made a move to get the door for him.

"What's that?" Dale asked, trying to balance a smile on top of the hesitation that the word 'favor' doused over him.

Rod chuckled at his reaction before putting him at ease.

"No announcements about this, no big deal," he put a hand on Dale's shoulder. "I'm just a parent helping out."

Dale breathed easier and gave him his word as he opened the door.

Rod exchanged as pleasant a goodbye with Dale as he did with Wendy on his way past her desk. She seemed to have overcome the resentment that colored their last encounter, or at least had groomed her ability to cover it.

The same could not be said for the other adults on campus the first day he reported for duty. Any doubts he may have had regarding his wife's assessment of the reigning attitude toward him and his family were squelched upon arrival. He had not been on site since the suspension ended, and he hadn't received so many dirty looks attempting to masquerade as blank stares since he used to stop by the grocery store in his filthy flannel shirt and jeans after getting off work from the fields.

The kids didn't express any hostility. They hardly noticed he was there. But Artie stuck by his side while the students played out their last few minutes before the first whistle. Rod wondered if his son had noticed the glances and was standing with him out of solidarity, or if Artie was in exile due to what had happened.

"You can go hang out," Rod encouraged him.

"I'm okay," Artie said.

They stood there together in the swarm of colored polo shirts, silently searching for safe places to rest their eyes amidst the vigorous screams, rubber balls splatting against pavement, and arguments over who was winning. Rod couldn't remember the last time he had felt so much like crying. Maybe out of happiness when Artie was born. If his son was taking some heat, he hoped he could take it for him by being there.

The whistle blew and the khaki stampede sprinted around them into the showroom. Rod was grateful for the wind that the herd generated as they sped past. It made him laugh and dried his eyes. Once everyone was inside, Artie tugged his Dad over for a kiss and walked in to join them.

Dale held up his end of the deal by making the morning announcements without a word in Rod's direction. Rod kept to the back of the room, which made it even easier to notice the heads turning to sneak a glare at him, from both volunteers and faculty.

The picnic bench he had in mind was available, on the route between the upper cluster and the main building. The rest of the volunteers were inside, either helping out in a classroom, or avoiding him by staying in the showroom or the garage. He laid out his work and pretended to do it. A text from Rita was the only task that engaged him. She let him know she was on her way and would like some help carrying in a box of supplies. He went around the side of the building when he heard her car pull in.

"You weren't kidding," Rod said as he met her in the parking lot.

"Stay cool," she reminded him, handing over the box.

On their way to the front door, they passed the mounted plaque commemorating all that he had done to establish the campus. Rod breathed deeply and stuck to their agreement that they wouldn't acknowledge the situation while on the premises.

He had no such agreement with Dale, however, who approached him after the morning recess and the two dozen nasty looks that came with it. Rod stayed seated at the picnic table to help him remain calm.

"Hey there, partner," Dale greeted him. "I know you've got work to do, but would you be up for helping me out with some P.E. classes today?"

Rod barely heard him.

"What the hell is going on here, Dale?"

"What do you mean?"

"Cut the crap."

Dale exhaled.

"I don't know for sure."

"Well what do you suspect is happening?"

"I did nothing to breech confidentiality. I told no one about the incident or the suspension."

"But somebody did."

"That seems to be the case."

"Was it Wendy?"

"I would vouch for Wendy's ethics over mine."

"Then who is it?"

Dale hesitated.

Rod got off the bench and stood squarely in front of him.

"Who is doing this, Dale? How do all these people know?"

"I have my suspicions."

"Is it one of the girls involved?"

"No."

"Their parents?"

"One of the parents."

"Which one?"

"And what if I tell you, Rod? What would you do with that information?"

Rod hadn't thought that far ahead.

"This bothers me, too," Dale said. "Maybe even more than you."

"I doubt that."

"Do you know what we are without you?" Dale was straining to keep his composure. "We are a small school. A small school in the middle of nowhere. And nobody gives a shit about small schools in the middle of nowhere."

They faced each other for an eternal few seconds before Dale spoke up.

"You've got a good plan. Stick with it. Let me handle the rest."

Rod nodded and sat down. He stared at the work in front of him and wondered if he would ever be in the mood to get it done. Dale left him with one more thought.

"Rise above them and they'll remember who you are."

Rod listened to Dale walk away and continued to look down at the tabletop, consumed by one more thought of his own.

He shouldn't have to remind them. They wouldn't be there without him. The grounds from which they gave him dirty looks were his creation. And if they insisted on hating him, they should thank him for the opportunity to do so.

Chapter Sixteen: Mia

The road to their father's condominium was for the most part a long stretch of highway that lent itself to silence. It connected their small farm town to the bloated one where he lived, and what lay between them was the kind of stark valley floor that made Mia wonder if the westward migration would have happened if the pioneers had the luxury of being able to see what their wish really looked like.

Zoey was usually the one to interrupt the stillness on occasion, from her position in the back seat.

"Why can't we fly on Daddy's airline to meet him?"

"We visit Dad when he has time off, so he's not flying, anyway," Mia answered from the front.

"It wouldn't have to be him flying the plane," Zoey countered.

"It's a small airline, honey, and there's never enough seats for passengers flying on a pass," their Mom jumped in to help.

"We could pay."

"Short plane trips between places no one wants to go to are expensive," Candice added.

"Daddy and Yael always take us someplace nice, where people like to go," Zoey pressed on. "We could fly there and meet them."

"Mom doesn't want to see Yael," Mia cut back in. "That's why we go to Dad's condo and then meet up with her later."

"Mia..." Candice sang.

"You wouldn't have to see her," Zoey said. "You could put us on the plane and we could fly by ourselves."

"I don't want to have to take care of you," Mia scoffed.

"You wouldn't have to. It would be a short flight."

"We're back to how much it costs again, honey," Candice reminded her.

"But you said it's not as much when you fly to popular places."

"She doesn't want Yael to pay for any more than she already does," Mia said.

"Would you stop bringing her up?" Candice murmured.

Mia could tell by the surroundings that they were getting closer to their exit. The compact skyline was not yet visible through the late winter fog, but the familiar indicators were building: the motor pool full of school buses locked away for the weekend, the public storage units, the scrap yard. Mia knew her Mom wouldn't fight back on any issue brought up at this point, because she wouldn't want to arrive at the condo flustered.

So Mia seized her chance.

"What have you got against honesty?" she asked.

"Where did that come from?"

"I know what you've been doing."

Her Mom looked genuinely confused.

"Maybe you could fill me in on what it is you think I've been doing."

"I know you've been calling around. Talking to parents about what happened."

"I haven't been calling to tell them what happened. I've been getting a sense of how satisfied people are with the school."

"And then you just happen to mention Artie."

"Is Artie in trouble again?" Zoey chimed in.

"No," Mia snapped.

"Sor-ry," Zoey elongated the word.

"I haven't called that many people," Candice defended herself. "Just a few that I know."

"You don't have to call that many people," Mia said. "All it takes is a few to get things started."

The cluster of midsized office buildings that composed the downtown area emerged from the haze, and as Mia suspected it would, their drive fell silent again.

A few turns after exiting the highway, they pulled in front of the slab of condos. Candice kept the motor idling while Zoey jumped out.

"Open the back, Mom!" she ordered before shutting the door.

Mia was about to open her door, but turned to deliver one more jab.

"I should have lied about what happened on the bus. I should have made up something that sounded harmless."

"It wouldn't have worked. Everyone's story would be different."

"They already are."

"They're close enough, apparently."

"Like you would know."

Candice sighed.

"It's best to tell the truth," she said.

Mia wanted to give her a long look, but couldn't bear to turn in her direction.

"I can't believe you just said that," she sneered, then climbed out of the passenger seat and slammed the door without saying goodbye.

"I got your suitcase for you, Mia!" Zoey waved her arms over both pieces of luggage as though they were prizes up for grabs on a gameshow.

Their Mom sped off.

"Hey," Zoey said. "She didn't say goodbye."

"She got a phone call," Mia pretended. "A work emergency. She said she's sorry."

Mia's plan had backfired. She was the one left trying to compose herself as she heard her Dad amble down the entryway.

"Hey there, bugs!" he greeted them.

"Daddy!" Zoey sprinted over to him and he knelt down to catch her.

"Where's Mom?" he asked Mia over Zoey's shoulder.

"She had a work emergency," Zoey answered instead, directly into his ear.

Mia nodded in confirmation.

"Okay," he said, still looking at Mia and not buying it for a second.

Zoey bounced from his arms.

"Where are we going?" she asked.

Their Dad stood up and playfully gripped his back in mock pain, though Mia suspected there was some truth to it.

"Maybe we're just staying around here," he fudged.

"Can we go to Applebee's?" Zoey pleaded.

"Why do I take you all over the place when all you want is Applebee's?"

"We don't have one in our town."

"Okay," he relented. "It's just the three of us tonight, anyway."

"Has Yael ever been to your place?" Zoey asked.

"Once."

"Where is she now?"

"Santa Barbara. We spent a few days there and she wanted to squeeze in one more. Tomorrow she's going to meet us at..."

He held for some anticipation to build.

"Where? Where?" Zoey hopped up and down.

"The snow!" he announced.

Zoey squealed with delight.

"I thought there wasn't any," Mia said.

"I called our favorite lodge with the sledding area. They've got just enough, and spring weather to go with it."

"Whoo!" Zoey cheered the news.

"Let's go, bugs!"

Zoey and her father jogged into the complex. Mia smiled, then realized the suitcases were still behind her on the curb. She picked up the baggage and walked where they had been.

Mia stuck with standard replies when her Dad asked about school, and realized she didn't have to worry about Zoey revealing anything she had overhead, either. Her sister had a limitless number of her own stories and arbitrary particulars she wanted to share.

Sleeping in the same room with her wasn't even a problem, as it often could be. Zoey's incessant talking throughout the evening, the gestures that accompanied it, and her frequent reenactments finally exhausted her so much that she fell asleep without the sound of her own voice that she usually needed in the way other people need the TV or radio on when they go to bed.

Mia lay awake on the futon on the floor of her father's guest room, to one side of the desk and office chair that were the only pieces of furniture, while Zoey slept on the other side. She surveyed the blank walls, listening to her sister breathe, thinking perhaps it was also the lack of stimuli that made Zoey drowsy.

By the time they reached the lodge the following day, Mia reckoned she was completely in the clear where recent events were concerned, as her Dad was too busy trying to placate everyone to go in-depth regarding anything.

Yael didn't even pretend she was happy to be there. She sulked in the lounge, drinking and watching cable news on the televisions that hovered over the bar and the deserted seating area, where she sat at a table with a basket of curly fries. Mia caught a glimpse of her while taking a bathroom break. She proceeded back outside before Yael noticed her, and reached the top of the hill that descended from the parking lot in time to see Zoey take a run on her inner tube.

To a certain degree Mia couldn't blame Yael. The snow was sparse and sprinkled with dirt. As Zoey planed out at the bottom of the hill, her tube came to an abrupt stop where the snow ended, a good fifty feet from the edge of the clearing. The woods looked neither wintery nor summery, caught in between, like their Dad.

"Yael got a call from her ex-husband yesterday," he confided in Mia as they stood atop the hill and watched Zoey trudge upward with her arm through the inner tube.

"Some bad news?" Mia was sincerely curious.

"His new wife is pregnant."

"Oh."

"And he always told Yael that he didn't want a family."

"That's too bad."

"I told her to stay in Santa Barbara, but she thought spending time with you and Zoey would make her feel better."

Mia laughed through her nose a little.

"What?" her Dad asked.

"So she could be reminded what a pain in the butt kids are?" she explained.

Dad joined her in a light chuckle.

"If that really was the idea," he said. "Then you should be flattered by her behavior. She must think you're pretty great and that she's missing out on something."

They watched Zoey work her way up. She passed the halfway point and gave them a wave. They returned it.

"Does she want to have a family with you?" Mia asked.

Her Dad looked out toward the woods.

"She's never said anything," he realized.

"What if she says something now?"

He continued to rely on the horizon for an answer.

"I don't know," he decided. "I think I could talk her out of it pretty easily."

Zoey reached the top and reported it.

"This is awesome!" she announced as a follow-up. "You wanna go down together this time, Mia?"

For the first time that she could remember, Mia wished she could switch places with her little sister. She had never felt that way when

Zoey was a baby being doted on, or when Zoey was a toddler who almost always got her way because Mia was older and was told she needed to start learning she couldn't always get what she wanted. But at this moment, in this parched winter forest, she was jealous that Zoey still found the conditions ideal.

"I would love to," she accepted the invitation. "I'll get in first, then you sit in my lap."

"Okay!" Zoey surrendered the tube and stood to the side.

"Here," their Dad offered. "Let me hold it steady for you."

Mia crawled into position and Zoey giggled in after her.

Their Dad got behind them.

"Ready?" he asked.

"Ready!" they said in unison.

"One...two..."

He grunted out the word "three" and shoved them over the side.

They bounced as much as they slid, the bumps and grooves of the hill hardly concealed by the threadbare blanket of snow. Mia screamed as much as Zoey did, and hoped for a childish moment. She hoped being in a ring together and sharing their voices would produce the magic necessary for her wish to come true, for the transformation to take place. They would reach the bottom and discover they had switched places.

Of course that didn't happen, but she lay there in the field on the edge of the snow with her head draped backward over the tube, looking at the trees and the sky upside down, feeling Zoey's laughter on top of her, and felt closer to her sister than she had in a long time. She could have stayed like that for hours, but in seconds Zoey popped up and was asking to do it again.

Mia detached herself from the ring much more slowly and took her place on the other side of it for the long walk up the hill.

She squinted up at the top and saw the distant silhouette of her Dad. He held still.

Mia waved.

He responded with a quick round of applause, then he headed back to the lounge for another round of negotiations.

Chapter Seventeen: Dale

From the beginning, he knew some families would pull their children. Turnover was a part of any school, and the issue about which he was least idealistic when he took the job at LOCA. You gained some, you lost some, hoped you came out ahead, and all of the above would be intensified as a new charter. He even accounted for the possibility of some sort of polarizing event to inflict heavy losses for a period of time that he hoped he would be able to keep short.

So when word was clearly spreading and opinions developing about his decision, he had already braced himself for the fallout. What surprised him was that the first wave of defections were from the ranks of the affluent. He had assumed they would try to outlast the meager levels to form what would amount to a free private school, as the exodus amongst the most vulnerable would amass over time.

The top-down insurgency made some sense when he thought of the world beyond their withered valley, and the role that the wealthy play in setting trends. It made even more sense when he considered the source of the Live Oak uprising. He imagined Candice was attempting to set herself up for life after the revolution at the same time she was fomenting it. And Dale was long past being in a position to disparage anyone for trying to bake themselves into the upper crust.

The families most at risk still played a role, but only as a cudgel for those coming in to announce their intentions.

"There are a lot of kids who seem to need more attention than they're getting," said Jo Jo, a mother whom Dale hadn't seen much of since her husband had fulfilled their volunteer hours with his electrical work on the building before the school opened.

"They will," he assured her. "Once we have our new high tech classrooms set up, the teachers will have more time to work with our gifted students, such as your Maddie, as well as those who may be struggling."

"I'm not really talking about that kind of attention," she said.

"You mean behavior, then," Dale confirmed.

"At our old school," Jo Jo nodded. "At St. Bonnie's, we had some kids like that, but they had people monitoring them. They had special classes they could go to."

"We'll get there," he said. "That's my background, after all."

"I know."

"And nobody wants to get that infrastructure up and running as much as I do. But we need to compile our evidence to demonstrate our need that leads to our funding, and then find qualified people to spend those funds on."

Jo Jo continued to nod, but as filler it seemed, rather than thanks to the point he made. She stopped nodding and made her pronouncement.

"I just don't think we can wait that long to feel like our daughter is safe."

Which is where every conversation with the initial evacuees ended up.

They had agreed that safety would be their theme.

Most fell on the safety net as their cue to exit, but some went so far as to say that rules were being applied differently to select students. If Dale pressed them for examples, they never mentioned Artie, so as to dodge accusations that they were violating any family's right to confidentiality, especially when that right belonged to a family so wealthy and powerful. They would instead reference a special needs student of some sort, usually Xavier, whose hulking presence and ongoing rivalry with the equally hulking Viv made him an obvious mark. The closest they would come to identifying

Artie is when Dale would bring up the high tech classroom and someone like Jo Jo would tie the funding to preferential treatment of certain students. Again, their marching orders prohibited them from naming Artie outright, so they would tiptoe through the accusation by claiming the computers would simply serve as a place where LOCA could plop all of the problem children and give them something to do, without having to address the behavior.

Dale wondered how long Candice's plan could sustain its momentum. He also realized that in terms of being able to stem its growth, Rod's plan would be of no help.

Not that it was a total failure. The Pluma doctrine was succeeding in its own way. Artie no longer bothered anyone, and he was never sent to Rod's table in lieu of the principal's office. Rather, Artie sat there voluntarily during recess and lunch, getting his homework done early, biding his time as quietly with his Dad as he did in class with his fellow students. The two of them were the steady presence Rod had hoped for. But their steadiness verged on lifelessness.

If Dale didn't have access to such information, he would have sworn Artie was being medicated. Whether it was Rod brooding solo, or the two of them indulging each other's solemnity, Dale was reluctant to approach their table. Others seemed to feel the same. Even Rita didn't spend much time with them while on campus. They were invisible and unavoidable, well-groomed echoes of broken people holding cardboard signs pleading for help. Dale made an effort at least a couple of times a day to talk with one or both of them, and it was like conducting a séance with ghosts that he could see but still had to lure into conversation.

During one of those contacts, Rod informed him that the dirty looks were fading, as were any looks in general.

Dale suspected as much with regard to their haunted picnic table, as he had also experienced a similar feeling of being the object of a disappearing act with a sizable portion of the parents since he had regained his bearings and started to venture out on campus more often.

They would avoid eye contact rather than express their hostility, and it usually served as a preamble for pulling their kids, amounting to a silent version of the evasive conversations he had with those who at least scheduled an office visit before leaving. One day a mother or father was pretending to spot something beyond Dale that provided an excuse to walk past him without saying hello, the next day their son or daughter was gone.

There was a sympathetic faction as well, those who had taken his side, but their overtures were almost as disconcerting. They lobbed him forced grins and thumbs-up signals, and their verbal support was far too lavish. They would tell him how courageous and brave he was, and thanked him for what he had done, which made him feel like a soldier getting off a plane to a hero's welcome when all he had done was work behind a desk, far away from combat. Others made him feel as though he had a grave illness with low odds for survival. They would put a hand on his shoulder or pull him aside and tell him how much he had to be proud of, that he had a cause worth fighting for, and they were rooting for him.

The students remained mercifully oblivious in great numbers, particularly amongst the younger ones, and provided a serene path for Dale on his hikes. They waved at him when he entered their classrooms, excited to see him, but perhaps even more excited to steal a moment that diverted their attention from their teacher or their work. He smiled back at them and silently suggested they return to what they were doing.

He threw the football around at recess, and shot a basket or two, and when running a game of kickball or capture the flag for a P.E. class, celebrated with the victors and shared in some good-natured gnashing of teeth with the vanquished.

He heard singing outside his office door after lunch one afternoon, and followed the sound onto the catwalk with a nod to Wendy as he passed by. Shirley Ojeda's Kindergarteners were marching around the showroom in a circle. They each had a word on a card, and would raise that card when the word was voiced in the song they were singing. The words were the type that often come up in children's songs, 'love', 'happy', 'mother', 'baby', and they sang a collection of greatest hits to give themselves plenty of opportunities to hoist those words. Dale drifted to the far end of the catwalk to keep from distracting them, and listened to their voices make their way through "Five Little Ducks", "Skidamarink", "You Are My Sunshine", and "Hush Little Baby", with Shirley maintaining the pace and belting out the lyrics loud enough to prompt those who forgot the occasional word, line, or verse.

He watched them until the circle was broken and turned into a wiggly line that Shirley wanted to straighten out before leading it back to the room. Dale focused on each kid for a moment as they jostled into position, imagining them as adults. They each had chosen a color to wear that day, and their choices appeared to represent all the available options, but so much about the rest of their upcoming days seemed so inescapable. One boy already carried himself like a very sweet, very lonely, very overworked man. A few spaces down the line stood a girl soberly waiting to fend off those who were drawn into idiocy by her looks, while the girl behind her was up for any attention that her friend didn't want. The boys who were as hyper as calves seemed destined to turn inward as they got older and become as sullen as bulls.

At the front of the line stood a brown-haired girl with a single pigtail on one side of her head. She looked up at Shirley, waiting for the order to walk, and spotted Dale. She announced her discovery by hollering "Hello Mr. Copeland!", which started a chain reaction. He waved back modestly, a bit sheepish at having been caught. As they receded from the open floor and gravitated toward their class, he hoped that most of his predictions would prove wrong.

Wendy greeted him back to the office with a reminder that they should start preparing for the state tests being administered later that spring.

"Maybe we'll begin with some announcements in the morning," he deliberated aloud. "Then we can decide in the faculty meetings how much class time we want to devote to test-taking strategies, and what those strategies should be."

"Performing well on these tests would really look good," she said.

Dale shuddered faintly.

"Let's just hope it still matters by then," he said.

Wendy smiled at him, and he couldn't quite decide if she was expressing sympathy or casting blame.

Chapter Eighteen: Candice

The whisper campaign was running out of breath. Nobody had transferred out of Live Oak for a week, and a couple of new students had transferred in. She took their arrival as a sign that the message was not reaching enough people beyond the confines of the campus. Almost all of the families who had departed from LOCA headed for St. Bonnie's, so word was not spreading in the public schools. She needed to start working her way down the economic ladder, but she had not made any acquaintances on those rungs.

Subtlety was no longer an option. It was time to put some distance between herself and the academy, and fill that gap with noise.

She didn't want to pull Mia without Kimmy, because she wanted it to be a joint effort, a show of solidarity between those victimized by the Plumas. And short of a press conference, she wanted to work together on a statement that they would send to the school, then be prepared to regurgitate it when people asked them why they left. They would still stop short of identifying anyone explicitly, but the implication would be even more obvious, and they would threaten to start using names unless Artie was expelled, and Rod forced to resign from the board.

"You could have pulled me right away," Mia curled into a ball on her bed upon hearing the plan. "But you had to stir things up."

"I didn't want to make any rash decisions," Candice maintained her stance in Mia's doorway. "I wanted to see how things played out."

"Whatever," her voice echoed in the shell she had created. "Just when I think it's over. It never ends."

"We're taking a stand."

"You're taking a stand. Don't expect me to say anything if anyone asks me why I transferred."

"What are you going to do, then? Shrug?"

Mia shrugged.

Candice sighed.

All the progress made over the fall and winter was collapsing. The sight of her daughter deflating all over again punctured Candice, and she braced herself with the first large object that came to mind.

"You could tell them that Mr. Benton resigned because of what's been going on."

Mia sat upright.

"What?"

"But what do you care?" Candice tried not to relish Mia's reaction. "You wouldn't have been in his class next year, anyway."

She backed out of the frame and took the door with her. By the time she gently closed it, she was already far less proud of herself, but neither was she compelled to go back in and ask Mia not to tell anyone.

When she drove up the gravel two-track at the Althouse spread to speak with Kimmy's grandparents, it was a weight bench that caught her eye amongst all the other discards tossed around the scorched property. It stood in a clearing ten yards to the side of driveway, halfway between the front gate and the house. The vinyl upholstery had faded to a light grey that left no trace of the original color, and the metal appeared to have been dipped in an orange powder. It was possible that the barbell was stuck in place, the weights not having been lifted in years. She couldn't imagine anyone walking that far to use it, or lifting while exposed to the elements. Candice decided it was the saddest weight bench in the world.

She trained her vision back onto the path. Kimmy's grandmother had just pulled in minutes earlier. She knew this because she had tailed Kile from LOCA to ensure that she would be home, and that Kimmy would not. Candice predicted that knocking would not be necessary, as the popping gravel under her tires would announce her arrival. Indeed, Kile was standing in her front door by the time Candice swung herself out of the Cherokee door.

"I know you," Kile chirped.

"Grandma i, yes?"

"You remembered!"

Candice nodded her way to a smile.

"Come on in, Candy," Kile beckoned. "It's a lot neater inside. Which ain't saying much, but at least Grandpa Kyle won't listen in on us."

Kile turned and raised her voice over the rusty jungle.

"Not that you'd be interested in a couple of hens clucking, right, Kyle?"

No reply came. She turned back to Candice.

"He worked at the state hospital for years. I think some of the loony rubbed off on him."

Candice offered a brief laugh as she entered and Kile closed the door behind her.

"Is this about Kimmy?"

Candice wasn't ready to engage the subject so quickly.

"I'm sorry," Kile backtracked. "Where are my manners...can I get you anything? Coke? Gatorade? A little early for a beer, I reckon."

"No thank you."

"Water? We've got a real steady well here. You'd never know there was a drought."

"I'm fine."

"Sure?"

"Really."

"Well then sit down at least. Don't make me feel like a total failure in the hospitality department."

Candice followed Kile's gestures to the kitchen table and sat in a chair that had the same upholstering as the abandoned weight bench.

"You'll have to excuse Kimmy," said Kile as soon as they sat down. "Wait, what am I saying? You don't have to do anything. But it would be nice if you could understand. We're doing the best we can, but with her Mom gone and Dad in prison…"

She completed her defense with a broad shrug. Candice was learning way more than she had expected, but she was just as surprised that Kile had stopped talking for a moment.

"Is that her Dad's weight bench outside?"

"Yes," Kile re-energized. "Yes it was. Would've been nice if he took his frustrations out with exercise instead of all that other stuff. He never used it much after high school. I told him after Josey died to get on it. But, there it is."

Candice lurched for something to say.

"I'm…really sorry."

"Long time ago, hon. Long time ago. And a lotta time left. So Kimmy…"

"Oh…"

"I know the girls haven't been spending time together, but that's just Kimmy. I think she makes friends just so she can fight with them later on. I can set my watch by her. Boy, did I just date myself. Who wears a watch anymore?"

She cackled and got up off her chair.

"So don't sweat it, Candy. Same old, same old. You sure you don't want a glass of water? I'm gonna draw one for myself, if you don't mind."

Candice shook her head. She waited for Kile to fill her glass and come back to the table, but Kile stood by the sink and punctuated each gulp with a satisfied exhale. When she took some time to inhale, Candice proceeded.

"It's not Kimmy's fault the girls aren't hanging out together."

"Well, there's a first. You sure about that?"

"Something happened to them."

Kile was about to chug the rest of her glass but stopped.

"What do you mean?"

"They were assaulted by one of the boys in their class. She didn't tell you?"

Kile followed through with a small sip before addressing the charges.

"You sure Kimmy didn't have anything to do with it?"

"Are you kidding?"

"I know my granddaughter."

Candice needed a moment to regroup and figure out how to respond.

"Even if she did do something," she decided to say, "assault is never okay. That's blaming the victim. Maybe she hasn't told you because she's embarrassed. Things went too far this time."

"Kimmy don't embarrass easily."

"That's how this whole thing got started. The same boy kept doing things and the girls were too shy to say anything. Kimmy finally did at one point, good for her, and it still wasn't enough to get this kid suspended. So it just got worse and worse and finally they had no choice. I can only imagine how bad it must have been to finally get him a suspension."

Kile leaned back against the counter.

"Who is this kid, anyway?"

"The son of the wealthiest man on the board. He practically built the school."

"Of course," Kile chuckled.

Candice saw an opportunity to present her case.

"Which is why I'm here," she leaned forward in her chair, stopping short of getting up and approaching Kile, which she figured would be a bit much. "It's not fair. And something should be done."

"What'd you have in mind, hon?"

"I'm going to pull Mia from the school, and would appreciate it if you would pull Kimmy, too."

Kile drooped into a single exaggerated nod before she spoke.

"Two students ain't exactly strength in numbers."

"But it's the two students who were involved. And it wouldn't be just the two of us. A lot of parents have already pulled their kids."

"Thanks to you?"

"I'm just the messenger. It's the injustice that convinces them."

Kile kept quiet and stared at the floor. Candice was as unsettled by her rare silence as she was by the fact that her pitch didn't appear to have stirred anything inside of her. She considered filling the pause with a few more gentle pleas, but resisted.

"I know that keeping Kimmy at Live Oak kind of messes with your case," Kile finally spoke up. "But I've got a kid to raise, and this school seems to be good for her."

"The school that subjects her to sexual assault by the people who run it?"

"I haven't seen any signs that Kimmy's gone through anything that bad."

"Well good for her," Candice sniped. "Wish I could say the same for Mia."

"Kids respond differently to things," Kile adopted a consoling tone.

"That doesn't change the things they're responding to," Candice resented Kile's attempt to play the role of the reasonable one. "Those things are what they are. And this is wrong, no matter how your granddaughter decided to react to it."

"You don't know what it was like before Kimmy got to Live Oak," she fell into a more desperate approach. "She went to just about every elementary school and burned every bridge there. I can't send her to the middle school. They're all in the same place now, all the kids from every elementary school. It would be like sending a cop to a prison full of people he arrested."

"Kimmy the cop?"

Kile laughed at herself.

"Maybe that wasn't the best example," she seemed eager for Candice to join her in lightening up.

Candice wasn't interested.

Kile moved back to the table and sat down across from her.

"I'm sorry, hon. I truly am. But are you really that surprised the game is rigged?"

Candice glared at her.

"So you're not going to do anything about it," she managed to measure her words. "And you're okay with it?"

"It's not my decision to be okay with it. That's just how it is. You ever been inside that warehouse up the valley where that online store ships all that stuff?"

"No," Candice was about ready to leave.

"They're always looking for seasonal workers. And I've done it a couple of times, made a little extra spending money for Christmas. Maybe if Kyle had taken a few more good shots from those lunatics we'd be getting a bigger check each month. But anyway, what you do there at the warehouse is stand by a conveyer belt and put stuff in boxes and roll them out to the shipping area. And you know who brings you the stuff?"

Candice shrugged.

"Robots!" Kile proclaimed. "Robots fill the orders. They're like those automatic vacuum cleaners, what are they called, Roombas? They're like those things, only with lifts on them, like Roomba forklifts. So you stand there in your spot and these things come rolling at you with bins full of stuff someone ordered, and you grab the right-sized box and slap the sticker on it and take the stuff out of the bin and put it in the box. That's it. Robots run all over the warehouse and you stay in one place. And when you do this, you just know that someday they'll probably have a robot that's doing what you're doing. I hope not, since I'm a person and all, but what I do know for sure is there's not a damn thing I can do about it."

"We're talking about our kids," Candice condescended.

"And we've got all the control in the world over them," Kile mocked her right back.

"We most certainly do."

Kile took a deep breath. Candice thought maybe she wasn't accustomed to anyone pushing back against her verbal walls. She hoped for a moment that Kile was reconsidering.

"I admire your spirit, Candy."

Her tone made it clear she was not leading up to a rousing declaration to fight by her side after all. Rather, it was a prelude to her final refusal.

"It's Candice," she corrected her.

"Candice. Sorry. I really wish you the best. It's good to have people who remind us what's right and wrong. But you might as well protest the sunrise."

Candice stood up and offered her hand.

"Thank you for your time."

Kile stood up and shook it. She also got in the last word, which came as no surprise.

"Worse things have happened to people who thought they had a lot more control over life than you do."

Candice mulled a variety of responses as their handshake waned. She was certain Kile would have a comeback for anything she said, and she had just enough restraint left in her to resist the lewd gestures that came to mind. So she nodded and turned to leave, not bothering to attempt a smile, since it wouldn't come out the way she wanted.

Candice drove down the driveway a bit faster than she had come up. She still noticed the weight bench, though, and as it floated into her passenger side window, the barbell looked like a pair of arms extended out from each side of the bench, which was the body. She stomped on her brakes. By the time she skidded to a stop, the glow of recognition had turned to shame. Of course Grandma i felt helpless.

She threw her arm over the passenger seat and looked behind her, ready to hit reverse and apologize. But the way back looked long now that she had it in her sights, and she wasn't very good at driving backwards. She checked in both directions to see if there was any place to turn around, but there were enough mysterious metal objects close to the road and to each other to give her pause, and make her wonder if there were things she couldn't see that would leave her with a flat tire. Besides, just because Kile had a problem with her son, didn't mean everyone else's kid should have to suffer. And why wouldn't she want to help other kids, in light of what happened to hers? Candice took a deep breath and drove forward again.

She spent the rest of the morning and early afternoon tending to renters in person and landlords on the phone, focusing on those tenants who paid their own way, and those owners who had but a house or two. She avoided a day of extracting government assistance from the poor and forwarding it to the rich. She never enjoyed such a transfer, but under the circumstances felt particularly susceptible to saying or doing something that could cost her dearly.

There was a hiccup involving a renter complaining about the owner stopping by with annoying frequency to check on the house, which was rare because so few landlords lived locally, but otherwise her job went smoothly enough to allow plenty of time to pick up the girls.

She parked along the curb of the frontage road leading to Live Oak, where she could see the rear blacktop and the meadow, while maintaining her stance of staying off campus. More than a couple of classes were outside, their teachers letting the kids run off their spring fever as the clock wound down on the school day. The sixth graders were one of them. Candice spotted Mia and Beatrice back on their customary bench. Their maudlin body language aside, the sight of them brightened up Candice a little, as it demonstrated that Mia was not completely back to where she started. At least she was able to hold on to the point where she met Beatrice.

Isaiah stood near the upper cluster of rooms, behind all the action. Thanks to his position, she didn't notice him at first. When she finally did, he appeared to be watching her. She told herself to stop being so self-absorbed, and shook her head with a slight laugh as she reached to turn on the radio.

Her phone pinged with a text alert.

It was from Isaiah.

The kids know I'm leaving, it read. *And they know why. I asked you not to tell anyone.*

She looked over and confirmed that he was in fact looking at her. There was no way to pretend she hadn't received the message.

Sorry, she wrote back. *I was upset. It slipped out.*

I had a story ready for them and for Dale. Now it's all damage control.

Just stick with the truth.

And then expect Dale to give me a reference when someone calls?

Why would you want a reference from someone you don't respect?

It looks bad if you don't have contacts from your most recent school. Like something bad happened.

Something bad DID happen!!!

She scowled out the window. Some kids approached Isaiah, who put his phone back in his pocket. When they left, he didn't retrieve it.

She re-sent the message. He ignored it.

She re-sent it again. He folded his arms into an obstinate pose.

She kept sending it until he cracked.

He snatched up his phone and started banging on it with both thumbs. When he finished typing, he made an exhibition of pressing "send".

Yes, and it had nothing to do with me! NOTHING!!!

Her heart thumped as she read his message. When she looked over at him, he held up his phone, and lowered his thumb onto the power button as though pressing a detonator.

She started the engine and pulled forward where the building stood between them so they couldn't see each other anymore. She spent her time waiting for the girls with her head leaning on the steering wheel, stuck between a cry and a scream, and stayed that way until she heard the bell ring.

When the girls climbed in, she told them they would be in a different school by the following week.

"Aw," said Zoey. "I thought we were going to wait."

Candice glanced at Mia, who had no reaction, much less a comment.

"Sorry, sweetie," she turned her attention back to Zoey. "There's no reason to anymore."

"Oh well," Zoey bounced back. "At least I get to see all my old friends."

"That's right," Candice started the engine. "And Mrs. Horst is a lousy teacher, anyway."

"What about Mr. Benton?" Zoey asked.

Mia looked at her Mom as if repeating the question.

"Mia's case is different," Candice answered. "She needs a better bunch of classmates."

"Which I'll be sure to find at the middle school," Mia spat.

Candice focused on merging into the flow of traffic so she wouldn't overreact to Mia's sarcasm.

"There's variety there," she said. "The kids from your old elementary school only make up about a quarter of the students. And you get a different teacher for each subject. They can't all be duds."

"Why not?" Mia asked.

"Law of averages."

"No such law."

"Who says?"

"Mr. Benton," Mia explained. "It's called the Gambler's Fallacy."

"Okay, then it's the Gambler's Fallacy."

"But a fallacy is wrong."

"Then maybe all your teachers will be great," Candice let her voice rise. "Every one of them a genius, a regular Isaiah Benton."

Her volume reached a level that quelled any further discussion, even from Zoey. The quiet continued as they entered the garage, the house, and their rooms.

Candice lay on top of her bedspread and stared at the ceiling, trying to decompress. Lately it had been moments like this when she would reach out to Isaiah for help in doing so. She reached for her phone and typed him a message.

I'm sorry.

After sending it, she rested the phone on her chest.

Within seconds it vibrated. She picked it up and saw a window on the screen. It said that she had been blocked by that number.

Her arms fell by her side, the phone bouncing off the bed and onto the floor.

"Everyone is a coward," she announced to the emptiness.

She felt naïve, like she was thirteen and all of the adults in her life had let her down. She hated the feeling. Once was enough. Yet it seemed to have become an annual event.

She sat up and spun her legs over the side of the mattress, reaching down for the phone. She opened the search engine and looked up the website for the county newspaper, checking the submission guidelines for sending a letter to the editor. They were easy enough to follow, but she wasn't sure if she had any paper of her own in the house, as she didn't want to sift through the girls' backpacks in case they caught her.

She found a long, narrow pad in a kitchen drawer from the real estate agent who had sold them the house. The woman's picture was at the top, with the company logo above her and a quote below her: "Your trust is my motivation." The transaction had occurred only a few years earlier, but since her husband handled most of its machinations, Candice could not muster any clear recollections of the woman smiling in the photograph.

The pad of paper did inspire memories of her ex-husband, though, which may have nudged her toward the introduction she wrote. She drew a few circles to rev up her pen, then started out by claiming to have plenty of experience with failed relationships, and that the relationship between Rodrigo Pluma and Live Oak Charter Academy was the latest example, in particular its principal, Dale Copeland. The narrow strips of paper left little room to write, so she had to flip to the next clean page rather quickly. This time the smiling photograph of the realtor reminded her of a ventriloquist, speaking the words beneath her through clenched teeth. So she made an analogy with Dale as a puppet, and Rod pulling his strings. She thought maybe she was enjoying herself too much, so she switched to a more distressing topic, and laid out the havoc that Arturo Pluma was able to inflict thanks to his father's influence, culminating in the assault on her daughter. As she pressed toward the end of describing what happened to Mia, the word "trust" jumped out at her from the realtor's quote as she flipped to the latest blank page, so she concluded the letter by addressing that very issue, and how the charter had violated the trust of the district and the parents who had put their faith in LOCA.

After dotting the final period as though spearing a fish with the pen, she dropped her weapon and slid the pad away from her.

She stared at it for a while.

Nothing happened, so she put it in her purse and brought it to work the next day, where she could type it up and send it in.

Chapter Nineteen: Rodrigo

"There's this perception people have about businessmen," he said to Dale as they sat in a deserted convention center conference room, both of them seated in the same row with a few empty chairs between them, and hundreds of empty chairs around them.

"And it's wrong," Dale smirked. "Right?"

"Very," Rod nodded with his whole upper body.

They had scheduled the trip long before any controversy broke, and decided to follow through on their plans to lead a breakout session titled, "The Best of Both Worlds: Forging Strong Relationships Between Schools and Businesses". Their spoken rationale for attending, as Rod framed it, had something to do with keeping promises because real men don't back out on their word. But their unspoken motive, the one informing their every interaction over the weekend, swirled with curiosity as to whether anyone in the charter community had gotten wind of their situation.

As interested as they were in people's awareness of the gossip that was sinking their charter, they grew hesitant when it came time to find out. They waited until a few minutes before the start of their presentation to dart from their hotel to the conference room, so as to avoid any mingling beforehand. When they were finished with the lecture portion of their session and it was time for discussion, some attendees lined up at the microphone in the center aisle to ask questions. Rod and Dale exchanged looks that were short of breath and silently agreed to stall until the next wave of sessions started at the top of the hour. Rod launched into an extended answer to the first question, hoping to also make it the last one. It wasn't easy, because the presentation as a whole had already been compromised by the computer deal falling through, leaving them with much less to talk about than they had planned. So Rod couldn't quite run out the clock, and they had to let a couple more people step up to the mic.

None of the inquisitors gave any indication that they knew what was happening in their valley. Or they did know, and were too polite or uncomfortable to say anything. To insure that the moratorium held after the presentation as well, Rod and Dale pretended to be much more preoccupied with organizing their supplies than was necessary as everyone filed for the exit to reach another session in some other room. One vaguely familiar colleague lingered for a moment, a woman with an administrator's fashion sense who claimed to recognize them from a previous event. "The tractor guys," as she put it. She expressed interest in talking some more about the subject, but Rod said they were hoping to catch a session in a distant wing of the convention center, and asked if she had a business card. She gave them one, got the message, and left the room.

Once it was down to the two of them, Rod and Dale took their positions amongst the vacated chairs to wait until the clamor in the corridors quieted down with the start of the next sessions, and to disguise themselves as audience members in the event any more strays came in looking for the names on the door.

"They think we're ruthless," Rod continued with the defense of his profession. "That we stop at nothing to make money."

"And it's just not true," Dale good-naturedly goaded him.

"Well, it's partially true," Rod acknowledged. "But it's not all attack, attack, damn it all, there's money to be made. You have to keep a level head. Rita says it's the same thing with artists. Not that she's a great artist, but she knows some. And she laughs about the way they're performed, attacking the canvas or the clay in a frenzy, like they're in a fight. But most of the time they just think about what they're doing, which isn't very interesting to imagine. Same with business people. The good ones don't always go all in. They think a lot. They know when to get out of a deal."

Dale looked over to see if anyone was lurking in the doorway beyond the rows of chairs. He confirmed that the coast was clear, and sighed.

"I guess we had to have this conversation at some point," he said.

"If I resign from the board," Rod provided details. "Maybe you can keep your job."

"You're the only vote I've got at the next meeting."

"But I'm the puppet master," Rod referenced the article written by Candice. "If I'm gone, they might put their faith back in you. My resignation is worth more than my vote."

They fell silent, and it was more quiet than Rod expected, as the noise coming in from the corridor had faded. The high ceiling seemed to rise even higher, and the empty floor seemed to sink.

"I've said it before," Dale stared ahead. "The job is nothing without your contributions."

"It's your source of income."

Dale shrugged and remained fixated on the same mysterious point somewhere in front of him.

Rod was about to offer some encouraging words about how much he mattered to the kids at the school, about how the job couldn't be measured in money, when Dale turned away from the distance ahead and back toward Rod.

"Did the computer deal really fall through?" he asked. "Or did you pull the plug?"

Rod took a deep breath.

"They had some concerns," he said. "And I didn't do much to ease those concerns."

Dale didn't seem very surprised. Rod felt a need to defend himself.

"The backlash was in full force," he explained. "I didn't feel like fighting to save a program for a bunch of people who hated me. Even then, I still felt guilty. Until the article was published."

Dale threw his head back and laughed.

"Yes!" he vented.

It was Rod's turn to look over at the door.

"Which reminds me," Dale settled down. "Have you heard back from your lawyers?"

"She never quite crossed any lines," Rod answered while making sure nobody was drawn in by the noise. "The editors at the newspaper probably helped her with that."

"Too bad," Dale hunched forward and wrung his hands together. "We can always go with my plan. But I have a feeling your lawyers would advise against it."

"Probably," Rod grinned.

Dale leaned back.

"What about Artie?" he asked.

"We're not pulling him this year. I can only wave so many white flags at one time."

"But next year?"

Rod exhaled slowly.

"Rita and I have to do some research," he said. "I know St. Bonnie's won't let us back in, and at this point I don't think there's a school in the district where Artie would feel comfortable."

"Boarding school?"

Rod nodded slowly, as though he should have been dragging along the word "Yup".

The lack of voices in the hall and intruders through the door convinced him they could exit the convention center unnoticed and make it to the nearest restaurant that Rod assumed was above the price range of the conference crowd. He assured Dale that lunch was on him and led the way.

They were spotted one more time along the sidewalk before reaching the safety of the "Please Wait To Be Seated" sign.

"Hey," waved the passerby in the necktie decorated with math equations. "The tractor guys!"

They offered him tight-lipped nods in motion, but laughed over it as they steadied themselves into a booth.

"But will they remember us when we're gone?" Dale asked.

"We?" Rod pried.

"Even if I do hold on to my job," Dale answered. "I don't think I'll be back on the conference circuit anytime soon."

Rod ordered a bottle of sparkling water for the table and asked Dale if they should order wine as well.

"Go ahead, but I don't dare. I may not stop."

"A glass of Sauvignon Blanc for me, then," Rod told the server, who recited the specials before leaving.

"Getting drunk on this trip would be so conventional," Dale said.

"It's just one glass," Rod pretended to be indignant.

"You can handle your liquor better than I can," Dale backpedaled.

They busied themselves with the menus. Rod glanced at the prices, then the surroundings, and finally his guest.

"Why did you decide to go so big when it came to LOCA?" he asked.

Dale looked up from his menu.

"What do you mean?"

"The conferences, the deals, the attention," Rod clarified. "Why was that important?"

Dale breathed in some potential reasons before choosing one.

"I saw an opportunity."

"For what?"

"Well..." he seemed to still be in the process of sculpting his answer. "To be a teaching consultant who actually teaches."

"What do you mean?"

"Maybe you didn't notice, Rod, but most of the people who move mountains at places like this don't spend much time in a classroom."

"I guess I didn't."

Dale seemed to grow more confident in what he had come up with.

"Read the bios on the brochures, in the programs," he wielded his menu like a Bible. "If any of them did teach, it was for a couple of years, maybe part of a Teach For America program, just long enough to collect some anecdotes and bide their time until applying for administrator jobs. But they saw all they needed to see, apparently, and now they have all the answers."

"That's unfortunate."

"When I look back on the first two or three years of my career, I feel like I should write letters of apology to my students. I didn't really feel comfortable until maybe a decade in. But that's just me, I guess. That's why I wasn't meant to be a guru."

The server arrived with the bottle of water and two glasses, and Rod's glass of white wine. She poured the sparkling water into the glasses and asked if they were ready. Rod ordered first, while Dale refocused on the menu and tried to make a snap decision.

"That sounds good," he gave up and went with Rod's choice. "I'll have the same."

The server walked away, orders memorized, menus in tow.

Rod lifted his wine glass and raised it toward Dale.

"To the voice of experience," he toasted.

Dale reached for his glass of water and raised it in kind. The first sip made him cough, as though he had inhaled on a cigarette.

"Forgot it was the bubbly kind," he explained after the short fit.

"And here I thought it was about money," Rod grinned as he put his glass of wine back on the table.

"The reason I choked?"

Rod laughed.

"The reason you wanted to make a name on the circuit."

"Sure," Dale shrugged. "I imagined making a little more money. At least for a while."

"Is there something special you need the money for?"

Dale shifted a few times on the upholstered bench and made it groan.

"Nothing in particular," he finally said.

"You sure?" Rod pressed him.

"I was trying to think of something. But I couldn't," Dale maintained. "I guess I just thought it would be nice."

Rod took a sip of wine and considered whether to continue the inquiry. He didn't believe Dale, and was sort of enjoying the hunt, but didn't want to ruin the poor man's farewell trip. He appeared to be withering under some self-imposed pressure.

"If anything does comes to mind," Rod told him after a satisfied exhale from relishing the wine, "let me know."

"I will," Dale nodded, his expression dissolving from tense to forlorn. "I will."

They sat in a silence that Rod thought appropriate, as Dale seemed in mourning for whatever it was he let pass. Rod let him break it.

"Come to think of it..." he said.

"Yes?" Rod encouraged him.

"That wine does look good."

Rod smiled and gestured for a server.

He thought of wine, good wine at least, as a token of the sophistication he was always striving for, but may never reach in spite of his success. It was a reward he would give himself on occasion that flooded him with a sense of fulfillment, wherein the world could end and he would simply think of how glad he was that the meteor didn't strike earlier in his life. But only up to a point. A few sips over the threshold and the floodwaters would run dark and moody, shrinking him instead of expanding. That was one of the best parts of the gift, how it challenged him to remember his limits, to bear in mind where he stood while making him proud to be there.

Rod had seen Dale drink a little bit during the renovation of the tractor dealership, when one of the contractors would head to the gas mart at sundown and come back with a case of whatever beer in a can was on sale. Everyone partook out of camaraderie, none more so than Dale, it seemed to Rod. The can was a prop to keep him connected to the guys on the crew, as he rarely saw Dale take a swig after the first one. The beer was typically awful, though, so Rod remembered thinking that it may have been a matter of taste.

Dale's reaction to the wine proved otherwise. He appeared to like the white well enough, with its chilly citrus flavor, but later, when Rod ordered a bottle of red with dinner at an even pricier spot even farther from the conference crowd, Dale clearly struggled with the tannins of a Cabernet that Rod considered a rather accessible label.

But he drank it anyway, and Rod could see a similar process to his own overtake Dale, the same feelings of contentment during the first glass, the same balancing act during the second, the back of the brain calculations over how much more he could get away with. It was their respective tones of voice that proved to Rod they were both tabulating their sip countdowns. Each would creep toward aggression, then slink away from it.

Rod felt each of them wanting to blame the other for the implosion. Rod wanted to tell Dale he should have had enough spine to stand up to his fatherly protectiveness over Artie. Rod's weakness was instinct, while Dale's was choice.

He also suspected Dale had more on his mind than blame during the frequent moments when he would stare at the table, that there were events and faces he was seeing that were not in his field of vision, for when he swirled the wine in his glass and Rod asked him if he knew why people do that, Dale replied, "Oh, was I swirling my wine?"

Such was the nature of what was actually spoken on their last night as colleagues. They traded opportunities to hold court in areas where they felt confident. Rod made speeches about great restaurants and the career of Hugo Sanchez, his favorite soccer player. Dale riffed on great books and why the United States was reluctant to embrace soccer. He avoided anything related to education, his real area of expertise, since that would inevitably circle back to LOCA and his mysterious reasons for using it as a springboard, reasons about which he had trouble telling lies, no matter how long he looked into a glass of swirling wine that according to him, wasn't really there.

"But what is really there?" was the kind of boozy meditation Rod indulged after sneaking down to the hotel lounge for one more glass of a more expensive vintage after they had retired to their rooms. "What is reality?"

He visualized a montage of what was real in his life, the fields worked, the cars driven, the buses ridden, the homes lived in, the men hated, the men admired, the women dated, the women he wished he'd dated, the early days with Rita, a variety of images of Lena, of Tony, of Artie, and wondered which of the stories attached to the images would be the ones he would end up telling over and over, which moments would survive the longest. And as the world currently in front of him disappeared as it had with Dale, the objects and the people and the room and everything visible through its windows vanishing under the weight of what was on his mind, he snapped back into the present with the terrible thought that such was the fate of everything and everyone.

The hotel was old, an historical landmark, and the lounge was just as old. A hundred years ago, a man sat at a table and sifted through what was clear to him while the world around him dissolved. Rod asked whomever or whatever was on duty in the universe who that man was. He imagined his question hurtling through space, and a surprisingly soft voice from the edge of existence answered back:

"Oh, was a man sitting there wondering what matters?"

Rod decided it was time to stop. He left his glass half full, nine dollars' worth of wine according to whomever set the price at eighteen, and concentrated with great care on his surroundings on his way upstairs, hoping no one recognized him one moment, then wishing someone would the next, and repeating the cycle until he lay down.

Rod was one of the first guests in the complimentary breakfast room the next morning. He didn't knock on Dale's door as he passed, preferring to spend some alone time sitting upright and sober at a table, rather than sprawled on an unmade bed with The Discovery Channel providing ambient noise.

Televisions still offered some noise, as cable news hung from the walls above the buffet and seating area. Rod sat and poured Raisin Bran from a fist-sized box into a Styrofoam bowl and decided to read the small cereal box rather than watch any of the interpretations of recent events.

"Tractor man," said a female voice reminiscent of the one who narrates GPS directions.

He looked up and found a sharp-featured woman who carried herself as though her clothes were still on a hanger. She appeared to be waiting for an invitation to sit down.

"I guess that's me," Rod replied. "Thank you for saying 'man' instead of 'guy.'"

"Sure. But I should have just gone with Rod Pluma. Mind if I sit down?" she tired of waiting for the invite.

"Go ahead."

"Barb Giusti," she introduced herself while arranging some plastic silverware around her scrambled eggs and coffee. "Vista Community Charter School."

"Mucho gusto," Rod shook her hand.

"Where are you headed today?" she asked.

"Home."

"You're checking out? There's some great people presenting today."

"I'm sure there are."

"I was disappointed I couldn't catch your session yesterday. I was conducting one of my own on effective long-term planning."

Rod laughed.

"Are you doing it again?" he asked. "We should probably attend."

Barb tried to laugh with him, but resorted to poking at her eggs.

"So," she finally said. "I hear your presentation wasn't quite up to your usual standards."

"You mean it wasn't as entertaining."

"No," she became abrupt.

Rod leaned back.

"I'm sorry we disappointed."

"I figured there must be a reason," she pressed on.

"Opening a business is easy. Running it is the hard part."

Barb was having none of his aphorisms.

"I looked you both up," she said. "Looked up your school."

"And did you find an article from The Valley Outlook written by Candice Ingle?"

"I did."

The memory of certain lines and words coursed through Rod as he searched Barb Giusti's expression for a sense of how she read it, but she revealed nothing.

"And did you find any other articles about me out there in cyberspace?" he asked.

"Other articles?"

"The ones about the businesses I founded, the charities I belong to, the millions of people I help feed every day?"

"I'm sure they're around. I just wasn't looking for them."

So this was to be his legacy, Rod thought. He would be the rich man who bought a school for his kid.

"It's been a pleasure," Rod quipped as he rose from the table.

"I'm sorry," she said. "I didn't mean to offend you. I was curious. You were so inspiring last time."

"I still am."

He passed by a television bolted to rods suspended from the ceiling, the screen angled downward toward its audience. It was broadcasting a foursquare of talking heads deciding what a famous person's body language meant in a photograph taken of them at an unflattering second of their life. Rod looked back to earth and noticed a basket of small, bruised apples that had probably been there for weeks. He resisted an urge to throw one at the show, and spent most of the drive home suppressing a variety of ways to lash out, keeping quiet instead and looking irritated, blaming it on a hangover for Dale's sake.

"Want to switch places?" Dale asked. "I can drive if you're not feeling well."

"I'm okay," Rod assured him, and eventually he produced a vision that really did make him feel better.

He imagined himself taking a chainsaw to the base of the post that held the plaque with his name on it in front of Live Oak Charter Academy, then using the post as a club to smash every window in the place. He replayed the scene on a loop, sometimes rewriting it so that he ripped the post straight from the ground, or held the post with the plaque facing him so he could see his name and the inscription as he wreaked his havoc. But he usually stuck with the original version, with a clean cut that was easy to wield with the plaque facing away from him so that his name was the first thing breaking through the glass.

"Good to see you smiling again," Dale remarked.

"Thanks," Rod suppressed a laugh he was certain would sound like a cackle if he let it out.

Chapter Twenty: Mia

Cleaning out her desk was the most difficult part of her last day. She felt as though she was being fired from a job. With Mr. Benton's permission, she stayed behind when everyone lined up for the walk over to the main building, but didn't want to start sweeping her pencils and notebooks and stray papers into the shopping bag she had wadded up in her backpack until her now-former classmates had filed through the door.

While they stood along the wall waiting for their procession to start, Mia sat alone at her desk. Most of the exchanges were light-hearted, as some of the goofier boys reached in her direction and pretended to blubber on about missing her, while the girls made pouty faces and gave her little waves. She worked hard not to laugh when Beatrice imitated the girls' attempts at sincerity, and discovered that the best way to keep from laughing was to notice that neither Kimmy nor Artie would look at her.

When the whistle blew and Mr. Benton opened the door, Mia kept her focus on the two of them. They were only a few students apart from each other, toward the end of the line. Kimmy was ahead of Artie, and she finally glanced at Mia as she reached the sunlight that poured through the opening. Mia had a feeling that the timing was by design, but it worked. Kimmy looked lovely as she turned and smiled at her. She seemed to apologize and wish her well all at once. Mia would have been more emotional if she hadn't been so surprised, but the emotions came seconds later when Artie took his turn in the sunlight. He couldn't quite bring himself to look at Mia, but a trail of tears on his cheek caught the light and shined it her way. She looked down as though the sun itself was in her eyes, and was glad there were but a few students left so that she only had to wait a few more seconds to cry on her own.

She did so for a good thirty seconds before unraveling the shopping bag and gathering items into it from inside her desk, while trying to compose herself before Mr. Benton came back. But when he returned, she was still breathing heavily, with her eyes and nose running at full sprint.

She apologized as he walked over and sat in the desk next to hers.

"Sorry for what?" he asked. "Being sad about leaving my class? I'd be offended if you weren't."

Mia laughed a little and tried to see through her tears if she had forgotten anything.

"I need to see if Zoey needs help," she explained as she stood up.

"You're a great kid," he said as he stood up with her.

"Thank you."

"And your Mom's cool, too. She's just going through a rough time."

"Why do I have to go through it with her?"

She started sobbing again and Mr. Benton hugged her.

"I've seen much worse," he said. "So much worse."

"I hate it when people tell me how good I have it when I'm feeling this way."

"I know. But it's true in the long run."

"And then they tell you it's a long run," she separated from him but kept hugging herself. "As if you don't feel bad enough. Wow, you mean I get to feel like this a bunch more times? Great."

Mr. Benton chuckled.

"And then they laugh at you," he chastised himself. "You do see my point, though, yes?"

She nodded.

"Sorry for hugging you," she said.

"Why?"

"I don't want to get anyone else in trouble."

Mr. Benton sighed until he ran out of breath.

"Grab your shopping bag," he finally said. "Let's take the walk one last time before I start crying, too."

Mia could see her Mom's Cherokee looming just above and beyond the campus on the frontage road.

Zoey was in the showroom pressing her face against the window as they approached, trying to earn some laughter.

"People are going to miss her more than me," Mia said.

"That's because they know deep down, she won't miss them," Mr. Benton answered.

Mia wasn't expecting anything so frank about a student from a teacher. And though she agreed with him, she felt a primal urge to defend her sister.

"She might," was the best she could come up with. "Some of them, maybe."

"You think that's a bad quality to have?" he asked her.

She turned toward him, once again surprised by something he said.

"You don't think it is?" she asked back.

"It can come in handy," he answered, then stopped short of the building.

She halted alongside him, but he put a hand on her back as a signal for her to proceed.

"You're going to be great," he told her.

Mia smiled as best she could, and as she made her way closer to her sister's funny face exhibit, she looked back before entering the showroom. Mr. Benton was staring out in the direction where her Mom was parked. He appeared to be deciding whether or not to wave, or maybe even walk over and say something, but he was deliberating in such a serene fashion, as though watching the ocean at sunset.

As she and Zoey walked up to their Mom's parking place, she didn't look back, but was hoping to hear Mr. Benton's voice asking them to wait up. When they crawled into the car, she peeked at the campus, but didn't see him anywhere.

He was done surprising her.

At the middle school the following week, she noticed that a lot of the reactions concerning her mother weren't what she had come to expect. Her teachers, in particular, regarded her mother as something of a folk hero.

When she met with each of them after class, their initial explanations regarding how they were going to handle her late arrival made enough sense.

"Since there isn't much work left," went the party line, "we'll just base your grade mainly on how you do on the state tests."

But then when Mia asked if she should bring in work from LOCA, or if they were going to contact Mr. Benton or Mr. Copeland, none of them found it necessary, and they would wrap up the meeting by asking Mia to "say hi to your mother for me."

She never delivered the greetings on their behalf. At first she withheld them out of spite. But her continued refusal was based on how much her mother was enjoying the fight. Mia hadn't seen her so happy in some time. Conflict seemed to suit her, give her a sense of purpose, and Mia didn't want to encourage that quality. Enjoying the agitation was enough. She didn't need to take pride in it.

The students, meanwhile, didn't take much notice of Mia. She drifted from class to class, as disinterested in making new friends as the established cliques were in expanding their ranks. She still hung out with Beatrice whenever she could after school. The middle school was in between the Live Oak campus and the shipping warehouse where Beatrice's mother worked, the "realization station". So on days when Candice allowed it, she would bring Mia's bike in the trunk on her way to pick up Zoey, and Beatrice would stop by the middle school on her bike and the two girls would ride to the warehouse together. Candice allowed it rather frequently, for as much as she relished her role as an agitator, when it came to the parts her daughters had to play, she harbored plenty of guilt for Candice to untie.

The bike ride was the best part of any day they were allowed to be together. The road leading to the realization station was sparsely traveled when there wasn't a shift change in process, and the land split by the road was flat, making for an easy ride. The ease inspired some maneuvers designed to ruffle the flatness and add curves to the straight line. Their signature move was to weave back and forth past one another in rhythm. If they were able to leave a trail of smoke that could be seen from above, their ritual would have left the shape of a rope that had unraveled.

After they finished doing their homework in the break room, they would look in on the warehouse with one of the managers, a combat veteran named Hector in the process of moving from muscular to rotund, who appreciated the change of pace that the girls threw into his shift. But they could only follow him so far. There was a line they couldn't cross, an actual yellow line painted on the shiny epoxied floor that ran around the entire perimeter. Hector told them the line was a mile and a half long.

For all the activity in the one million square feet, the space operated at a low volume. It was all hum and hiss. Viewing it from Hector's office provided a drone's eye view, but little difference in terms of sound. Even when on the floor, everything seemed to be happening through a window. Hector took a lot of pride in his work, but explained that much of the pride was grounded in surviving his previous work, and managing to adjust to a civilian job with less difficulty than a lot of his old co-workers.

"I never think of soldiers as co-workers," Beatrice said as they stood in Hector's office with him and surveyed the floor and its hundreds of gliding parts sneaking around beneath them.

"There's actually a lot of them here," he added. "Well, mostly their spouses, from the base. But a lot of vets who were stationed there and came back to the valley when they retired."

"I never think of anyone wanting to live here," Mia said.

"You should see where a lot of the other bases are," Hector chuckled. "This is the Garden of Eden compared to them."

The girls were not comforted by the thought that their hometown wasn't as bad as much of the rest of the world. They revisited the idea the day after Hector broke the news, as they worked on their pre-Algebra homework in the empty break room.

"We'll just have to aim for the nicer parts," Beatrice concluded as they considered their future in such a world.

"Maybe it's comfort," Mia offered. "People get used to a place."

"Like you," Beatrice said.

"Me?" Mia dropped her pencil into the gulch between the pages of her textbook. "Do I seem satisfied to you?"

"I mean when it comes to school. You adjusted quickly."

"I was just relived to get out of Live Oak."

"Aw..."

"You know what I mean. I was starting to feel like Artie."

"Son of Satan?" Beatrice likewise surrendered her pencil.

"Daughter of Shiva, destroyer of charter schools."

"Shiva's male."

"That's right. Sounds so feminine, though."

"We need more kick-ass goddesses."

"Speak for yourself. Try being raised by one."

"Come on. You said the teachers love her, and the students don't care."

"Most of them. Do you remember a girl named Eve? Seventh grader at LOCA?"

"I think. She's at the middle school now?"

"Yeah, and pissed about it. She's cornered me a couple times and bitched about my Mom convincing her parents to transfer her."

"So," Beatrice looked on the bright side. "It's just one."

"But if the charter closes, I'm screwed. I'll have dozens of Eves coming at me, all the time."

"The teachers will have your back."

"Sure," Mia scoffed. "That'll help. A teacher's pet on top of whatever you call the thing I've become thanks to my mother."

The door to the break room opened and a woman whose mascara blended into the darkness around her eyes flashed them a split-second smile before fetching a flattened bag of microwave popcorn from the pile in a shallow basket next to the oven.

The girls weren't ready to return to their homework, but didn't want to talk while the woman stripped away the plastic and put the paper shingle behind the smeared door of the microwave.

"If that happens," Mia picked up the conversation as the oven started to breathe, "if the charter closes, maybe Artie and I can finally bond."

"Not unless you go to boarding school with him."

"What?"

"That's where he's headed next year," Beatrice explained. "No matter what happens to LOCA. Some school in San Francisco, I think. That's the rumor."

"So he may not be going?"

"No, he's definitely going. The rumors are about where the school is. I don't think his father wants anyone to know."

Mia stared at the pencil nestled in the shallow chasm of her math book. She heard the popcorn start to thump into the sides of the bag as it spun around.

"How convenient," Mia deflated. "I wish we had the money to run away and hide."

The sound from the oven was accompanied by laughter from the woman who pushed the button.

"Ain't the first time you're gonna wish that, honey," she cackled.

Mia and Beatrice looked at each other as the popping grew louder and closer together, bunches of kernels bursting at once while the bag absorbed the blows. Mia looked down at her pre-Algebra, then Beatrice looked at hers.

The oven stopped and its bell rang.

They took the bell as their cue to start working again, exchanging weary grins as they did.

Chapter Twenty One: Dale

People talked about him at the board meeting as though he wasn't there, but they would still look at him. They would take their turn in the public comments line, which was longer than it had been for any previous meeting by far, and read their passage they had written or try to remember what they wanted to say about why Dale Copeland should retain his position, or why Dale Copeland should be released from it, and regardless of their stance, they would look at him after they were done. If they were supporting him, they would wink or nod in his direction. If they were in support of ousting him, they would glance over with an apologetic smirk or practically subliminal frown.

The board members did much the same. During their public exchanges, they referred to Dale in the third person, none of them addressing him directly except with their eyes when someone else was talking.

Before the meeting was adjourned, Dale was finally spoken to in the second person by the interim member who had taken over for Rod, a placid bookkeeper who was most likely chosen under the assumption he wouldn't do anything other than keep the seat warm until the next election.

"Is there anything you would like the board to know, Mr. Copeland, before we begin our private deliberations?"

Dale shook his head, and as soon as people started to stand up, he hurried to the door in the back of the room.

To his relief, he heard no voices flagging him down as he trotted to his truck. He wondered why he had bothered coming in the first place. As he suspected, his heart and lungs had seemed to migrate entirely into his neck and head, leaving the rest of his body numb, and his ability to hear or remember anything overwhelmed by the throbbing that pounded him above the shoulders. He recalled the term "good man" being used frequently, often as a qualifier.

"He's a good man, but…"

"Good man, but…"

"But…"

When Wendy told him the board president was on the line the following morning, he was pelted with the same onslaught of feelings and lack thereof.

He asked her to take a message.

She jotted down enough notes to compose a memo, while saying "okay" and "mmm-hmm" a dozen times each. He felt guilty for putting her through that, and walked out to her desk so he could apologize the moment she hung up.

"That's okay," she stayed seated and reviewed her work, perhaps as an excuse not to look at him.

He watched as she tapped her pen under every other word in every line and worked her way down. He was about to try and read what she wrote, but thought that would be rude.

"So what's the verdict?" he asked.

She took a deep breath and started with news about the school.

"They're whittling down to Kindergarten through fifth grade. The contract with the district emphasizes fill rates rather than raw numbers, and most of the defections this year came from sixth through eighth. We can blame the losses on kids wanting the full middle school experience."

"The full middle school experience?"

"I know it sounds horrible at our age," Wendy clarified. "But they haven't gone through it yet. They're curious. Sports, cheerleading, a different teacher for each subject. That sort of thing."

Dale wasn't wholly convinced.

"If that's how they want to spin it," he shrugged.

The other news loomed. Neither was sure how to get there. Dale decided to make the move, since Wendy was kind enough to take the message.

"And who's going to take over?" he asked, assuming that if the news was good, it wouldn't have been difficult for her to deliver.

"They've offered you another job," she said.

"Really?"

"Special Education Coordinator."

"They invented a job for me."

"They had to create it at some point. They said the pay would be comparable to the same position in the district."

"I would hope so," he exhaled a quick laugh. "It's not a hard offer to match. Am I supposed to stay on as principal for the rest of the year?"

"They'd like you to resign, effective on the last day of school. If you'd rather take a leave of absence until then, they've got Ken Bedrosian ready to jump in. Otherwise he'll officially start as the interim principal on the first day of summer while they search for a permanent hire."

"So much for Ken being vehemently opposed to the charter."

"I guess he hasn't developed any hobbies in his retirement."

They smiled at one another, decades of shared experience passing between them. Then Wendy seemed to remember something that made her uncomfortable, and appeared to search for an invisible wall to hide behind.

"Is there something else?" Dale asked.

"Well...no"

Dale pulled one of the chairs away from the wall and sat down beside her desk.

"I'll take the job," he said. "Or use it as leverage to get my old job back with the district."

"It's not that."

He knew it wasn't. He let her work her way up to what she wanted to say.

"They would 'like' you to resign," she said. "That's a direct quote."

Now he remembered.

"How could I forget?" he leaned back in the chair.

"You're not into that sort of thing," she smiled.

Which was still true for the most part, as his excitement at possibly forcing the board's hand had already turned to dread at the thought of actually pursuing the matter. But he had spent a lot of the previous year trying to reinvent himself, and promoting that new version to convince others, if not himself, that he was well-versed in the art of the deal. He wondered if he had come so far as to take hostages, or if recent events were enough to demonstrate how unfit for business he was.

"They're depending on you to go quietly," Wendy said, picking up on his apprehension. "You're good at this job. And you have a three-year contract."

"I'm surprised Rod didn't remind me of my contract situation when everything started to fall apart. We talked a lot at that last conference."

Wendy snorted, then explained herself.

"You're surprised Rod didn't remember something about someone other than himself?"

Dale felt as though he had lost the right to comment on anyone's ambition.

"I thought you were mad at me," he said.

"I was," she shot back. "But not enough to think you deserve this."

Dale appreciated both her candor and her respect. But none of his feelings at the moment could escape the pull of what beckoned.

"Would a buyout leave them with enough to hire a replacement?" he deliberated aloud.

"They could limp along with Ken for a while," Wendy speculated with him. "Or string along a couple other placeholders until they got out from under it."

Dale couldn't bear to sit any longer. He stood and paced in no particular pattern, moderating a debate between the positions in his head.

Wendy stood up and steadied him.

"Go home and talk to Alma and Jonathan," she said. "I'll handle things here today."

"Thank you."

As soon as his words stopped vibrating, he felt incapable of doing or saying anything else. He stood there trying to muster the energy to leave. Wendy hugged him, which filled him up enough to make it out the door and down the stairs to the parking lot.

Once behind the wheel, he put his hands behind his head and arched into a ball as though waiting for a bomb to drop, and fueled up on a minute of his own heavy breathing to start the drive.

Alma said very little when Dale led her through the circumstances.

She gave the impression of nodding when he explained the board's decision, and she may have actually nodded when he told her what they had requested of him. A look of surprise mildly made its way across her face as Dale told her about his contract situation. He remembered that the idea behind a longer contract for the principal was to provide some stability amongst the one-year contracts for everyone else, and to insure they had some administrative consistency to get the school up and running.

"And since I was so busy doing all those things to fulfill the contract," he addressed the reason why he had never mentioned it to her before, "I never thought much about the contract itself."

Which led him to the possibility of a buyout, which inspired her to make a noise. It was a quick hum, followed by more silence.

"We could buy the house for Jonathan," he tried to coax her into saying something. "And have enough left over to start some sort of nest egg he could eventually live off."

She finally consented.

"People may think you deliberately tanked in order to force the issue," she offered.

"I'm getting used to people thinking things about me."

She fell back into silence.

Dale joined her, willing to wait as long as it took for Alma to provide some more guidance.

When she spoke at last, it was to suggest that he talk to Jonathan about what loomed, since the decision revolved so tightly around him. Then she changed the subject.

Dale though it best to take his son to a place where Jonathan thrived, where he was at peace.

They didn't need to make reservations at a campsite. They knew of a few spots in the woods off some side roads, a few thousand feet above the valley, from their years of searching for sites that allowed them to truly get away from the world of manufactured stimuli. He went with the safest site, the one sitting on a plot of land that belonged to a friend of a friend. It was not as beautiful as the others, but they would run no risk of being discovered.

Jonathan never seemed to prefer any particular site, anyway. It was Dale who cared, or Alma, or their daughter when she was younger and still camped with them. They were the ones who ranked the settings, who differentiated between those trees and these trees, this creek and that creek. All Jonathan needed was nature. He said so once through the instrument Alma had invented. He said the natural world took him back in time to a place when nobody talked much, and nothing made noise other than wind and water.

Jonathan bolted from the truck the moment they came to a stop in the clearing by a small stream that trickled its way through the drought. He stood by the narrow shore with his fists clenched in front of him, as though sinking a winning putt or free throw, and not wanting the celebration to end.

Dale kept an eye on him as he pitched the tent and dug the fire pit a little deeper out of respect for the dry surroundings. The pines were still green, though, and moss still clung to the boulders, offering a mirage against the scarce backdrop.

When his work was done, he sat on a toppled section of trunk and watched his son for a while. Jonathan's fists were still drawn forward, but raised a bit higher, and he rotated slightly back and forth while looking up, nothing between him and the God he was either thanking or cursing.

Dale entertained an absurd thought that maybe the best thing for him would be to build a shack here, or someplace like it, and deliver supplies every few days and check in on him. The life expectancy would be short, he mused, but the quality would be high from Jonathan's point of view. It was one of those ideas that quickly starts to fray upon thinking through the logistics. Dale brushed it away, and plotted a delicate method of saddling his son's revelry with a rundown of what was happening back in their tiny slice of civilization, and the decision those circumstances were merging toward.

Dale got the interruption started by asking his son to help gather some firewood. Jonathan unclenched his fists and spread his palms downward, sweeping them slowly around as he walked the perimeter where the forest stood, as though his hands were a metal detector or a pair of divining rods designed to help him find wood instead of loose change or water. He would bring a single piece every time he found one, rather than stack them in his arms. Dale appreciated this system, as it allowed him to keep track of Jonathan without hovering. Even when he started to venture into the pines on his search for the next piece, Jonathan was never in the woods' grasp for more than a matter of seconds before reappearing with a rotten chunk or skinny branch with the needles still attached.

When the sun set and fire reached its peak, Dale further paved the night with speech by commenting on how good the hot dogs were, and the beans, and then the hot chocolate, which he hoped wasn't too hot, until he had gathered the strength to lower the shield from in front of his son.

"Thanks for coming up here with me, Jonathan," he started lowering it with some small talk. "It's been too long."

Some doubts quivered and kept him from proceeding. He wondered if he was really doing his son a favor by treating him like an adult. He wondered what was so great about that. A lot of people seemed determined to avoid it. But Jonathan was an adult who never had the chance to decide if he liked being one or not, and maybe he would welcome the burden rather than feeling like he was a burden. If Dale couldn't give him a house, he could at least give him that chance.

"I've been so wrapped up in work," he looked into the fire as he continued, "in getting things going for the school, for us, for myself. Mostly for myself, I suspect. I have a very strong suspicion. Even bringing you up here is kind of selfish. I want your opinion on something, even though I already know what I should do. I want you to make me feel good about that decision, or give me an excuse to do what's tempting, so I can say that I'm doing it for my family."

He turned away from the fire and looked over at Jonathan, whose attention remained on the flames that kept the tics and idiosyncrasies at bay.

"So, no pressure," Dale watched Jonathan watch the fire. "You'll give me what I need either way. I'll appreciate whatever you have to say. See? Now I even feel better about bringing you up here. I'm getting so good at spinning any situation in my favor. So good. 'Good,' 'good,' 'good.' They constantly said that about me at the board meeting, the one where they ended up canning me. Proof that if you say anything often enough, it loses meaning. 'Good man,' 'good man,' 'good man'..."

The fire snapped out a burning ember and Jonathan laughed. Dale smiled and nearly laughed with him.

"I notice you do that a lot. Say something over and over and over. That must be why. You can beat the meaning out of it, beat it into submission. One less word flying at you. One less expression to make sense of. I totally understand. I get it."

Jonathan settled back into a staring contest with their source of heat. One of the logs popped again, and he repeated the expression "A poppin' good time" for about a minute straight. Dale couldn't place where the words may have come from. "A poppin' good time." Perhaps it was a line from a series or a movie, or the hook to a commercial that he had since forgotten, or didn't notice to begin with, as it meanwhile captivated his son. Maybe Jonathan had strung the words together on his own. The "good" made sense, but Dale tried to think of a time during another camping trip when he said something about the fire popping. He couldn't make the connection, and was left with another unsolved mystery inside Jonathan's mind.

Dale let it drift away and join the other forgotten puzzles. He rubbed his back against the log behind him and waited until it was clear that Jonathan was done talking before he continued to explain the situation.

"Anyway, back to the part about being canned. That's not entirely true. And that's where you come in. I know I didn't bring the instrument. That's on purpose. All you need to do is listen. I'll follow up when we get home. I don't know how to use it as well as Mom, anyway. And you know how I feel about the 'Yes' and 'No' cards. I just want to plant what's happened lately into that fascinating head of yours, let you in on what's going down amongst those of us who can supposedly communicate with each other."

Dale was drawn back to the flame as well. The night air started to put on some chilly weight, and it felt good to face the warmth in full.

"The charter wants to fire me, but I have a contract. So there's a chance I can force them to pay me for the remainder of that contract, more or less, to get rid of me. Or I can accept a different job they've offered me, at less pay, and have the awkward privilege of continuing to work with those who asked me to leave."

He looked over at Jonathan, who appeared quite serious, no longer reveling in the peaceful accompaniment that nature offered. Probably because his Dad was interrupting it, Dale thought. Though he had faith that maybe the lack of civilized noise allowed Jonathan to really concentrate on what he was saying.

"I could just leave altogether, I suppose. Bail and look for a new spot, maybe get my old job back, who knows? But your opinion on the buyout is really all I'm asking of you. The other jobs, and wherever they're located, that's just rearranging the furniture. I want your thoughts on the buyout. I know this may be a lot to ask, but you're an adult, and it affects you. And I know it seems like an easy decision on the surface, at least I hope we've raised you well enough for the right way to seem obvious, but bear in mind what we could do with that money. Any one of those houses we toured could be yours. We could start a trust that would pay your living expenses when we're gone. We could accomplish everything I intended to build over the span of many years with one swing. One slimy, drawn-out swing."

The volume of the world seemed to lower from where Dale sat. The thickening air muffled the sounds of the forest, and the fire barely hissed. Jonathan looked beautiful in the orange glow of the firelight. A still photograph of him at that moment, at that angle, would cause women who saw it and didn't know him to ask if he was single, and men to tell themselves that women want more than looks in a man.

"I'm sorry," Dale said. "I've let you down. I shouldn't have done this."

Dale wasn't sure whether he was referring to the past year or just that night.

"There was so much happening, so many things that seemed okay, because they were getting me where I needed to be, to do all the wonderful things I was going to do."

The hush that had fallen over their campsite persisted, and Dale felt as though his voice had become too loud for it. He stopped to gauge where he needed to be, and could hear the stream fighting its way to a larger body of water so many miles away.

"I've heard so many people say the same thing," he matched his voice to that of the stream. "They say having a special needs child made them a better person. And I thought I was the same. I was so proud of myself. I was getting so much out of having you as a son that I started to feel guilty. I wasn't sure I could make it up to you."

He stopped and listened to the water again, which now seemed to be running straight through him.

"Now I know I can't. And I'm not the person I thought I was."

The fire snapped once softly, then unleashed a loud, crackling stream.

They both flinched and smiled.

Dale went with the flow and lightened his tone.

"It was all a crackin' good time, until it wasn't."

"Poppin' good time," Jonathan corrected him, then continued to correct him while Dale chuckled.

They each quieted down and Dale wanted to talk with him some more, but he already knew what needed to be done.

So he told Jonathan about those things that had seemed okay, the events that inspired him to overreach, and the people involved. He speculated on what may have motivated them, what circumstances they faced and what they hoped to achieve, for Dale could only speak for himself, but he wanted to stay up late with Jonathan and tell stories, and he wanted the stories to mean something. He was convinced there were lessons to be learned from the lives of Rod and Artie, of Candice and Mia, of everyone involved, at least during the brief time he knew them, and the small window through which he was able to observe them.

Dale kept clutching to the belief that Jonathan's sober expression indicated he was listening intently to his ideas on how everyone ended up in their respective corners. But then a blue jay would bounce onto the nearby branches and screech at them, or the fire would spew another ember, and Jonathan would react with such glee that Dale wondered if Jonathan welcomed the distraction and was telling his Dad in his own way to shut up. Or perhaps, he hoped, the goose to Jonathan's senses further amplified his appreciation of their conversation, or what Dale liked to think of as a conversation.

He clung to the latter explanation and proceeded. He imagined out loud what the future might hold for the players, what the fallout might be for Candice and Rod, how Mia and Artie might adjust to their new schools, and how the other people in their lives may be affected.

He projected as far as he could, then started to tire. Jonathan was still alert, however, which Dale found encouraging.

"You may be wide awake, son, but I'm about to nod off," he announced as an overture to prepare their tent for bed. "Forgive an old man for not being able to keep up with you young folk."

He crawled into the tent and made sure that Jonathan's sleeping bag was spread out with a pillow on top for when his son was done watching the fire, then slid into his own and watched his son's silhouette projected onto the tent wall surrounded by the swirling lights of the flame.

And when Dale awoke hours later to find the light and shadows no longer dancing together, and the air much colder without the fire to stave it off, he also felt Jonathan closer to him than normal, curled up inside the cocoon of his own sleeping bag, lying in the fetal position, his head and knees burrowed into the side of Dale's sleeping bag.

For warmth, most likely.

For all the different kinds of warmth, Dale hoped.

Chapter Twenty Two: Candice

A few people had told her they read her article, and a few others had left some comments in the thread beneath it on the website. The comments were innocuous, along the lines of "Nice work", "Wow. Din't now this wz happening", with just one troll, who called it "winey bullshit", and a comment promising that if you clicked on the link provided, you could make five thousand dollars per month working from home just like his cousin.

The scant recognition had initially been a disappointment, which she was able to brush off thanks to the action her words inspired. Eventually, though, she grew nostalgic for that lack of acknowledgement after the board came to their decision, and a rash of newfound attention formed around her. The number of people who approached her didn't rise much, but the number who appeared to recognize her did. It didn't occur to her that the increased awareness was leaking into the comment thread under her article in the Valley Outlook, since weeks had passed since its publication, until one day her co-worker, the one so fond of enormous cups of soda, mentioned between sucks from a straw how long the list of tirades was becoming as they ate lunch in the office.

He assumed she had already seen the recent additions, and panicked upon realizing that he was bearing the news.

"Forget I said anything," he squeezed in before a suppressed belch got away from him.

"Are they that bad?"

He took a moment to arrive at something to say.

"Don't look," he said, "If you can find a way to resist. Please. Not that we're great friends. But nobody should talk to anyone like that."

The thought of his reaction helped her stay away for most of the day.

After the girls went to bed, though, she found herself visiting the website and searching to see if anyone had written a letter to the editor in response to her piece, now that the charter had announced its plans to downsize.

Her article was the first hit on the list of search results, of course, which spiked her adrenalin flow.

She scanned the results and saw no other articles or letters related to her name, so her pulse softened.

But this also meant that everyone so inclined to respond was piling on in the comment thread, where names weren't required, which caused her nerves to throb all over again as she hovered over the hit with her name on it.

She took a deep breath and tapped it.

The words she was so familiar with appeared. She had pored over them so many times on her own, then with the editor, and then out of pride after they were published.

She scrolled down and stopped just before the end, where the accomplished words crossed over into the chaotic ones. The expression on her office colleague's face came to mind and held her up. His rotund face had suddenly looked gaunt at the thought of what lay below. But she wanted to see how tough she was. She wanted to challenge herself.

"I'm not scared," she said out loud, and pushed the 'page down' button one more time.

The move made her dizzy. She needed to catch her breath and focus to see what was on the screen:

"Comments for this article have been closed."

Her relief was again short-lived.

Having worked herself up to see them, she felt cheated, and laughed at herself over such an odd reaction.

But the sensation didn't go away. She was aware of the interpretation which said that someone was trying to tell her not to look. But she had made her pact. She had put herself out there, and she wanted to see the results.

It was too late to call the editor, she realized, so she called him the next morning from the middle school parking lot after dropping off Mia.

She was told that once the comments are closed, they disappear from their network, and he didn't know how to get them back.

He also told her that before they shut down the thread, he sent a copy to the sheriff's department.

Candice assumed she said "What?" very loudly, but apparently that had only happened in her mind, for after a while, the editor asked if she was still there.

Since she hadn't really said anything, she started fresh with a more pertinent question.

"Why?"

"Well," he stammered. "Because I thought maybe you hung up. Or dropped the phone."

"No," she shivered back into the conversation. "I mean, why did you send them to the sheriff's office?"

"They were, you know..."

"I don't know. Tell me."

"They were...bad."

"Oh my god," she clutched her forehead. "There's that word again. Bad, bad, bad. Everything is either good or bad."

"Fine," the editor growled. "They were alarming. They were disgusting. They weren't fit for human consumption. Shall I go on?"

"No," Candice apologized. "I appreciate that you care. Thank you."

He may have said "you're welcome", but she hung up before she could find out. She was in the process of feeling guilty about cutting him off as she looked up the number for the Sheriff's Department.

Her guilt vanished, however, the moment she tapped it and heard the phone ring on the other end.

The person who answered passed her to the chief on duty, who then passed her to someone they claimed was the deputy in charge of her case.

A deep female voice greeted her and told her that the comments were evidence.

"But nothing has happened," Candice said.

"In case something does," the voice was as steady as it was low.

"So I can't have them?"

"We would prefer not give them out."

"But it's for me. Potential victim over here."

"It's not really a legal matter. We just think you'd be better off not seeing them."

"Who are 'we'?"

"Me," the woman said. "I think you'd be better off not seeing them."

"If I had checked the site yesterday, I would have seen them anyway."

"The editor pulled them two days ago."

Candice sighed.

"If I had visited the site two days ago, I would have seen them anyway."

The voice paused, which Candice imagined didn't happen very often.

"Okay, ma'am," she finally said. "If you come to the office, I'll make sure you receive a copy."

"The main office in the county seat?"

"Yes."

"You're going to make me drive forty-five minutes each way during business hours to get them?"

"I'd prefer you picked them up in person."

"Why would anyone want them besides me?"

The deputy paused again, but this time merely to exhale before giving in.

"What's your email address, ma'am?"

"Candice Ingle, all one word, at Cada Casa Management dot com."

"That's reassuring."

"Why?"

"Confirms your identity."

"I could just be sending them to this Candice person as a prank," she jabbed.

The deputy ignored her quip and wished her a nice day.

Candice drove to the office to check her email.

Nobody was there, as she suspected. Her colleague was most likely making some rounds amongst the rentals, and the manager, if she came in at all, wouldn't appear until the afternoon.

She accessed her account as quickly as possible, trying to bypass the heightened heart rate and shortness of breath that had consumed her during the previous night of toying with the idea of looking. But the dread kept pace. Her fingers shook as she fumbled passwords and quivered into a few wrong turns thanks to some unsteady clicking.

The first item listed in her inbox was indeed from the Sheriff's Department, with the subject heading "Copy of Threats".

She hesitated. It occurred to her that this is how the world would end someday, not with a bang, but with a click. She let go of a nervous, one-syllable laugh, then clicked.

The comments splattered onto the screen, and her nerves were severed.

Her brain perceived the words, but it could only send a message about them to her stomach. She was a torso full of nausea, her limbs untethered.

The first couple of entries were the only ones she read in full. She could only bring herself to scan the rest. Key words and phrases rose from the thread and filled her with more bile. Nothing surprised her about the language itself. Typical brain-dead slurs against women were thrown about. She just wasn't used to being the object of them.

A contributor who dubbed himself "Constant Common Sense" was the first to turn the aggression sexual, which the others used as permission to do the same. It became an escalating frenzy of degradation and rape. She eyed the scroll bar to see how much farther down she had to go, determined to get to the bottom. They put every part of her body in play. She had a vision of herself in chart form, like a poster behind a butcher's counter that illustrates what part of an animal the cuts of meat are taken from. And unlike the standard quality of the initial smears, their enthusiasm for violence inspired shocking levels of creativity. The depictions remained sexual only in the most technical sense.

An admonishing written voice would occasionally pop in with appeals to decency, but it was of little use, like saying "bad dog" to pack of wolves. Those from the scrum who bothered to acknowledge the interloper would merely train their howls on them, at which point Candice imagined herself screaming, "Forget about me! Run! Save yourself!" And by coincidence the dissenting voice would give up and disappear.

When she reached the last violent screed, she read every word of it, then leaned back in her chair and tried not to throw up.

It was like everything associated with the past year, and admittedly some of the years before, in that something was going to end badly, but she morbidly pursued it anyway.

She wondered how many of the authors she had met before, how many she really knew, and how many had nothing to do with the school, or her, and were just seizing an opportunity to anonymously rage against a woman they didn't know while imagining one they did. Their voracity and speed convinced her that those who were strangers had programed alerts to let them know when their favorite deviant word combinations were being used somewhere on the web, so when they got an email notification directing them to a link where "choke, piss, face, smear" was billowing, they could pick up the scent and join the hunt.

The rest of the day proceeded in a way she hoped wasn't a prologue for how the rest of her life was going to feel. She was scared. Men with whom she had always been perfectly comfortable made her uneasy. Even those she couldn't imagine would ever do her harm made her wonder if they could have written any of the comments, or if they harbored the same thoughts but were blessed with restraint. She even refused to have a cup of coffee with the sweet old man at The Oasis who looked after his grandkids in his apartment, once he mentioned that the kids were with their mother, who took the morning off to register the oldest for Kindergarten.

As the day extended into several more, she made some progress in her efforts to stop reading every male mind she encountered, but not as much as she would have hoped. The stream of words she had absorbed gathered in her head like a cold she couldn't get over. Thoughts of a world without civility or law pressed on her throat and the roof of her mouth. She was irritable, but unwilling to share what clung to her. She imagined how histrionic it would sound, how easy to disregard. Dismissive waves of the hand came to mind when she found herself on the brink of saying something, thousands of condescending hands flopping in her face.

Afraid of the effect her twitchiness may have on her daughters, she negotiated extra time with their father as school ended and plans for the summer took shape. Her ex was reluctant at first to take on any additional days, until she confessed that it had to do with her mental state, which seemed to offer him a sort of victory. He tried to sound consoling, but there was a smug undertone that undermined whatever genuine concern he had, and made it all the more difficult to see them off into his arms when the days came, as much as she knew it was for the best.

He agreed not to say anything about her condition to Yael. He vowed not to tell the girls, either, though Candice suspected they already knew she had seen better days.

The time alone served her well. She took care of work and of herself, and in the routine found security.

Eventually she found serenity.

And she found it in the words of her tormentors.

The "Copy of Threats" remained in her inbox. She held onto it with the idea that when she could read the words without despair, or at least far less of it, their loss of power would signal a cure. The copy had worked its way down the inbox list as other emails arrived that Candice needed to keep, until the copy wasn't visible any longer.

But it was still there.

She tried to read them once a day, and by late summer the results started to show in how often she forgot to do so. There wasn't so much a decrease in fear and sadness, but a rise in satisfaction.

She felt as though she was offered a glimpse into the depths of what people are capable of. The murky water had been cleared for her so that she could see the bottom without having to jump in. It started to feel like a blessing in deep cover, a twisted privilege. She used its shocking ability to enlighten as a way back to a place before the charter, and beyond that to a place before so many of the other events that wadded up her nerve endings. She was alive in a heartless universe, and in the face of its indifference, she gave it a shrug.

She saw Alma Copeland at the grocery store and didn't feel the least bit uncomfortable. Unlike Alma, who tried to avoid her.

Candice respected her wishes for a few laps through the aisles, but by the fourth time they crossed paths, the ruse had become too absurd to carry on.

"Hello, Alma."

"Oh, hi Candice!" she overreacted.

"How are you and Dale holding up?"

Alma looked as though she had taken a punch from the casual manner that Candice had thrown at her.

"Well…" she wobbled. "All right."

"Glad to hear it."

Alma paused and regained her footing.

"Is this some sort of victory dance?"

"I'm just wondering how you're holding up."

"In spite of all you've done?"

"Yes," Candice easily maintained her sweet surrender. "In spite of it all."

"It's been tough," Alma started to get emotional.

"I understand."

"Do you?" she snapped. "Dale gets angry letters and emails."

"People still write letters?"

Alma was once again caught off guard.

"The older ones," she relented with a slim chuckle.

"Any death threats?" Candice asked, as though it was an item on her shopping list.

"No…"

"Rape? And lots of it?"

"Why would anyone threaten to rape Dale?"

"I just thought since he and I are both being attacked over the same issue, that maybe the threats would be the same."

"We haven't been threatened."

"We?" noted Candice. "They mention you in some of the letters?"

"No, not really."

"I didn't think so. Because if they did, then maybe you'd know what I'm talking about."

Candice almost offered her a glimpse of the glimpse she had been granted. She nearly paraphrased some of the most harrowing acts, positions, and implements that had been brandished at her. But her newfound place in the cosmos prevailed. She instead wished Alma a good day, and to say "hi" to Dale for her.

It felt like gloating, Candice thought as she walked away, though she hadn't said anything that would lead Alma to believe that's what she was doing. Even if Candice was proud, it had nothing to do with any changes she instigated in the schools.

For when the new academic year started, and the charter was down three grades while the district was up five dozen students, it didn't trigger any feelings of accomplishment, other than satisfaction at having made it through another year, with a new one on the way.

She was working, raising children, breathing, moving, and when she held still, it was to delight in some passing moment that nobody else would remember.

Chapter Twenty Three: Rodrigo

He remembered when Artie was in Kindergarten, maybe first grade. He would listen at the door to his son's room and hear him perform scenes from stories he was making up as he went along, adopting all the voices and acting out all the movements. His plays were a mashup of reality and fantasy, the plots borrowed from movies he had recently watched, their characters replaced with the names of his classmates. So it wasn't Woody and Buzz trying to chase down the moving van at the end of Toy Story, it was Artie and Claire desperately warning and encouraging each other, or Artie and Joaquin, or Artie and Lindsey.

The names Artie used were kids who didn't really play with him, as far as Rod knew. He wasn't around enough to monitor many playdates, but he heard about the patterns from Rita, and given the few kids who played with Artie, combined with the number of names he used in his one-man shows, it was mathematically unlikely that they were all friends in real life.

But his son admired them enough to write them into his fantasies. They were, after all, the princes and princesses of the valley, destined to inherit whatever money could be squeezed from it, so Artie's admiration was understandable.

Rod surveyed the new slate of classmates at the boarding school as he and Rita visited on Parents Day, and he wondered what sorts of stories these rejects could be written into, if Artie was still so inclined.

Sending them to such a pricey hideaway seemed to be part of a scheme by the parents to spend all their money before the kids could grow up and blow it all. They reminded Rod of those infamous siblings of famous people when they were younger, already being trained to stay in the background and not embarrass the family. At the previous schools his kids had attended, Rod could at least imagine a harmless adulthood for most of the students, even if that future was dimly-lit rather than bright. But this group had a potentially fatal dose of money to go with the halting personalities that were so hard to watch.

He and Rita looked at one another frequently with no expressions. None were necessary. This was the way it would have to be until college.

Artie seemed happy enough. For the first time in his academic life he was not an oddity. Rod and Rita reminded themselves of his default rise in standing as they went to dinner afterwards and almost drank too much.

"So where does being the cream of this particular crop get you?" Rod asked after they decided not to order a second bottle of wine.

"Someplace where they use the word 'eccentric' in front of your accomplishments," she leaned back and appeared to ponder her buzz as much as their son's prospects. "Eccentric billionaire, eccentric owner, eccentric board member."

"What if you end up with no accomplishments?" he enjoyed being able to cover their concern with laughter. "What if you're just eccentric?"

Rita contemplated the possibilities.

"Then you're reclusive," she decided.

"A reclusive eccentric."

"That's redundant," she chided him.

"An eccentric reclusive?"

"Recluse," she corrected him, then giggled. "Remember what your English was like when we first met?"

Rod warmly nodded, but was still considering where the wealthy weird wound up.

"You need money to be a recluse," he speculated.

"You do."

"Otherwise you're homeless, or a vagrant."

"A hobo," Rita added. "Or whatever the kids call them nowadays."

"You don't know? You spent all that time with them in the classroom."

"It wasn't a subject that came up."

"Half their family members are homeless. They just don't notice because they see them on the couch or the floor."

"Maybe it's too sad or scary for them to think about."

"Nobody wants to face anything," Rod shook his head and rummaged around the bread basket to see if there was one more piece hidden inside the napkin.

"Sorry," Rita sneered. "I should have led a discussion while they were making those Q-tip skeletons for Halloween. 'And speaking of scary thing, kids, how many of you had a drunk uncle on the couch this morning? Maybe a meth head aunt? Does she have teeth like a jack-o-lantern? Let's use her as a model. But not as a model for your life! Say no to drugs!'"

"That's about how it goes," he muttered, not finding anything in the folds of the napkin. "It's all talk. Woe is me. Poor me. And nothing happens."

"We're getting gloomy, Rigo."

"Nobody does anything."

"We should go."

"And when someone does do something, people try to tear them down. That's their idea of an accomplishment. Rip those who get things done."

"I understand."

"I had all of the above and more. I had drunk uncles. I had aunts and cousins with their own recipes for meth."

"But you overcame."

Rod spread his arms in acknowledgement.

"Why can't everyone be like you, Rodrigo?" she said in lieu of applause, then waited for him to finish his curtain call.

"Why can't they?" he let his arms drop.

Rita looked as though she had more to say, but buried her words with a sigh instead.

"We've got that breakfast reception tomorrow morning in the cafeteria," she said at the conclusion of her exhale. "The 'Bon Voyage Breakfast'. Let's get plenty of rest and start fresh."

He tried to recharge the fun they had been having while paying the check and helping Rita with her coat, but he was talking to himself. Her reminder and her advice were the last words she spoke for the night, and a sunrise was his only chance to be in good company again.

They did play nicely with the other parents the following morning, most of whom they had avoided the previous afternoon. They sat a table with a husband and wife who owned some assisted-living compounds in Costa Rica for American retirees, and a nanny who was attending Parents Day on behalf of her employers, who were on a Rhine River cruise.

"Who's watching the other kids while you're here, then?" Rita asked her.

"Colton is an only child," she replied.

"Well, then, if you don't mind me asking," Rita prefaced, "why do they still need a nanny?"

"I guess I'm mostly a house sitter now," she seemed to suddenly realize. "But when something like this comes up, or Colton's in town for the holidays, I put my nanny hat back on."

Meanwhile, the assisted living moguls didn't take long to hand Rod a spiral-bound prospectus and try to convince him to invest in what they presented as their "growing empire." Rod grinned and nodded his way from wariness to hostility that he concealed well enough to inspire a compliment from Rita.

"The only reason I didn't stab him with my fork is that it took me so long to wrap my head around what he said," Rod admitted. "People in Costa Rica are easy to screw over?"

"Maybe we don't look Latin anymore," Rita joked as they milled from the smell of eggs in the cafeteria to the campus courtyard, which barely concealed the scents and sounds of the city on the other side of the walls. "We're bleached by success."

"And that's how white people talk to each other?"

"He could have been talking about the old Americans who move there."

"If that's the case, I'm in," Rod snickered as he tossed the booklet into a trash can they passed.

"Aw," Rita mocked. "I wanted to see if screwing people over was part of the literature."

"You're welcome to sift through the garbage if you'd like."

The school bell rang, which sounded more like an alarm, and the students started to flood the courtyard, their bustle drowning out the traffic noise from the surrounding streets. Artie materialized from the horde and approached.

"This is the 'bon voyage' part, I take it?" asked Rita.

"I guess so," Artie shrugged. "The staff probably wants us all in one place so they can make sure nobody tries to kill their parents on school property."

Rita raised her eyebrows at him.

Artie shifted into exaggerated cheer.

"Or they want to see all the warm, touching moments that take place."

"All five of them," Rod muttered.

"Not helping," Rita glared.

"Five might be too high," Artie fed off his father's jab.

"I'll bet the staff takes bets," Rod reached into his pocket for a money clip full of cash. "See if you can get in on the action. Take the under."

Rita smacked his hand with the money in it. He grinned and put it back.

Artie smiled, too.

But then his lip started to quiver.

"Honey," Rita gave her son a hug.

"I'm sorry," Artie said as he turned his head to the side so his words wouldn't land in her coat.

"Don't be," she rubbed his back. "This is a new adventure."

"A chance to see things we've never seen before," Rod added.

Rita didn't appreciate his contribution.

Rod lip-synced a disbelieving "What?"

"We're proud of you," she turned her attention back to her son, who had turned his face inward again to muffle his sobs. "You've been through a lot, and you're stronger than we ever imagined."

Rod put his hand on Artie's shoulder, but it felt arbitrary, as though he was checking their temperature rather than joining the moment. He let his hand slide off and he watched them.

Artie unraveled himself from his Mom, inhaled some sniffles, and turned to hug his Dad.

"Oh," Rod said. "Does this count as two moments?"

Artie giggled briefly. Rod looked at Rita to confirm that this time she enjoyed his joke as well. She seemed okay with it. Before he could cajole her into a more approving look, Artie's voice rose between them.

"I'll try to be more like you."

Rod stood a bit more straight.

"Like me?" he stared down at his son.

Artie looked up at his father and nodded, then hugged him again.

Rod thought of the night before when he had wished for a world full of people like him, and remembered the silence from across the dinner table that greeted his solution.

He focused on the top of Artie's head and avoided eye contact with Rita.

Artie stepped back and did his best impersonation of bravery, but was too young to pull it off convincingly. Rod was able to share the moment with his wife while still avoiding her gaze, as she reached for his hand and clutched it while their son blended back into the wash of boarders.

He continued to shy away from her sight all the way to the airport, pretending to look at what was outside the window. She may not have been looking at him, either, but he suspected she was. He imagined she was staring at him the whole time, waiting for her chance to pounce at the slightest glance with a facial or verbal expression that summarized what was wrong with the way he saw the world.

His son was never going to be like him, no matter how much he tried.

His other kids never even tried.

And as their plane climbed above the city, he considered the millions of others below, submerged in the skyline, who didn't even know who he was, and never would.

Reaching the space above their homeland later on offered a chance to feel full of himself again. He had been involved with nearly every patch of the furrowed checkerboard that spread beneath them for hundreds of thousands of acres. Some he had worked, others he had managed, and still others he had owned. Reviewing his geographical work history from the air had always been a source of pleasure.

"Everything looks so small," said Rita as they started their descent.

She said the very same thing at some point during every airplane ride they had ever taken, but this time he suspected it was supposed to mean something.

They flew over the most recent addition to his patches of familiarity, the slightest of them all, and it seemed to stare up at him with the same look he assumed Rita had been trying to give him.

Live Oak Charter Academy stood like a walled city that would not surrender. He had conquered all the surrounding land, but the center of ideas, the cradle of thought, would not yield.

Rod kept his eyes on the campus until it disappeared behind them as they drew closer to the ground.

He finally looked at her for the first time since Artie hugged him.

"I was thinking it all looks so vast," he said.

She smiled at him as they touched down.

The landing was not very smooth. Her smile wavered during a couple of bumps, but it was still there when they slowed down and taxied to the little terminal where no one was waiting for them.

Chapter Twenty Four: Mia

She made a pact with Beatrice before seventh grade started.

They were comparing schedules in Mia's room. Her mother was making up for sending her daughters to their father so often over the summer by offering a week's work of playdates and room service before the first day of school.

They had math together second period.

"If things are as bad as I think they're going to be," Mia told her, "I'll let you know by not sitting next to you in math."

"It's only second period. You really think you'll be able to tell after just a couple hours?"

"Yes."

"Okay..." Beatrice was staggered by Mia's certitude. "But why does it matter if we're seen together?"

"You're not going to want to be associated with me."

"I'm your friend."

"We can still hang out together after school, at the warehouse. My Mom will drop me off. One good thing about what's happened is she'll do anything to make it up to me."

Mia tilted her head back and raised her voice.

"Right, Mom?"

Footsteps padded down the hall and reached the bedroom door.

"What's that, hon?" Candice poked her head in.

"Beatrice and I were hoping to do our homework in the warehouse again this year. Can you give me a ride?"

"You don't want to ride your bikes?"

"We can't be seen together."

"Why not?"

"Well...you know."

Candice opened her mouth wide and nodded slowly.

"Ah," she agreed. "Of course."

"So is that a yes?"

Candice thrust up her thumb and smiled.

"Can I get you two anything?" she offered.

"We're good."

"Okay, then. Let me know if you change your minds."

She leaned in a little farther, then pulled herself up by the door frame and launched herself back into the hall with a "wee" sound.

"Is she on medication?" Beatrice asked as the footsteps faded from earshot.

"I don't know what's up," Mia pondered. "I thought maybe she had a new boyfriend, but she swears she's not seeing anyone."

"Maybe it's an affair."

"Whatever it is, she's keeping it a secret."

And within minutes of day one at their newly-integrated middle school, it was clear to Mia that the girls should keep their friendship a secret as well. The Live Oak refugees were furious at having their school taken from them, and according to their murmurs and stares, believed Mia had taken it from them. The only other person they seemed to be aiming their hatred at was Kimmy.

Mia thought it best to make the same deal with Kimmy as she had with Beatrice, if only to spread the anger and hopefully thin it out.

"We'd better stay away from each other," Mia said to her in the corridor when they found themselves walking side by side for a few paces, as though they were being chased by an angry mob and decided to split up. She thought maybe Kimmy wouldn't understand why she would suggest such a maneuver, but Kimmy agreed with a wide-eyed nod.

Their classmates did not accept the terms. The ex-LOCA students lumped the two girls together, blaming them for everyone having to re-enter the district, and they quickly managed to convince most of the others to join the movement. Their line of reasoning went that the school was more crowded than it had to be thanks to them.

Kimmy pushed back by saying to anyone who harassed her that really the snotty LOCAs were just bitter about having to mingle with the low class again, and couldn't pretend they were superior anymore. Her tactic backfired, though. The ex-LOCAs appropriated Kimmy's message as their own, claiming her low-class theory in fact revealed her feelings rather than theirs. And since they had the numbers, they only had to persuade a few before it spread amongst the many who didn't want to fall outside the bubble of convention.

Unlike Kimmy, Mia didn't counterpunch her tormentors as the exile developed momentum. She remained stoic, with the thought that maintaining dignity may count for something.

"Dignity?" Kimmy admonished her. "In a middle school?"

They started to sit together at lunch by mid-September, realizing all they had during school hours was each other. They were giving their classmates what they wanted, a more convenient way to glare at them both, but it was worth it to be able to deflect the scorn together.

"That's just what I call it," Mia admitted. "I don't know how to defend myself, and the word 'dignity' sounds good."

"It does," Kimmy agreed. "I missed your honesty."

"Thanks," Mia said.

She scanned the faces, all of whom appeared to talk with their mouths full, and wondered if she was being paranoid or if half of the crumb-covered lips really were talking about the two of them. She'd catch a pair of eyes squinting their way in disdain, and the eyes would turn away toward the other chewers. Then one would gargle a comment through a swamp of dough in their mouth, and the others would laugh as shards of food would fly.

"Well?" Kimmy asked.

"What?"

"Did you miss me?"

Mia tried not to smile as she kept quiet.

"Dignity," Kimmy cracked.

Mia broke into a brief smile and they surveyed the leering faces together.

"I feel like a zoo animal," Kimmy said.

"Like a couple of pandas they're hoping will mate," Mia played along.

"And we're both girls."

"And they're too stupid to notice."

They chuckled and Mia looked for Beatice.

She saw her sitting near some typically disapproving classmates, trying to keep her emotional distance from the clique.

"I feel more sorry for Beatrice than us," Mia said.

"Do you talk to her?"

"Sure. We still do homework at the warehouse. Nobody can see us there."

Kimmy whipped her whole upper body in Mia's direction.

"All this time I thought you were just as lonely as I was."

"It's been like two weeks," Mia shrugged.

"That's a long time for a seventh grader."

"Sorry."

Kimmy exhaled and returned to staring at the masticating gallery.

Mia did likewise and found Beatrice making inquisitive eye contact with her. Mia shook her off.

Beatrice rose from her seat.

Mia facially implored her to sit back down.

Beatrice headed their way.

Mia held her breath.

Beatrice arrived and stopped in front of their table.

"She knows about us now, doesn't she?" Beatrice asked Mia while gesturing at Kimmy.

"Yes," Mia sighed.

"Might as well join you, then."

Beatrice sat down in the seat across from them with her back to the shocked and delighted crowd, many of whom stopped chewing in honor of the moment.

"She's just going to use that information against us at some point," Beatrice continued.

"Only if you really piss me off," Kimmy deadpanned.

"Just as well," Beatrice straightened up. "I'm as much to blame for Live Oak as the two of you."

She breathed deeply and let it out, appearing to reach beatitude by the time she was done.

"So?" Kimmy sniped. "It's not like you confessed to anything. Everyone knows you told Mr. Benton."

"But I never became a target. It's not fair."

"That's because you don't have a psycho mother like Mia does, and you're not a bitch."

"Like you," Mia confirmed.

"Like me," Kimmy obliged.

"I'm a narc," Beatrice said. "A snitch."

"You were concerned," Mia reached across the table for Beatrice's hands.

"Love you, too," Beatrice locked fingers with her.

Kimmy rolled her eyes.

"Barf," she subtitled.

"Come on," Mia scolded her. "Our numbers just increased."

"We need to stick together," Beatrice added. "It's us against the world."

She let go of Mia's hands and turned to catch her first glimpse of the hostile flock from her new perspective.

When she turned back toward Mia and Kimmy, she appeared to have lost all feeling in her face.

"Oh my God," she said. "What have I done?"

"You can pretend you came over to make fun of us," Kimmy offered. "It's not too late. We'll play along."

"Is it always like this?" Beatrice flicked her head in the direction of the masses.

The girls nodded.

"I'm sorry I didn't cross over sooner."

"Aw, see Kimmy?" Mia said. "She's a great teammate."

Kimmy tried to smile, but it came across as more of a pout. She caught herself, then shifted in her seat before making an announcement in the form of a question.

"But does she know how to make all of this stop?"

"And I suppose you do?" Beatrice answered.

"Is there a computer in the warehouse you have access to?"

Mia and Beatrice looked at each other.

"Hector's office?" Mia suggested.

"Yup. But we've never used it," Beatrice reminded her.

"We can ask," Mia said.

"I'll ask Hector," Kimmy cut in, suggestively emphasizing the "I".

"He's our friend," Beatrice said. "We don't need you to stick your ass in his face."

Mia covered her mouth and bent over to squelch her laughter.

"Yeah," Kimmy groused. "Great teammate."

"All I'm saying is that we're pretty sure we can use the computer," Beatrice backtracked. "Why can't we use one here, anyway? Or your phone. I assume you're looking for web access."

"Web access that can't be traced to us."

Mia sat up and wiped away some tears with the back of her hand as she exchanged a glance with Beatrice.

"What exactly are you thinking of doing?" Mia asked.

"Can I come with you to the warehouse?"

Mia and Beatrice shrugged at one another.

"Sure," Beatrice said.

"Now can you tell us?" Mia tried again.

"You'll see," Kimmy grinned. "These people are gonna forget we even exist."

The girls considered her pronouncement.

Beatrice spoke up first.

"I actually like the sound of that."

"Me too," Mia said. "If you said 'these people are gonna remember our name,' I'd be nervous."

Though when Hector left the girls in his office the next afternoon and told them not to trash the place as he shut the door behind him, Kimmy remarked, "It's not this place we're gonna trash."

"Whoa," Beatrice raised her hands in harmony with her eyebrows.

"That sounds a lot more dramatic than the way you sold it yesterday," Mia piled on.

"Relax, you ninnies," Kimmy waved them off as she sat down in front of the computer. "You're the ones amping up the drama."

She clicked into the web and started typing her way around.

"Did you notice Hector checking me out?" she said as she worked.

Mia and Beatrice slapped their foreheads in spirit.

"Let's see..." Kimmy thought out loud. "Should we use Facebook, Instagram, Tumblr, Yik Yak?"

"For what?" Beatrice asked.

"Our page. It's mostly going to be pictures. I guess any one will do."

She clicked on "create account" and started to fill in the blanks.

"Whose email address is that you're using?" Mia asked.

"I opened it last night under a fake name."

For the name of the page, she typed in "The Dirt Mill" and asked the girls if they liked it.

"We can't answer that if we don't know what you're doing," Beatrice snapped.

"Oh, wait," Kimmy ignored her. "It needs the name of the school, too. Can't forget the bait."

She made the addition, and then in the text box devoted to a motto or description, typed, "Not your typical school website."

"Now let's take a group selfie and use it for the logo," Kimmy reached into her pocket and pulled out her phone.

"What?" Mia squawked.

"You said this was supposed to make them forget we exist," Beatrice said.

"I'm kidding," Kimmy put the phone down. "Jeez."

She left the picture box empty and activated the site.

Then she opened a new tab and logged onto a fellow student's website. She selected and copied a photograph of two popular eighth grade boys, Luis and Darren. They were posturing for the camera, playing up their image as two of the best athletes in school.

She tabbed back to The Dirt Mill and posted the picture on the new page as its premiere entry. Then she wrote a caption:

"Who would win in a fight between them? Vote below. Check back for updates and results."

The girls bent over each side of Kimmy to get a closer look.

"Oh my," Mia was transfixed. "Now I get it."

"Are people going to find this?" Beatrice asked.

"As long as one does," Kimmy said. "They all will."

"So they vote," Beatrice was still putting it together. "Then what?"

Mia jumped in.

"Whoever loses the vote throws the first punch."

"You catch on so fast," Kimmy leaned over and pulled her in for a hug.

"Come on," Beatrice remained skeptical.

"It may take a little while," Kimmy stood up and stretched. "But it will happen. Just like I knew Hector would check me out."

"Please," Beatrice rolled her eyes. "Guys are easy to predict when it comes to girls."

"Everyone is easy to predict when it comes to their egos."

And she was right.

"By God," Beatrice admitted. "She was right."

The two boys were rolling around on the dried grass in center court, locked together and unable to get any leverage into their punches. Mia and Beatrice were a few rows back on the far side of the crowd that was gathered around cheering them on.

"How many days was that?" Mia asked.

"Four, I think."

Kimmy waltzed up behind them.

"Abracadabra," she whispered.

"What did you get for the final tally?" Beatrice asked her.

"Luis eighty-seven, Darren sixty-five," Kimmy answered.

"That makes sense," Mia said. "Apparently Darren jumped Luis."

"It was hard to get an exact number," Kimmy clarified. "Some people didn't actually vote, but their comments made it pretty clear who they favored."

"I had Darren a little closer," Beatrice said. "About eighty to seventy."

"Would this have worked if they tied?" Mia asked.

"There won't be any ties," Kimmy said. "Somebody will always win."

Beatrice turned to her.

"So there's more of this coming?"

"Lower your voice," Kimmy grinned. "I'll see you at the warehouse this afternoon."

The next time it was two girls, Angelica and Lisle, with the question of who was prettier. Kimmy had to search a little harder to find a picture of them together, but found one deep in the archives of Angelica's page. It was a selfie of them hugging each other cheek-to-cheek in the backseat of a car.

"People are going to start making their pages private," Mia speculated.

"Maybe a few of them," Kimmy acknowledged. "But people like attention."

"Not the kind we're giving them," Beatrice countered.

"Any kind of attention," Kimmy maintained.

And there was a certain excitement in Lisle's voice when she approached them at morning recess two days later and asked them if they thought she was prettier than Angelica, and then gave them a rundown of the things Angelica said to her after the poll question was posted on The Dirt Mill, and who was siding with Angelica, and who was siding with her, and the things Team Angelica members were saying about Team Lisle members.

Angelica, meanwhile, was no less animated when she approached them at lunch that same day and provided her side of the same stories before dashing away to lobby some other students to her cause.

"We need to close this poll," Beatrice muttered.

"Give it one more day," Kimmy muttered back.

"I'm not sure I can stand one more day," Mia sided with Beatrice.

"That's what makes it great," Kimmy snickered. "Nobody else can stand it, either."

So they gave it another day, which is all Angelica and Lisle needed to seal their newfound hatred of one another, and alienate themselves from most of their friends.

"Shouldn't we post the results of the Angelica-Lisle vote before moving on to the next one?" Mia asked Kimmy as she scrolled through the official school website looking for candidates.

"Does it matter?" Kimmy asked back.

"Angelica was lapping her," Beatrice offered.

"If those girls weren't so hard to listen to, I'd say that round was too easy," Kimmy cracked as she rolled the mouse over a page of pictures as though it was a shooting gallery.

A shot caught Beatrice's eye.

"Hold on," she said. "What about those two gamers who tutor math in the homework club?"

The photo of the boys featured them standing in front of a white board filled with algebraic equations.

"What would the poll question be?" Kimmy asked out the corner of her mouth.

"Who's smarter," Beatrice replied.

"Who would vote?" Kimmy followed up. "Besides them and their mothers."

"Lots of people," Beatrice maintained. "They're really rude. You go for help and they make you feel like an idiot."

"So all those people who go for math help," Kimmy snickered. "That's gotta be, what, ten, twelve people?"

"They are pretty icky," Mia chipped in.

"The people who go for math help?" Kimmy asked. "That's mean."

"No..." Mia started to explain.

"I know, I know," Kimmy waved her off. "Look, I'm sorry those two dweebs made you feel like crap in the homework club. But this has nothing to do with brains. This is jungle stuff we're dealing with. Who's strongest, who's prettiest, who's the biggest slut, who's got the biggest dick. We only post a question about who's smarter if it's with a picture of the two dumbest kids in school. This needs to hurt!"

Kimmy appeared to surprise herself with that final thought.

Mia wanted to look over at Beatrice, but waited until Kimmy settled back into her search.

"Besides," Kimmy added before Mia and Beatrice could telegraph anything to each other, "if we go after some brains, they might push back and start looking into who runs The Dirt Mill."

The office grew quiet. In the warehouse next to them, on the other side of the window, there were thousands of orders being filled, going out to thousands of different places, but all they could hear was the computer hard drive, and Mia was certain she could also hear Beatrice's thoughts.

"People are going look into that at some point, anyway," Mia said. "If they haven't already."

"I haven't heard anything yet," Kimmy stayed focused on the screen. "Have you?"

"Well, no," Mia admitted.

"They're too busy thinking about themselves," Kimmy explained. "If they knew who was in charge, they'd ask when it was their turn to be on the page."

"That's not what the teachers and the principal are going to think."

Kimmy leaned back and exhaled at the ceiling.

"Okay," she regrouped. "I was saving this for later, but if it will make you feel better..."

She opened a tab and went into her own site and grabbed one of her many selfies on display. She pasted it onto The Dirt Mill, then went back into the other tab and looked up Eve's site, the girl who had been harassing Mia last year, before it became fashionable.

Kimmy copied a picture of Eve and pasted it next to her own on The Dirt Mill.

She typed, "Who's the bigger bitch?"

Beatrice laughed and Mia said "Oh my God."

"That should buy us some time," Kimmy smiled.

"Who do you think's going to win?" Beatrice asked.

"Oh, I fully expect to run away with this," Kimmy answered.

The trio shared a laugh.

"And when I do," she continued, "I'm going after Eve. Really play it up with every ounce of pretend anger in my body."

But when they posted the results days later, and Kimmy followed through on her promise to further divert any suspicion away from them, her anger seemed very real.

She shoved Eve down the hall several times in succession, punctuating her shoves with accusations of rigging the bitch contest.

"Should we step in?" Mia asked Beatrice as they watched the fear widen in Eve's eyes while Kimmy appeared to gain strength with every push and every charge.

"You go first," Beatrice suggested.

"That would be kind of ironic given my history with Eve."

"All the more reason."

Mia glanced at Beatrice and acknowledged her point.

She took a deep breath and walked away from the safety of the gathering crowd. She reached Kimmy's side and played the voice of reason by putting a hand on her shoulder and telling her it wasn't worth it.

"What the fuck do you know about anything?" Kimmy hollered at Mia, then brushed her off and continued to go after Eve even harder.

Mia groaned, gathered herself, and made a more assertive attempt by stepping between them.

Kimmy barreled past her and tackled Eve as the crowd bellowed.

The burly history teacher on morning yard duty, Mr. Fabregas, broke through and pulled Kimmy off of Eve. Before he escorted her to the principal's office, he looked over at Mia.

"Bring her to the nurse," he barked while pointing at Eve, who sat on the ground checking herself for damage.

Mia watched Mr. Fabregas and Kimmy walk away, hoping for some sort of signal from Kimmy, a turn and a wink perhaps, to let her know it all truly was an act. But that would be a dumb move, she realized, and tended to Eve.

"I don't need the nurse," Eve stood up and snapped.

"You sure?"

"That bitch didn't hurt me. She's all show."

Paranoia splashed across Mia.

"What do you mean by that?" she asked Eve.

Eve dismissed her with a grunt and turned to find some friends in the dispersing crowd.

Mia turned to find Beatrice approaching.

"Did you hear that?" Mia asked.

"Yeah," Beatrice arrived. "I didn't know we had a nurse."

"No," Mia shook her off. "The thing about Kimmy being all show."

Beatrice leaked air and smirked.

"That's just bitch contest talk," she said. "Looked pretty real to me."

"Almost too real," Mia nodded. "I hope she didn't oversell it."

The principal bought into her performance. She suspended Kimmy for a week.

Mia and Beatrice found the first day of her suspension quite relaxing. Kimmy wasn't there to spur them on to the next scheme, but Kimmy's schemes had bought them the peace they were able to enjoy.

As she predicted, nobody was paying them any mind. All conversations rotated around the fights and arguments breaking out at regular intervals since the debut of The Dirt Mill. And indeed, none amongst the students seemed concerned about the source. If anything, they appeared grateful.

As evening fell on her first absence, Kimmy called Mia at home.

"I can't talk for long," she said. "I'm grounded. But Grandma is out in the grass looking for Grandpa. Could take an hour, could take one minute."

"I can't believe they grounded you."

"Yeah, well even they have their limits, I guess," Kimmy spoke in brisk, hushed tones, as though held captive. "Can't say I blame them."

"Great performance yesterday," Mia complimented her.

"Thanks. Hope I didn't freak you out."

"Maybe a little."

"Sorry about that. Had to keep up appearances."

"Naturally."

"Speaking of keeping up appearances," Kimmy pressed on. "I need you and Beatrice to post a poll on The Dirt Mill tomorrow. It'll look suspicious if the site stops while I'm out."

"Oh," Mia hesitated. "Sure."

"Come on," Kimmy noticed the pause. "You've seen how I do it, and it's already logged in on Hector's computer. If you need to re-enter the password, it's 'upskirt911.'"

"Okay."

"Remember to use two people who have some popularity. Nobody from the shadows. Leave them alone. No one cares. And nothing sexual. I think I may have said something about big dicks once, but that was a joke. If it starts to look like it's run by some kiddie porn adult, the police will get involved. And in that case, poor Hector. Even if we confessed, that's the kind of accusation that's hard to live down once it's out there."

"No dicks. Got it."

"Or best ass," Kimmy added. "Anything remotely pervert. Hold on..."

Mia heard the phone fade from Kimmy's mouth momentarily.

"Dang," she growled back onto the line. "I think Grandma found him. She might be talking to herself, but I can usually tell the difference. Gotta go. Thanks for doing this."

"Sure."

"It's good to know we've got each other's backs."

Then she hung up before Mia could respond, which was just as well. Mia felt stretched by the idea of having Kimmy's back, and if Kimmy had listened to her waver, as Mia did earlier in the conversation when asked to post something on the site, it would have added up to an easy case for Kimmy to make regarding the ambivalence of Mia's loyalty.

"Everything has to do with backs," Mia pondered aloud as she and Beatrice rode their bikes to the warehouse the following afternoon. "I've got your back, you went behind my back, you stabbed me in the back. Everyone is obsessed with what goes on behind them."

"Do you not want to do this?" Beatrice asked.

Mia pedaled for a dozen rotations. They came upon the barren road that connected the last neighborhood in town to the realization station.

"We wouldn't be able to do this if it weren't for her," Mia finally said.

"Riding our riding bikes again," Beatrice clarified. "Out in the open."

Mia nodded.

"She cleared the way."

"So let's do this," Beatrice started to swerve back and forth across the empty pavement. "We know the question, we just need to figure out whose pictures to post."

Mia joined her in swerve formation.

"Sorry," she called ahead to Beatrice. "I'm spaced out today. Are we going with 'Who will get pregnant first?' or 'Who won't finish high school?'"

"Pregnant," Beatrice hollered back over her shoulder.

"That's not too sexual?"

"I don't think pervs are interested in getting anyone pregnant."

"Just thinking of Hector."

A pair of trucks rose from the horizon in front of the warehouse. They were single file, but not lined up perfectly, so they could see them both. Beatrice pulled over to the side, knowing that Mia didn't like riding past the big rigs that drove back and forth from the loading docks, even though the road offered plenty of room.

Mia stopped next to her. They straddled their bikes and watched the rigs gain speed as they gained distance from the warehouse.

"You think she might actually pin this on Hector if it comes to that?" Beatrice asked.

"I wouldn't be surprised if she tried," Mia replied.

They shielded their eyes as the trucks passed and scattered grit in their wake. Mia thought she saw the second driver wave, so she waved back with her available arm.

When the volume of the engines had suitably faded, Mia picked up their conversation.

"Once we do this," she said, "we're in. We can't claim it was all Kimmy and we were just bystanders."

"I'm sure she knows that, too."

They remained standing halfway between the town and the realization station.

"What if we do get called to the principal's office or the sheriff at some point?" Mia asked herself as much as she asked Beatrice. "What's the right thing to do?"

"Deny everything."

"If they give us a chance to give up Kimmy," Mia mixed in a wrinkle.

"Which I have a feeling would happen," Beatrice added.

"She helped us," Mia said. "She made our lives easier."

"By making others miserable."

"That's what I mean."

"A lot of those people were making our lives miserable," Beatrice reminded her.

"Was it that bad? We were pretty good at laughing them off."

"How long could we have done that?"

"It would be a lot of laughing," Mia acknowledged.

"Laughing too much hurts."

They stood some more. The trucks were long gone, and the only sound on the road was the wind blowing over it.

"Maybe no one will ever find out," Mia said.

"We're smart enough," Beatrice joined her in that thought. "We'll pull the plug before anyone gets around to an investigation."

Mia remembered a dream she had about Artie the night before, or maybe it was the week before. She may have had it more than once.

She dreamed she was invited to a popular girl's birthday trip to Disneyland, and asked her Mom for some spending money. Her Mom was excited for her, and gave her more than enough. She used the money to take a bus to San Francisco instead. Artie snuck out of school and took her to lunch and a bunch of shops and to dinner. His parents arrived at the restaurant and interrupted dinner. They were very upset. They had surveillance video of them in every place they had been, sitting at tables and walking down aisles and past shelves. They had records of everything they had purchased, recordings of phone conversations, and a satellite map with bright lines marking their paths. Everything was documented. Her Mom showed up and couldn't stop laughing, which made Artie's parents even more upset. Mia and Artie looked at each other without any idea how to feel.

Mia considered telling Beatrice about the dream, but they had been standing for a while.

It was time to move on and see what was to become of their decision.

Chapter Twenty Five: Dale

Jonathan was having a good day.

He ordered his nachos on his own, pointing conclusively to the item on the takeout menu, and he was still happy about the rain. Everyone else seemed to have grown tired of it already, even though three straight days of rain barely started to make up for what was needed.

Dale had yet to reacquaint himself with carrying an umbrella after so much time away from one, so he had dashed from the truck to the restaurant, while Jonathan stopped short of the door and stood under the drops with his head back, as though relaxing in a hot shower after a hard day's labor. Dale had to come back out and nudge him onward to keep him from getting soaked.

The furtive stares aimed at them appeared less pitying than normal. Their fellow diners seemed to appreciate Jonathan's enthusiasm for the storm, perhaps being reminded of how grateful they should be for water.

Dale pretended not to hear when their number was called, and Jonathan was alert to that as well. He shooed his Dad in the direction of the counter, to which Dale feigned offense and told Jonathan to get it himself.

And he did.

When he arrived back at the table, Dale noticed he only had the nachos on the tray.

"Where's mine?" Dale asked.

Jonathan sat down and started eating. Dale looked over and saw the young woman who often served them holding his order and smiling. He smiled back and went to retrieve it.

"Did he tell you to do that?" Dale asked her.

"Not exactly," she said. "He just took yours off the tray."

He chuckled and rejoined Jonathan at the table, who continued to ignore him.

"Fine," Dale said before digging in. "I deserved that."

Jonathan laughed in a way that sounded like someone imitating laughter, which was good enough for Dale.

They ate in silence for some time before the door opened and a group of four men came in shaking themselves from the rain. They all wore matching windbreakers that sported the logo of an ag company on the breast. Three of them paired the jacket with jeans and work boots, while one of them wore slacks and dress shoes.

That one was Rod.

Dale made no gesture to attract Rod's attention, but braced himself for the possibility of Rod seeing him. He was relieved to hear the party order their food to go, but tensed up as they sat at a table in the dining area to wait, with Rod taking a seat that put Dale in his line of sight. He breathed easier again when they started to talk and Rod failed to notice him, but then the lack of recognition started to irritate him. He looked at Jonathan while being acutely aware of what was going on at Rod's table.

The area in his peripheral vision occupied by Rod came to a standstill. Dale figured he had been spotted. He continued to look at Jonathan as the figure of Rod rose from its table. It was on the move, and there was no use pretending any longer. Dale averted his eyes from his son as Rod approached.

"Dale Copeland!" Rod held his arms open while he walked, but reduced his gesture to a handshake by the time he arrived.

"Hello, Rod," Dale stood up and shook the hand.

"We were on our way out to Stanton Ranch," Rod released his grip so he could gesture in the direction they were heading. "Now that the prison's open, they don't want to farm the land next to it. Like prisoners will escape all the time and take their workers hostage or something. We were kind enough to offer our services. I told my guys we had to stop for burritos on the way. The burritos here are like a magic potion when you're getting ready to negotiate."

"They are good."

"So what are you up to?"

"I'm back with the district," Dale said. "The woman they hired to replace me didn't work out. I don't think they wanted me back, but the talent pool wasn't very deep."

"Selling yourself short, as usual," Rod waved him off.

"It's a hard job to fill. Even harder in a place like ours."

"You're the best anywhere. They're lucky to have you."

Rod looked down at the table and saw Jonathan.

Dale took note.

"This is my son," he said. "Jonathan."

"Nice to meet you, Jonathan."

Rod appeared to wait and see how Jonathan responded before making any moves. Jonathan didn't respond at all.

"Rod is one of the people I worked with at the charter school," Dale explained in his son's direction. "He was the head of our board. There wouldn't be a charter school if it weren't for Rod."

Jonathan jerked his head slightly to one side. They waited to see if anything else was forthcoming.

He scooped up some cheese with a chip and took a loud, crunching bite out of it.

"Well," Rod said, "nice to meet you, Jonathan. I should go up and check on our food. Can I borrow your Dad for a moment?"

Jonathan nodded slightly, but it may have been coincidence.

"I'll be right back," Dale said, and followed Rod to the front where people milled around the soda machine waiting for their orders.

Rod found a relatively open space and pivoted.

"Why didn't you tell me?" he asked just above a whisper.

"About what?" Dale played dumb.

"Your son."

"I told you I had a son. And a daughter."

"But you didn't tell me about his…I don't know. Condition? Challenges? What am I supposed to say?"

"It's not something we go around announcing to people."

"We worked together for almost a year."

"And I learned right away that you hate it when people ask for things."

"What does that have to do with this?"

"Because it's hard not to tell someone about Jonathan without feeling like you're asking for something," Dale explained. "Sympathy, pity, praise, help."

"Money," Rod added.

"Money," Dale agreed. "If they're the type who has money."

"You're different," Rod assured him. "You've earned the right to ask."

"For what?" Dale asked. "Sympathy? Help?"

"You know," Rod grinned.

The young woman behind the counter called out a number.

"You're right," Dale confessed. "I know. But I don't agree."

"Stop the modesty already. You're overdoing it."

"I'm not being modest," Dale said. "I don't agree that people have to earn the right."

"They do if they want my money."

The young woman behind the counter called out the number again.

"And they earn it by not asking," Dale confirmed.

Rod chuckled and wagged a finger at him.

"You didn't talk to me like this last year," he narrated his gesture.

"I wouldn't have earned your approval if I did," Dale said.

Rod ceased all playfulness and charm. He sized up Dale as though meeting him for the first time.

The woman called the number again.

One of the men from Rod's table arrived.

"Mr. Pluma," he said. "That's us."

Rod looked over at the other men with whom he shared a logo. They were standing by the table, waiting for him with patient smiles.

"Sorry," he said, forcing himself back into the highest level of charisma he could manage. "Just talking to my old friend here. Catching up a little."

Dale nodded and played along.

The man politely returned the nod while keeping his focus on Rod.

"We shouldn't keep the Stanton family waiting," he reminded him.

"Of course," Rod agreed.

He moved toward the counter and brandished his wallet as the trio reconvened behind him.

"I've got this," he announced.

The men offered various forms of gratitude.

After paying, Rod handed the bag to one of them and faced Dale.

"Good to see you again, Dale," he offered his hand.

"Good to see you, too, Rod," Dale shook it.

"If there's anything I can do, let me know."

Dale covered his impulse to laugh with a smile that may have been a bit too broad, for Rod appeared to notice its expanse.

"Thank you," Dale withdrew his hand from Rod's. "I will."

He watched the four of them walk out the door and break into a trot through the raindrops.

"Anything," he said as he rejoined Jonathan. "You hear that? He'll do anything. Our troubles are over."

Jonathan was done eating. He had wadded up a paper napkin into a ragged ball and was batting it back and forth on the tabletop.

"What a ballgame!" he exclaimed. "What a ballgame!"

Dale watched him for a while.

"Did I ever thank you?" he finally said.

"What a ballgame!" Jonathan repeated.

"Thank you for helping me make the right decision about the buyout and the job. I really appreciated your help."

The paper ball made its way to and fro.

"Bumping into Rod just reminded me," Dale continued. "He was one of the people I talked about around the campfire that night."

"What a ballgame!"

"So anyway, like I said. Thanks."

Dale dug back into his food. It was cold, but still tasted good.

Jonathan finished his game a few bites before Dale finished his meal.

The drive home was quiet. The hills were already turning green, having waited so long for some water, and the raindrops had knocked off most of the frail autumn leaves from the trees. The rhythm of the windshield wipers and heat from the defroster seemed to make Jonathan drowsy.

He revived when they pulled into their driveway, and was in the house before Dale was out of the car.

Dale assumed he would be in his room with the door shut, settling in for a nap. He planned on checking to see if he needed anything before he fell asleep.

But he entered to find Jonathan at the kitchen table with the instrument placed squarely in its center. He was staring at the instrument, which meant he wanted to use it.

"I don't think Mom's home," Dale said before calling Alma's name a couple of times.

"Nope," he confirmed. "I'll let her know when she gets back that you want to do some writing."

Jonathan tapped an open hand on the table, as though patting a dog on its back.

"Me?" Dale asked.

He gave the table one last forceful pat and stopped.

"You don't like it when I use the instrument," Dale reminded him. "I'm too slow. That's what you say."

Jonathan brought his hand down one more time.

"All right," Dale said. "If you insist. Let me get some paper and a pen. I need help remembering where we are and where we've been."

He retrieved the tools and sat down next to his son. They hadn't worked together on the instrument for a while, so Dale was rusty. But after sliding it around beneath Jonathan's fingertips for several letters and forming a few words, he reached a decent stride, from which a sentence materialized on the paper Dale used as his palette.

"I want to understand what happened," Jonathan said.

"When?" Dale asked. "Or, where?"

He realized Jonathan wasn't done with his sentence yet. Dale apologized and waved his arms in front of him as though clearing a white board with an eraser in each hand, then started playing the instrument again.

"At the charter," Jonathan continued.

"I told you what happened," Dale said. "On our camping trip. And in bits and pieces a bunch of other times."

He was getting the hang of adding in the prepositions and articles of speech to make Jonathan's sentences flow, and anticipating what word he was trying to spell.

"You told me what happened to you," his son replied.

"I told you about the others," Dale maintained. "Like Rod, the guy we ran into at lunch. I even made up stories by the campfire about what may have been going on in their lives."

"I said I want to understand."

"Understand what?"

"Why people do what they do."

Dale hesitated. He kept the instrument away from Jonathan while he considered his answer.

"Only they know for sure," was all he could come up with.

Jonathan eagerly gestured for the instrument. Dale obliged, and Jonathan's hands flew around the contours of the letters as Dale transcribed.

"We should try to understand," it said on the next line of the paper.

"We?" Dale asked.

Jonathan undertook a more confined version of the same gesture Dale had used earlier, wiping an imaginary board clean with both hands.

"Something new?" Dale wondered aloud, then fed him the instrument.

"Something not in my voice," Jonathan said.

Dale stared at the latest line they had written together.

He couldn't quite figure out what it meant. He was about to ask, but Jonathan was already flowing back to work on the instrument. Dale rallied the pen back to the paper.

Jonathan brushed his hands over the topography of the board, which seemed to move with less guidance from Dale, as though his son was casting a spell on its peaks and valleys.

"People used to smile at them when he took his son out to lunch," he wrote.

Dale caught on and caught his breath.

His son proceeded.

"Back when Jonathan was a child..."

Dale delivered the words and tended to them, making sure their place in the sentence and on the page was secure.

Also by Sean Boling

The Current Mr. Orr
Devin's Best Afterlife
Once in Two Lifetimes
Revenge and Wellness in the Sweet Hereafter

Standalone
Cut Flowers
Abraham the Anchor Baby Terrorist
Pigs and Other Living Things
The Summer of Our Foreclosure
Satellite Campus
A Charter to That Other Place
The Latest Version of My Love Story
Show Them What They Won
The Name Field
Should
Moral Adjacent
Over Here We Have

About the Author

Sean lives with his family in Templeton, California. He teaches English at Cuesta College.